HOW TO BE A BADASS DETECTIVE

HOW TO BE A BADASS DETECTIVE

HOW TO BE A BADASS DETECTIVE™ BOOK TWO

MICHAEL ANDERLE

DISRUPTIVE IMAGINATION

LMBPN Publishing
PMB 196, 2540 South Maryland Pkwy
Las Vegas, NV 89109

First US edition, June 2021
ebook ISBN: 978-1-64971-819-8
Print ISBN: 978-1-64971-820-4

THE HOW TO BE A BADASS DETECTIVE
BOOK TWO TEAM

Thanks to our Beta Team

Kelly O'Donnell

Thanks to our JIT Readers

Daryl McDaniel
Wendy L Bonell
Veronica Stephan-Miller
Deb Mader
Dave Hicks
Diane L. Smith
Zacc Pelter
Debi Sateren

If We've missed anyone, please let us know!

Editor
The Skyhunter Editing Team

To Family, Friends and
Those Who Love
To Read.
May We All Enjoy Grace
To Live The Life We Are
Called.

CHAPTER ONE

Mother LeBlanc laid a hand on James' forehead, which was warm. He was developing a fever as a side effect of his injuries, their long and harsh journey, and their lack of access to proper medical care. He needed bed rest, away from the elements.

But he was alive. And they had, at last, found shelter.

Samantha came up. Her brow was furrowed in concern, and she was haggard. She was nothing like her usual vivacious, flirtatious self. Her long hair was disheveled, and she had barely done anything to put it back in order.

"How is he?" she asked. "Once we get him inside, I'm sure his chances will improve."

LeBlanc nodded to acknowledge her, though she kept her eyes on James. "He's getting sick, but his injuries are better. If we can remain hidden at this place of yours for a solid week or more, I imagine he will make a full recovery." Befitting the age in which she had been born—long, long ago—LeBlanc had a formal and archaic way of speaking, and her voice was still tinged with a New Orleans Creole accent.

The dark look in Samantha's eyes suggested she was not optimistic. After the loss of Damian and Zacharia, she had grown more protective of James than ever.

"Let's go in, then. If the neighbors see us and ask too many questions, we can always erase their memories later." She gestured at the house.

The eleven of them had detoured west to a rural area in north-central Pennsylvania, where they had buried Zacharia in the woods. Heading east again to Wilkes-Barre where Samantha had a second house that no one seemed to know about was a risk, but it was one they had to take. For James' sake, if nothing else.

Josiah Kane pointed out, "There are no visible neighbors anyway. I'm assuming the privacy of this place is part of why it's your *second* home. There is no one around to see while you work out on your treadmill at night in a sports bra and hotpants in front of an open window with a strong backlight on."

He'd said it with a teasing undercurrent of dry humor, and Samantha, despite herself, smiled. "I hadn't thought of it that way, but you're right. The place is...dull."

Mary Mitchell stepped forward to pick up one end of the makeshift stretcher on which James lay. "Dull is exactly what we need right now, I'm afraid. We've all had more than our fill of excitement. Shall we?"

LeBlanc and Mitchell picked James up and carried him across the lawn, which was surrounded by high walls covered with ivy. Tall maple and oak trees provided further cover from the sight of the surrounding neighborhood with their reddening leaves. Samantha went to the front doors and unlocked them with a small brass key.

Ezeudo, their new recruit and therefore the only person present who was not a member of the North American Council of Thaumaturges, walked alongside the stretcher, glancing between the slumped and groaning form of James and the place that would hopefully provide him with a safe haven.

The house was not palatial, falling a thousand or two square feet short of what would qualify as a mansion, but it was far from small, with two stories and at least three, perhaps four bedrooms. The magic users might be cramped, but they would manage.

Ezeudo asked, "What kind of heating do you have here? James will need to keep warm." Though he had lived in Europe for years before coming to America, he was originally from Nigeria, where winter did not exist. The threat of cold weather was something he'd learned to take seriously.

"Oh, um," Samantha began, "I don't recall, actually, but we'll figure it out in a moment. If there are any problems, I'm sure we of all people can manage."

Ezeudo nodded. Despite all he had seen lately, it was easy to forget just how powerful the council members were.

Although, compared to the Orthodoxy, perhaps not powerful enough.

They brought James in through the small foyer, then, under Samantha's direction, carried him to the guest bedroom on the ground floor. The house had a musty but not unpleasant fragrance, as homes that had long sat disused often did. It could also use a good dusting.

Ezeudo and Rufus Mayer helped LeBlanc and Mary pick James up slowly and carefully from the stretcher and lay him on the bed. LeBlanc pulled the covers over him, being cautious not to aggravate his chest wounds. He had taken three molten spears to the chest. If one or two minor factors had been different—if the injury had been infinitesimally worse—he would have been dead by now.

James' eyes twitched and then opened, and he let out a long moan. "Where am I?" he asked in a hoarse voice. "Did everyone make it?"

LeBlanc, standing over him, wondered how much of his memory remained intact. He had regained consciousness long enough to speak at Zacharia's makeshift funeral, but he might have forgotten about it.

There was no point in being delicate. "Everyone is here except Zacharia and Damian. We are at Samantha's home away from home in Pennsylvania."

James looked sad. "Yeah. I remember about Zacharia now. Goddammit. I'm sorry I brought it up." He lifted a hand and rubbed his eyes. "And Pennsylvania isn't far enough. Ideally, we should be in, like, Oklahoma or something by now. Did they destroy my house, by the way?"

Amanda Moore moved closer to the bed. "We performed a scrying spell last night to check on the Orthodoxy's movements. We didn't dare look too closely so they couldn't trace the spell back to our location, so we only saw your house from afar. Bird's eye view, about a quarter-mile to the west."

Mary added, "It seems they have chosen to occupy your estate for the time being, perhaps to raid it for valuables and rest and gather their strength. Thus far, they do not seem to be in a great hurry to hunt us down. Humiliating us by driving us out of New York appears to have sufficed for the time being. They will undoubtedly come back to finish what they started and soon, but we should have time for you to recover."

James blinked. "You're all taking a massive risk for my sake, you realize. I appreciate it but don't all get killed just because of me. Where are my glasses?"

Hugh Buchanan smiled. "We have no intention of being wiped out."

Twisting around and fishing inside her blouse, Samantha produced a case about the length of a hand and opened it. "Here you are, James." She produced his glasses, unfolded them, and handed them over.

He slipped them on. "Oh, right, I remember this place. We were here for a week, um, that one time. Fun stuff."

Samantha blushed but leaned closer to him and squeezed his hand.

LeBlanc cleared her throat. "James needs his rest. Let's gather in the living room to talk, and when there's time, perhaps we can have tea or coffee."

As the majority of them strolled out of the guest room, LeBlanc sidled up to Ezeudo and said in a low voice, "Samantha and James were once in a relationship, which is not unusual since Samantha has had *many* relationships. They rarely speak of it for various reasons that are none of our business, but you ought to know. She is taking his injury harder than I'd expected."

Ezeudo rubbed his hands; the sun was setting, and it was growing cold. "That makes sense. I am closer to him and you than the others, though I am becoming fond of all of you. What has been happening is not something I wish to see any more of."

"None of us do," LeBlanc agreed. "You are taking it better than we are. Your work for charitable organizations in trouble spots around the globe has probably hardened you, at least somewhat, to violence and tragedy. It has been a long time since we of the council have seen anything like this happen, particularly in our own home territory. Not so long ago, we were concerned with day-to-day matters and how best to run our organization. Now, we are fleeing and fighting for our lives."

She shook her head, and her dark eyes looked somewhere beyond the broad living room window.

Although Ezeudo had been born with the gift of magic and had taught himself to use it in certain basic ways, it was only since he'd come to America with LeBlanc and James that he had begun to receive formal training. He was advancing rapidly, but there was still much work to be done.

Still, despite his limited experience, he had been developing one of the secondary abilities that came with the full unlocking of one's thaumaturgic potential: enhanced perception of the emotional vibe given off by others, including those who were good at hiding their feelings.

Though they were trying to be stoic, every one of the council members, including the normally even-keeled LeBlanc, was on the verge of being overwhelmed by grief and fear.

He wondered how long the council had reigned supreme and unchallenged in America. How long it had been since not just one but two of their members had been killed in battle, and half the rest wounded, with all the survivors hounded and scattered from their places of authority.

Samantha remained in the room with James for a moment but called to them that there was probably old tea and cups in the kitchen. LeBlanc went off to do the brewing while the others settled in the living room. Those still nursing wounds took the couches and armchairs while the rest leaned against the walls or brought in wooden chairs from the dining room.

Crystal Green, who was one of the better healers amongst them, though none of them were specialists, announced to the rest, "As LeBlanc mentioned, James will require at least a week to recover, and that is if we do our part by helping him along with restorative magic as well as mundane medicine. Samantha tells me, though, that she has almost no emotional ties to this place, which will make it harder for the Orthodoxy to track us here. And there are no records of its existence in James' library."

Lauren Jones commented, "Well, that's good. But James mentioned the time he and Samantha spent here, and it seemed to affect her. We'll have to cleanse the emotive vibe *that* may have created."

"Good point," Mary agreed. "We will do so tonight before we sleep."

LeBlanc returned with a tray and half a dozen small porcelain cups from which steam rose. "I'll be back with the second round. Help yourselves." She set the cups on the coffee table and went to gather the remainder. "There. I think we all could use this. It's a small comfort but an excellent one, I'd say."

No one disagreed. Samantha emerged and took one of the

cups into the guest room for James before coming out and joining the others for the discussion.

Ezeudo sat and listened, contributing little. To some extent, they regarded him as comparable to a younger brother tagging along with the older boys. His presence was tolerated, but he was not truly one of them. Not yet, anyway.

Still, they seemed to respect him. He had done as they'd asked during the awful battle at James' mansion, helping them all without quailing when the fight turned against them. His intervention had helped save James from dying on the scene.

No one was in agreement as to what their next course of action ought to be. Everyone was still recovering mentally, physically, and emotionally from their defeat.

"So," Amanda persisted, "when do we counterattack? If we move quickly, we might be able to strike them before they've prepared for their next maneuver. We could eliminate them, or at least do heavy damage, while they're still complacent and overconfident."

Since Zacharia had passed away, Amanda had become unusually strident, almost vicious.

LeBlanc, Lauren, Mary, and Rufus exchanged glances. Hugh Buchanan sat impassively, and the others frowned.

LeBlanc took the initiative. "I do not think," she began carefully, "that it would be wise to launch a counteroffensive at this time. We were not able to pick off as many of their troops as we'd like, and they still outnumber us by a large margin. What might be better is to rally the minor covens or lull the Orthodoxy into greater complacency by spreading the rumor that we've fled the country and are languishing in exile on another continent."

"Perhaps," Rufus said. "We certainly do not want the minor covens to swear allegiance to our enemies. They would be able to provide the Orthodoxy with substantial information about our movements and assets, or might even find themselves conscripted in the war against us."

Josiah Kane grimaced. "They already made it perfectly clear that they wish to stay out of this. Perhaps when they see how brutal the Orthodoxy truly is, they will change their minds, albeit too late for our friends."

LeBlanc added, "It is possible that some of them will offer us tacit aid, if not explicit. But for the most part, we might be on our own for the time being. The Orthodoxy is stronger than we expected, almost *too* strong. It is not over yet, but we need to...recover."

Watching them, Ezeudo was more certain than ever how dire the circumstances were. As Mother LeBlanc had said, there was always hope. But even for her, hope seemed slim indeed.

Milena unfolded her razor blade. Traditionally, the procedure called for a ceremonial knife; for novice practitioners, it helped them extract the maximum amount of energy from their subjects. But Milena had been doing this long enough that any blade would suffice for her purposes, the sharper, the better.

The man on the table moaned through the rag stuffed in his mouth, which had been secured with tape wound around his face. He was also blindfolded, and his arms and legs were strapped down at the wrists and ankles.

Milena turned her head toward him. "Be silent, please. There is no point in trying to speak. Nothing you could say would have any effect on what is to come. And it will be over quickly; you will not suffer more than is necessary. I am a professional."

She looked at the razor again, then ran its blade quickly through the flame of a black candle and washed it with pure water from a silver pitcher. The spell worked best when there were few if any contaminants interfering with the mingling of steel and blood.

Not many witches still practiced the form of magic in which

Milena had chosen to specialize. She was among the last true experts, which was part of what made her so valuable to the Orthodoxy. Within the last nine years, she had finally secured a seat on their highest council. Though the youngest and newest member of the elite, she was officially the equal of those who ranked just below Grandmistress Anezka.

She held the razor by her side and used her free hand to open the little black book on the stand to the appropriate page. The tome was bound in jet-colored steerhide, and its writings and etchings were a curious dark rusty-brown color.

The passage to which she had turned described an ancient spell—dark, potent, and long-forbidden in polite magical society. It was the type of witchcraft that instilled fear in the common populace and had in the dim past led the human authorities, religious and secular, to pursue long campaigns of persecution against the arcane and thaumaturgic arts.

But it was *useful*. And since the Orthodoxy had pledged to protect all witches from harassment by the normal majority, Milena had no fear of retribution. Her secrets would be safe as long as the coven's victories continued.

Which they would, thanks in part to what she was about to do tonight.

Milena turned around and looked at the man. He was naked and covered with sweat, which was a product of his fear since the room was chilly. He was an average-looking man in early middle age, perhaps forty, with dark hair and brown eyes. Tension went through his body and he pulled against the straps, writhing and struggling in vain.

Milena's red lips parted in a smile. "Calm yourself," she said. "Again, it will be over soon. You will feel very little of this."

The table was made of stone, with slots beneath its surface that were originally intended for thick rope or chains. In the modern age, tough elastic straps worked better still. There were also smooth indentations or channels carved into it that directed the subject's blood away from his body so it could be put to good use.

Certainly, the man was not doing anything remarkable with his life. He was a standard expendable person with a *slight* sensitivity to magic, but not enough for him to have become a warlock of any degree of accomplishment. Still, his faint trace of the gift meant his blood would add more power to the spell than if he had been a thoroughly mundane specimen.

His whimpering and thrashing grew more frenetic as she approached. "Think of it this way," she explained in a soft, soothing voice. "Your vitality will bring life, strength, and success to others. You are contributing to something greater than yourself—a world in which magic is...safe."

She cast a light charm of calming on him. It was important that he remain conscious for the sacrifice to have its full effect, so the spell only relaxed him enough to where he ceased trying to escape and accepted his fate.

Then Milena raised her hands and spoke the incantation for the blood rite. Most of it was in languages so old they bore no resemblance to the Indo-European roots of her native Russian, coming as they did from dark prehistory when magic was both stronger and more fearsome.

Finally, she bent over the victim, the razor in her hand, and completed the work.

The man's death was messy and painful but relatively quick. Such was the witch's expertise that he passed out from severe blood loss within a matter of seconds, and his body died a few seconds later. The only part of him that retained any life force was the warm red fluid.

His blood flowed down through the channels and into the small obsidian fountain that lay beside the altar table. Given how much denser and stickier blood is compared to water, it did not flow as freely, so maintaining the fountain was a full-time job.

Each day, Milena had to rejuvenate the heating spell that kept the volcanic stone nice and warm to thin the blood and keep it pumping through the fountain's channels to spill out the mouth of the squat, leering gargoyle perched atop the rock formation. From there, it ran down into the basin, gurgling, before being cycled back through. The hydraulic function of it was simple. The magical function was more complex, though, and when it was in operation, the fountain glowed faintly with a mixture of deep reds and bright greens.

Each member of the Orthodoxy, before their commencement of hostilities with the North American Council of Thaumaturgy, had added a drop of their blood to the fountain, leaving it there to be mingled with the fresh infusions from various sacrificial victims, and thus was the bond of power maintained. The fountain sent charges of power to the contributing witches, increasing their strength by a factor of at least thirty percent. Closer to fifty in some cases.

It also granted them easier access to certain types of magic that most covens had deliberately obscured behind the veil of time and ignorance.

Milena herself was among those who received the benefits, though she had not participated in the fighting thus far. Her role was one of support, and she performed it well.

Sighing as the newest boost in power began to take effect, making her feel warm and energized, she turned away from the pale, unmoving corpse and went back to the stand where the book lay to clean her razor blade and contemplate the tasks to come.

The fountain required the blood of one full-sized human to replenish itself approximately once every five days. Those with a tinge of magic were better, but normal people would usually suffice.

Milena would have to begin the search for another subject within the next forty-eight hours. It occurred to her that once the Orthodoxy had achieved total victory and held dominion over the continent, they would have access to the various local covens' records. That would make it far easier to track down persons who would make good sacrifices should the fountain become necessary once more to put down petty rebellions or defend their new territory from challengers.

"There is always the need for war, it seems," she reflected. "But such is the way of things. And I am a professional."

CHAPTER TWO

Chris stared in wonder at the package on the counter. "You know, I had only heard about maple sugar candy, like, once or twice. I thought it was a Canadian thing."

Kera shrugged. "Vermont is close enough to Canada, and it's not like there's a shortage of maples. It's technically not the season for it, but they sell it year-round."

As the counterman rang up the sale, Chris nodded at the obvious insight. "Touché. In fact, now that you mention it, I don't think I've ever been this far north. I half-expected it to be nothing but a frozen wasteland that belongs on a Scandinavian metal album cover."

Kera pointed out, "If we stay long enough, it will look that way, but it's a couple months off yet. Of course, I have no intention whatsoever of remaining in my mom's clutches for *that* long."

The guy running the shop, a big, friendly-faced balding man, looked at them. "You're from around New York, aren't you? Winter up here sometimes sets in a month earlier than it does down there."

Kera smiled and shrugged. "Technically Connecticut, but if Vermont can be 'close enough' to Canada, I guess Connecticut can be 'close enough' to New York. Plus, my parents have a townhouse there. In the City, I mean."

"Oh, nice," he replied, accepting the money. "Well, you came at the right time. Lots of folks from the cities down south head up here for the leaves."

Chris quipped, "*Way* down south. We live in LA, though she's from the Northeast originally."

"Oh." The man handed them the candy. "Bet you're already missing the weather back there. I've been thinking about retiring to California when the time comes."

Kera laughed. "The climate is nice, to be sure. Not sure I'd consider LA a good retirement spot, but it's not like it's the only place in the state. There are much quieter towns if you look around for them."

They said goodbye and headed outside to the family car they'd taken, a silver Prius, where Kera's mother would be meeting them any minute now.

Kera exhaled. Her tension and aggravation must have been obvious. It was absurd, she knew, since she, Chris, and Mom had been getting along surprisingly well. Nothing too terrible or embarrassing had occurred.

So far, anyway. Kera's father had been present most of the time, and he tended to impose a degree of sanity on the proceedings. However, he'd sat out the trip up to Vermont, so Kera feared it was only a matter of time before Mrs. MacDonagh dropped the hammer and demanded detailed reports on every single aspect of Kera's and Chris' existence.

"Man!" Chris exhaled, looking at the scenery. "It's weird seeing so many trees. Everywhere you look, if there aren't buildings, it's just trees, trees, and more trees. I guess I've been in SoCal too long. Makes me a little claustrophobic, even though it's pretty."

He slipped a hand around Kera's waist, and she joined him in enjoying the moment while they waited. "Yeah, that makes sense. We used to come up to random places in the rustic parts of New England every autumn, so I'm used to it, though it's been a while. Makes me more nostalgic than anything."

Chris nodded. "My parents went up to Oregon sometimes. Slightly different type of forest, but still, tons of greenery. It's been a long time since I've seen the place, though. Oh, which route are we taking back to Danbury tomorrow? Same one?"

"Eh," Kera replied, "let's not. I'd rather see different stuff each way. Plus, we took the longer route on our way up, and I think everyone would rather get home a little quicker."

After securing their reservation at a hotel in Rutland in south-central Vermont, they had driven up via I-84 east through half of Connecticut before switching onto I-91 in Hartford and following it the rest of the way north through Massachusetts and then along the state line between Vermont and New Hampshire. It had taken about four hours.

Kera planned to take the more direct westerly route back, which would save them perhaps fifteen minutes. Not much, but better than nothing. It involved taking US-7 south-southwest and then getting onto 22, which would lead them down through the easternmost part of New York state before finally getting back on I-84 and returning to Danbury.

After that, they would spend only one more night at "home." She and Chris would board a plane for Los Angeles the following day.

Chris pulled her close to him and she obliged, resting her head against his shoulder.

"So," she asked, "have you had a good time so far? Also, we should dig into that candy soon. Maybe not right now, but definitely soon."

He moved it away from her as though he were protecting it. "Noted. And yes, I'm glad we did this. Your parents aren't so bad, really, and it's been nice and interesting seeing where you grew up and whatnot. The vibe is a lot different back here, aside from everything still being, well, American. Also, since we discussed the driving route back to Connecticut, I'm still trying to cope with the way everyone refers to highways as just 'I-69' or whatever they are. Like, I had no idea that the rest of the country *didn't* call them *'the* I-69.' Weird."

Kera laughed. "Technically, Californians are the weird ones, but I guess everything's relative. And oh, hell. Speaking of *relative*..."

Mrs. MacDonagh had appeared without warning at the far end of the lot, swinging a paper shopping bag by its loop handle and adjusting her unnecessarily large floppy hat and sunglasses. She looked like a New Yorker vacationing in Florida in the summer, though it was all of sixty-five degrees out. By LA standards, the weather was a touch on the cooler side.

Chris waved as the woman approached. "Hi, Mom. We got some maple sugar candy."

Kera's mother adjusted her glasses again. "Oh, did you? I suppose I shouldn't be surprised, given that Kera has always had a sweet tooth. She used to devour cookies on a daily basis. I suppose it's for the best that she was always active, or she might have gotten fat on us. Dear," she added, looking at Kera, "you are *eating*, aren't you? You're still young enough that your metabolism can excuse how thin you are, but I can't help worrying that you might have grown obsessed with your figure. You're not experimenting with anorexia or bulimia, are you?"

Chris briefly struggled to keep a straight face, but after a second or two, he made a sputtering, snorting sound that turned into guffaws of laughter.

Sighing, Kera said, "No, Mom. I eat a healthy diet and get plenty of nutrition. I'm naturally thin, I guess, plus I get plenty of exercise. That's all."

Getting himself back under control, Chris affirmed, "Plenty

of nutrition. Yeah, that's one way of putting it. This girl can and does eat. Believe me."

Mrs. MacDonagh was now only about ten feet away. "Well, that's good then. Wait, that isn't a double entendre, is it? If it is, please don't admit it. The thought just popped into my head that it might be, and I'm afraid I said it out loud before I thought about the consequences."

Kera put a hand over her eyes and allowed her face to droop toward the pavement. "No, Mom. I eat a lot of food to keep my energy up. High caloric needs due to my activity level, that's all."

It was true, of course. In addition to needing to refuel because of her martial arts training and workouts, performing magic burned a ton of fat.

Up close, Chris could see the resemblance between mother and daughter, notwithstanding Mrs. MacDonagh being half-disguised by her hat and shades. Both were thin, on the taller side of average, and light-complected with fine features. The older woman's hair was blonde, as Kera's was, though Kera had begun dyeing her hair black shortly before they started dating.

Kera's mother showed them her purchases: a nice little wood carving of a fish which she planned to keep on her mantel and a framed photograph of the fall color, which she insisted Kera take back to LA.

"Oh, thanks," Kera responded. "You didn't have to get me anything, but I appreciate it."

Mrs. MacDonagh smiled. "Don't mention it. Besides, it cost far less than the rest of this trip, and we can afford it."

Good point, Kera thought. *But formalities are formalities. I wonder how Chris feels, seeing how, well, loaded we are? He comes from a lower-middle-class background and probably doesn't have much experience dealing with rich people, particularly not older-money types from the East Coast. If he's met any millionaires, they're likely the tech-startup or entertainment variety that is endemic to Cali.*

Mrs. MacDonagh took the wheel. Kera had offered to drive,

but she hadn't driven a car in a long time since she preferred to get around on Zee, her Kawasaki Z-900. Chris drove a Jeep which was probably twice the size of the sedan.

The drive from the little satellite village back to the city of Rutland did not take long. Chris marveled all the while at how rustic, underpopulated, and small-town-oriented Vermont was. Rutland was among the larger cities in the state, yet it would barely qualify as a proper suburb within the greater LA metro area.

Their hotel was a major chain but a good one. By Kera's recent standards it was luxurious, though her mother regarded it as barely adequate. "I suppose," the older woman murmured as they settled back in, "that if we'd wanted top-end accommodations, we should have either waited for something to open up at one of the nice places or perhaps gone all the way up to Burlington."

Kera took off her light jacket. "This place is nice. You're just spoiled."

"Well," Mrs. MacDonagh conceded, "you *do* live in a warehouse, so I suppose your standards have lowered somewhat. Have you done anything to make it more homey? I suppose you can only improve the interior, though. People out on the street will look at it and see a warehouse, no matter what. Have you thought about moving into a nice condo?"

Kera whispered to Chris, who was sitting on one of the beds and taking his shoes off, "Remember, when the time comes, you know what to do. Finish me off quickly and cleanly. It's better this way. I'll see you in the next life."

"Noted," he whispered back. "There may still be hope for your survival, though."

They would be on a plane within the next twenty-four hours, so she was willing to consider that he was right. Today was the first day her mother had gone all-in with the sanity-shredding verbal prods and nettlesome comments. Plus, she hadn't pried too much into Chris' life and career or the status of the detective agency, either.

Kera tried to relax.

Her mom asked, "You two are making fun of me, aren't you? Well, young people always do that. I only ask questions because I care, you know. What would you like for dinner? I'm debating whether to see if room service here is decent or look for a nice restaurant in town."

They ended up ordering a fairly basic but quite good chicken dinner from room service and ate it while watching TV. Mrs. MacDonagh had a separate bed in a smaller room attached to the suite and she retired there to read, leaving the young couple in their own room.

As they lay together, winding down toward sleep, Kera's phone buzzed. Frowning, she pulled it out and looked at the screen. It was Mr. Kim.

I miss the Kims, she admitted to herself. *Kinda late for them to be texting me, but they probably forgot they're multiple time zones earlier than I am at the moment.*

To her surprise, Mr. Kim had messaged to inform her that he had a gift of sorts on the way. Apparently, a friend of his and Mrs. Kim's, a "psychic researcher" and scholar of the occult, had a book on magic they wanted to loan her. The man in question lived in White Plains, New York, which was only a short way from Danbury. He wanted to drop it off at Kera's parents' house tomorrow before she left.

She texted him back. **Thank you. Tell him that we should be back by about 1 pm. There's a gate on the property. Tell him just to push the button and say he has a book for me. I'll tell my parents. Looking forward to seeing you guys again soon.**

She pressed Send, then summarized the exchange for her boyfriend.

"Interesting," Chris mused. "In this day and age, you'd think they would direct you to a website or an ebook, so if they're having to loan you a hard copy, it must be pretty legit stuff."

Kera furrowed her brow. "That's what I'm thinking also. Well, it might be crap. Just because something is rare doesn't mean it's actually *valuable*, except as maybe a novelty collector's item. It could be some half-assed vanity publishing project from the occult craze back in the 1970s or the late nineteenth century that does a better job of seeming spooky and mysterious and portentous than of conveying useful information."

Still, she trusted the Kims' judgment. They, too, had the gift, and they chose their friends wisely and carefully.

"I suppose we'll find out soon enough," said Chris. "Gives you something to read on the flight back, if nothing else."

The drive back to Connecticut had been nice enough. Kera's mother, as though making up for lost time, needled the couple for more information about their personal and professional lives, to which Kera responded with the bare minimum of words necessary to be polite while giving away as little as possible.

However, they also talked about old, embarrassing stories from Kera's childhood, or fun stories from Chris', or the scenery around them. Northern Appalachia was beautiful. Kera found that the rolling hills and forests became repetitive after the first hour or two, but Chris enjoyed it.

At last, they arrived back at the MacDonagh estate. It was an old house, though not that old by the standards of the region, having been built in 1892 and renovated twice: once in the 1950s and again in the 1990s when Kera's parents took over ownership. That had been three or four years before she was born. It sat on six acres of land, not a vast expanse, but large enough for their purposes and certainly more elbow room than most non-rich people had.

It was 12:53 in the afternoon when they pulled up at the gate. A black Camry was parked to the side and a man stood beside it, holding a small rectangular parcel wrapped in brown paper.

"Who," Mrs. MacDonagh wondered, "is that? Wait, it's probably the man you mentioned with the book. Pardon me, dear, but I'm not used to having strangers waiting for me at my own home. Are you sure—"

Kera interjected, "I trust the Kims with my life, and that's not an exaggeration. If they recommended this guy, everything should be fine."

"Oh, all right." Mrs. MacDonagh stopped her Prius about fifteen feet from where the man stood.

Before her mom or her boyfriend could object, Kera unbuckled her seatbelt and hopped out. In the extremely unlikely event that the man did turn out to be threatening, she was perfectly capable of taking care of herself. She'd left her Glock home, but between her hand-to-hand fighting abilities and her ever-growing talent for thaumaturgy, she was far from defenseless.

Of course, Mrs. MacDonagh didn't know her daughter was a witch.

"Hi," Kera greeted the stranger. "I'm Kera, and I'm guessing you're the guy the Kims mentioned?"

He was a short, balding man, possibly Indian, with thick spectacles and a pink shirt rolled up at the sleeves to reveal incredibly hairy forearms. "Yes, hello. I have a book for you. Mr. Kim mentioned that you are a personal friend of his and also a private investigator. He said that a recent case of yours dealt with what might have been ceremonial magic of this type."

Kera frowned. It was safe to assume he was talking about the combination of art thefts and murders committed by the madwoman known as the Alchemist. It had been an unpleasant business, and Kera was happy not to have thought about it for the last week.

"Yes," she replied in a hesitant tone. "May I see the book?"

He began unwrapping the brown paper. "Of course. It's old and rare and valuable, however, so please be careful with it. You may read it, and don't worry about wearing gloves, haha, but please wash your hands and return it to its sleeve when you are done. You may keep it as long as you like, but when you are finished, please mail it back to me. My business address is written on a slip of paper within."

"Sounds reasonable." Kera watched as the book, which had a glossy black cover, emerged. On the front, in Gothic red lettering, were the words *Sacrificial Magic*. Her skin crawled.

"Okay, I get the picture. Yes, this might be, um, useful."

She accepted the parcel and thanked the man again. He clearly wanted to stay and chat and she indulged him for a minute or two, then excused herself on the grounds that she had to prepare for her trip back to the West Coast. That had the virtue of being true.

Kera got back into the car and the Prius glided up the driveway, the gate closing automatically behind them. The man continued to stand there, waving at them.

Chris said, "Seems like a friendly guy."

"I guess." Kera had rewrapped the book before returning to her place in the backseat. "Did Dad want to do anything else today before we leave tomorrow?"

Her mom pulled into the garage, which was big enough to hold four vehicles, though at present, they only had three. "I'm not sure. Perhaps you could ask him? He might be busy, though, and I believe he wanted to have a nice dinner together tonight."

They got out and entered the house through the interior door in the garage, taking their shoes off immediately with the aid of Mrs. MacDonagh's reminder.

Within, Kera's father met them and led them into the sitting room, pouring everyone a cup of coffee and asking how the trip went.

His oversized PC screen displayed what looked like the tail end of a business meeting via video call. Waving his hand at it, Mr. MacDonagh commented, "Ignore that. The important stuff's over with, and I forgot to close it."

Kera's dad was a paradoxical man, strongly built but given to poor posture, with a handsome face combined with small, narrow spectacles that she never thought quite suited him. He gave off a simultaneous impression of nerdiness and masculinity. It occurred to her, with a brief flush of red to her face, that much the same could be said of Chris.

They summed up the trip, which hadn't been all that eventful but pleasant enough. Toward the end, Kera asked her father, "I know you probably won't have time, but I might as well throw it out there. Want to go shooting? We haven't done that together in forever."

Mr. MacDonagh's smile was bittersweet. "I'm sorry, hun, but as you guessed, there won't be time. Are you *able* to go shooting in the People's Republic of California?"

"Yeah, believe it or not," she replied.

Chris raised a hand. "I can confirm. We and her friend Stephanie have been to the range probably half a dozen times in the last couple of months. I even bought a .357 Magnum. Of course, you can't own 'assault weapons' out there, but any gun is better than none."

"True," Mr. MacDonagh agreed. "And with Magnum rounds, you don't need as much capacity, anyway. Just make sure you can hit what you're aiming at and tame the recoil enough to get a follow-up shot if need be. Kera, are you still a Glock fangirl?"

"Yep," she stated. "Though these days they have a lot of competition since every company wants to get in on the market for striker-fired polymer pistols. But it's what I'm used to."

Mrs. MacDonagh cringed. "Is it really necessary to talk about guns in so much detail? Ugh. Though I suppose with you being a private eye now, you might have to carry one, Kera. You know that your father and I support you in starting a business, but we hope you're not getting involved in anything too dangerous."

Kera sipped coffee to give herself a second to think of a response. *Oh, you have no idea. Our first attempt at a low-key art theft case turned into hunting down a goddamn serial killer. And that was an improvement over waging war against organized crime.*

Chris covered for her. "Yeah, we solved a case involving a stolen painting. It's impossible to completely avoid danger since, after all, criminals don't like being caught, but we're trying to avoid anything too nasty and also sticking to non-confrontational techniques."

The elder MacDonaghs nodded, satisfied.

Good job. Kera sighed with relief. *He's really getting the hang of saying stuff that sounds reasonable without giving away too much real information.*

She added, "Yes, and Lia and Steph are looking into what our next case will be. I told them to stick to low-risk incidents. We're also trying to avoid sleazy stuff like chasing around people's cheating spouses and whatnot."

They chatted a bit longer about finances and bookkeeping. In the middle of the conversation, Kera caught her mom looking at the brown paper parcel.

"Oh, Kera. What did you need from an occult bookstore? Something to do with your art case?"

Her abdominal muscles tightened. "Uh, yes. Plus, I just have an interest in historical books on weird stuff. It's interesting."

Her mom leaned back, then continued talking. A moment later, Kera got up to use the bathroom. When she returned, her mother had unwrapped the brown paper and was browsing through the book.

Fuck, Kera thought and practically sprinted to the couch. "Hey, now," she began.

Chris held up his hands. "Don't blame me. I suggested waiting until you got back to ask permission, but, well..."

Her dad had gone into the kitchen to check on the roast he had in the oven, so Kera and Chris were on their own.

Mrs. MacDonagh's face was strained and aghast, and her eyes were wide. "Good Lord, Kera, this is horrifying. It includes *diagrams* showing how to perform human sacrifices. When I was younger, there was a big scare over stuff like this, you know. Most people assumed it was just another silly moral panic, but maybe we were wrong. Why on Earth would you want to—"

"*Mom*! I said it was morbid curiosity, okay? Books like this sell for a lot, so if I can resell it at a profit, that's that much more money that can be put into the agency."

Her mother closed the book and put it back in its paper sleeve. "If you say so. But please don't tell me you've gotten yourself involved with a cult or anything like that. You know, California was where the Manson Family—"

Kera snatched the book. "No, nothing like that. I want to make the world a better place. Sometimes it helps to, well, understand the uglier side of life, so you know what you're dealing with."

Chris stood up, and the two of them seized the moment to head upstairs to the guest room, which had formerly been Kera's bedroom.

Once on the second floor, Kera confided, "Honestly, I'm about as squicked out as she is after that crap with the Alchemist. I imagine the Kims meant well, but this," she wiggled the book in the air, "is the *last* thing I want to think about. I was just starting to feel normal again."

"Understandable," he said. "And I'm sorry I didn't physically restrain your mom from picking up the book."

She chuckled. "That would have taken more balls than any man can be reasonably expected to possess."

In the back of her mind, however, her natural curiosity was growing and already threatening to overwhelm her reluctance and revulsion. She wanted to read the book. If her face was going to be rubbed in such scary stuff, she might as well understand it. It never hurt to learn more about new types of magic.

CHAPTER THREE

Chris had already passed out. He had rolled over on his side, facing away from Kera, and was hogging most of the covers, but she didn't mind. Sleep had proven impossible; she was too accustomed to her months-long pattern of being a night owl, and her brain was demanding she satisfy its hunger for info and stimulation.

So as not to disturb her boyfriend, she read by the illumination of a small pocket light. It was barely sufficient, but she made do. The book demanded careful, meticulous attention, anyway. It had been published in 1972 and was written in a somewhat dry, old-fashioned, and long-winded style she would have thought more appropriate to fifty years earlier.

Then again, the knowledge it conveyed was thousands of years old.

The book was framed as a scholarly study that drew upon sources gleaned from all over the world. Ancient traditions practiced in obscure parts of the world. Extinct religions of antiquity. Occult cults that had once been considered more or less legitimate but had since dissolved due to scandal or suppression by the authorities. True-crime cases and individual testimony and hearsay.

As a purely academic work, it was exhaustively and meticulously researched. Quite impressive.

However, it included a wealth of detail on how sacrificial magic was performed, both the more benign varieties that involved offerings of fruit, grain, minerals, or ceremonial objects and the malevolent type that required killing animals or people.

Between the glut of serial killers in the 70s and the "Satanic Panic" of the 80s, Kera wondered if perhaps the book had struggled to find an audience due to the possibility of legal repercussions or at least massive controversy, boycotts, and the like. That might explain its rarity.

She examined an illustration showing a dog tied to a tree, about to be vivisected by a group of hooded figures holding curved knives.

"Charming stuff. Light bedtime reading," she mumbled to herself. Chris did not stir.

To give her eyes a rest from having to read things that didn't illuminate themselves automatically, she set the book down on her nightstand, marked her place with a slip of paper, and picked up her phone. She had no new messages or missed calls, so she opened the Internet and browsed a news site.

Her eyebrows rose. Apparently, there had been a major volcanic eruption in Iceland earlier in the day. One of the active volcanoes that geologists had been keeping an eye on lately had made second-page news here and there for months before finally graduating to the top story once the caldera blew its lid.

Vivid photographs of the scene showed bright reddish-orange lava streaming down the black slopes of the mountain, while above it, dark-blue and ash-colored smoke rose in fuming clouds, setting off lightning storms within their shadowy depths. It was both frightening and beautiful to see as a still image. She wondered if there was video footage.

There was, and watching it, she got a feel for how powerful the Earth was in relation to humans. Even humans with magical powers.

"Damn," she muttered under her breath. "Maybe someone should have sacrificed something to the volcano gods to keep them appeased. A goat, a bag of Skittles, a virgin, or whatever. Might have worked. Stranger things have happened."

As she browsed the comments on the news stories and videos, it occurred to her that she was wasting time and ought instead to be shutting things off, relaxing, and trying to sleep. They needed to be up fairly early, and if she passed out within the next half hour, she could still get a respectable six hours.

Despite feeling groggy from the sleeping pill she'd taken two hours ago, she was still weirdly alert, though. And as long as her mind kept wanting to find external things to focus on, it made sense to go with the volcano story. It made for a nice distraction from the creepy and depressing subject matter of the book.

Then her problem-solving skills—the detective mindset she had been gradually developing since winter and particularly since she had decided to go into business for herself—went into overdrive. The two subjects she had been contemplating began to overlap, leading her to strange and disturbing conclusions.

Her spine went cold. *What if there have been unsolved murders that actually were human sacrifices, whether performed by witches or other people who are batshit crazy? The Alchemist proved that it can and does happen. Probably not often, but it's no longer just an urban legend. Ick, why did I think of that?*

Over the course of the strange current year, experience had taught her that quite a few things most people considered myth were real and true. There were dark secrets buried within the deep fabric of the world or obscured by the fog of time. Based on everything she had learned, it would be farfetched to assume that dark-magical sacrifices *hadn't* used regular disappearance cases as cover.

She put her phone to sleep, then leaned back in the bed and rubbed her eyes as her head sank onto the pillow. There was nothing she could do about all of the world's problems, especially those in the past. She had to get some shut-eye, and once she was back in LA, she could return to work and continue making the planet a better place to live.

No sooner had her eyes drifted shut than they shot back open and she sat upright, snatched her phone, and reopened her mobile browser. She went to the website for Hartford-Brainard Airport, from whence she and Chris were scheduled to depart tomorrow.

"Fuck," she muttered, and Chris stirred beside her. Ignoring him since he didn't fully wake up, she kept reading.

The Icelandic eruption had filled the skies over the North Atlantic region with soot and ash and smoke. It was spreading rapidly and would have a severe effect on visibility by late morning. As a precaution, all flights at the airport—and, Kera guessed, at all the others in the area—were grounded until further notice.

She groaned and blanked the screen once more, turning the phone face-down on her nightstand.

Oh, shitballs, she lamented. *I love my mother and all, but she's going back into acting like, well, she's a private investigator herself who has been tasked with finding out every last detail of what Chris and I have been up to so she can pass judgment on it and then offer "advice" on how everything we're doing is wrong.*

If we have to spend another goddamn week here, I won't be able to get through it without a lot of alcohol. Or some Xanax. Possibly both. Then Mom will start pestering me about having addiction issues.

There had to be another way.

"Stop!" Mother LeBlanc barked in an abrupt tone of irresistible command. "Do not move." She held up a hand, palm facing outward, to emphasize her words.

Ezeudo did as he was told, freezing in place. At first he had thought it might be a trick or a test, an attempt to get him to make a mistake so she could lecture him about developing more fortitude of mind to resist compulsive-voice spells. But it did not take long for him to notice that a spear of molten metal and plasma was hovering in midair about two feet behind him, aimed at his left kidney.

LeBlanc swept her hand aside, and the fiery lance scattered into cooling droplets off to the side. "You need to work on your defenses," she pointed out. "Not all attacks come from where you can see them, regardless of where your opponent may be standing. Let us discuss your progress before we continue."

Frowning, Ezeudo tried to relax. The rush of battle, albeit only sparring, had set the blood to pumping in his temples, and his thoughts raced at warp speed through his skull. He breathed in and out, willing the world around him to slow down.

It didn't help that LeBlanc had used *that* spell to make her point. Three molten javelins much like the one that nearly skewered him had brought James to the brink of death. Ezeudo had been the one to cradle and heal him in the instant after it had happened.

He dismissed the magical shield he had conjured in front of himself and asked, "Was that necessary? I do not wish to be reminded of what happened last week."

"Yes," LeBlanc asserted, "it *was*, to ensure you grasp the importance of keeping yourself alive. I am not trying to mock you or imply that I somehow blame you for what happened to James. You were the one who saved his life. But I am definitely trying to scare you into improving your combat abilities."

Ezeudo flexed his hands and rolled his head around on his neck, continuing the gradual process of relaxation. "I understand.

But if I am honest, I ask that you not do that again. It is all still fresh in my memory. I need nothing to remind me."

They stood in the center of the backyard at Samantha's second house, where they had remained for the last seven days. Thus far, the Orthodoxy did not seem to have tracked them to their new sanctuary, but there was a growing sense that time was running out. Sooner or later they would be discovered, and their enemies would move in to finish the job they had started at Damian's villa and James' mansion.

The plot of land on which the house stood was nowhere near as large as the grounds of James' vast estate, covering only about two-thirds of an acre. Still, the rear lawn was large enough to make for a decent sparring field. LeBlanc had covered the property with cloaking and deafening spells before they'd begun. Nothing they did would be visible or audible to anyone from the street or from the neighbors' windows.

Ezeudo was tired and hungry. They had been practicing battle magic all morning and into the early afternoon with no more than a couple of five-minute breaks, and he needed rest and replenishment. He said as much, then added, "But before we have lunch, please tell me what you are most concerned about. You know that I *want* to learn. James and Lauren considered me a good student."

"Yes," LeBlanc confirmed, "and they were right. Chief amongst your problems is the simple fact that you have no meaningful experience in combat, least of all the kind thaumaturges and witches engage in. Yes, I recall you saying that you sometimes carried a handgun while doing aid work in war zones, but it is not the same thing."

The tall Nigerian grimaced. "I suppose that is true. I have never been involved in fighting. I try to *avoid* fighting and convince others to do the same. I hate violence."

LeBlanc gave him a soft, sad smile that was surprisingly full of sympathy. "Most of the time, and under most conditions, that is a good thing. But when others are determined to bring violence to us, regardless of how we feel about it, we must be prepared for it. To fend it off if nothing else."

On some level, Ezeudo still had not accepted that it was *necessary* for the council and the Orthodoxy to fight one another to the death. His whole career had been oriented toward ending wars and conflicts and bringing aid and relief to the people who were not involved in the fighting but suffered from collateral damage, artificial famines and pestilence, and other such horrors.

When he had first agreed to accompany James and LeBLanc to America, they had seemed like odd but ultimately reasonable people. The rest of the council, likewise. And the United States was a more peaceful country than many others.

But since they had received the challenge from the Orthodoxy, the rhetoric the council had been using had reminded him of the hopeless, fatalistic arguments made by those responsible for the suffering he had spent years trying to ease. They *presumed* that an endless cycle of retribution and counter-retribution was inevitable and created a self-fulfilling prophecy by so doing.

However, he had not been personally involved in the wars or feuds he had overseen. No one had ever been looking to kill *him;* at worst, he had been threatened for meddling in their affairs. Now, the Eastern European coven regarded him as part of the council and would seek his death alongside those of the others. There was no reasoning with them. He had seen how ruthless they were.

It disturbed him that despite his efforts to resist such ugly thinking, he was starting to understand why some of the people he had counseled had been so willing to fight, to die, and to kill.

Ezeudo swallowed the spit building up in his mouth. "I am willing to do what I must to protect myself and my friends, though I do not like it. The thought of taking these people's lives, even if they would do the same, gives me no sense of pleasure or satisfaction."

"Again," said LeBlanc, "that is commendable. But your willingness to do it, regardless, is now required. I am sorry it has come to this, but the Orthodoxy will not stop until every last one of us meets the same fate as Damian and Zacharia. And though I hate to say it, perhaps James as well."

Her student shook his head. "I would like to check on him. Samantha has been doing more than she should. Others should take up the duty of healing some of the time."

He paused, then added, "Are we *certain* that they mean to pursue us and hunt us down? Would it not be possible for us to go underground, as I believe the expression goes? They might be satisfied with having killed two members and taken over our chief gathering spot. They can declare themselves supreme and dismiss the rest of us as unimportant fugitives."

The cold, hard look that set into LeBlanc's eyes surprised him. He knew beyond any doubt that the answer he was about to receive would *not* be what he wanted to hear.

"No," she stated. "That is not an option. It is not realistic, it is not probable, and it is not even being considered. And there are two reasons for this. One, you seem to have some grasp of. The other has not yet fully impressed itself upon you, though you have seen or heard of the evidence of both."

Ezeudo was not shocked. That there might still be a chance to sue for peace, if only a wretched sort of peace, had seemed a slim hope. "Tell me, then."

The Creole woman extended her hand and raised a finger. "First of all, the Orthodoxy's track record indicates that *total elimination* of the competition is their standard operating procedure. They said as much in their challenge—that to back off would cause them to lose face and appear weak, which might invite similar challenges from other covens. If they have not been in a hurry to crush the rest of us, it is only because they are busy with something else. Quite possibly, something which will improve their chances to destroy us. A temporary halt on their part is not the same thing as a suggestion that they want a truce."

"Gang logic," Ezeudo grumbled. "The thinking of warlords."

"Exactly. We may abstain from such a barbaric worldview, but they are under no such compunctions." LeBlanc raised another finger. "Second, what the Orthodoxy seeks is dominion over all of North America. This would mean that not only the various minor covens but the *entire population* of the continent would be subject to their way of doing things. I will assume that it is unnecessary for me to elaborate."

Ezeudo hung his head. "There is no higher authority to restrain them. You are right. They would have free rein to act as they please, so I suppose it is different from when one country attacks another or mistreats its own population and must then face pressure or sanctions from the international community. Or a national government, in the case of feuds between criminals."

LeBlanc nodded. "Yes. The only way to expose them to 'outside pressure' would be to unveil the entire magical underworld to the general public, and that would put *all* of us at enormous risk. Even if the human authorities were to grasp that we are far better stewards of the magical disciplines than the Orthodoxy are, the public outcry might well convince them to pass sweeping measures to either suppress magic altogether or to bring it under the tight control of government forces."

Rubbing his chin, Ezeudo could find no good counterargument. "So, then. The dozen of us, and the few dozen of them, must agree to kill one another to spare the rest of society the pain that would come with their being involved."

"Basically, yes," LeBlanc shrugged. "Well, if we win, we will *continue* to spare the rest of society. Barring the occasional depowerment of rogue casters or memory-wipe, of course. But it's entirely possible that the Orthodoxy will prey upon the general public for their own benefit. On that cheery note, shall we head inside and have lunch?"

Ezeudo strode forward, and side by side, they strolled back into the house.

Those of the council who were in better condition were not present. Either they were scouting the surrounding area for threats or rumors of threats, or in other cases, they had gone shopping for various useful supplies or paid visits to the lesser covens closest to eastern Pennsylvania to explain to them what had transpired.

There had been a healthy debate as to the wisdom of splitting up since the Orthodoxy might be lying in wait to pick them off one by one. Ultimately, they had decided that there was little choice if they wished to accomplish everything that needed to be done over the course of a mere week or two.

Besides Ezeudo and LeBlanc, the only other people in the house were Hugh Buchanan, Samantha, and James.

Hugh was sitting in an armchair reading a book on military tactics. He lowered it and looked up as the pair came in. "Ah. How did it go?"

LeBlanc reported, "Reasonably well, but Ezeudo has more to learn. He's a committed and diligent student with substantial magical potential, so he certainly *can,* but he lacks certain types of tactical awareness, as well as the necessary kill-or-be-killed mindset. Ezeudo, pardon me for speaking about you in the third person while you are standing right next to me."

The Nigerian spread his hands. "It is all right. And yes, what she has said sounds accurate. I am not a fighter by nature, but LeBlanc has convinced me that there is no escaping the battles to come."

Hugh made a low sound in his throat and inclined his head. "That is a fair assessment. I briefly saw the end of your match out the window. Always watch your flank, young man. Danger can come from any direction."

Ezeudo nodded. He was forty years old and did not think of himself as "young," but then again, Hugh looked at least seventy and, given how long thaumaturgists seemed to live, may have been far older.

"How is James?" Ezeudo asked. "And for that matter, how is Samantha?"

Hugh gestured vaguely toward the guest room. "They are getting by. See for yourself if you wish."

LeBlanc went into the kitchen to prepare lunch while Ezeudo headed for the first-floor bedroom. Within, he found Samantha leaning over James, who lay unconscious under the covers. It took him a moment to realize that she was engrossed in a healing spell.

Reaching out with his expanded consciousness, Ezeudo realized that she was faltering. The combination of stress, general exhaustion, and giving too much of her own energy toward the charm was pushing her to the brink of collapse.

Samantha, he said in his inner voice, linking his mind and his power aura to hers, *I am here. I'm somewhat tired too, but allow me to help a little.*

She did not respond in words, but he felt her gratitude as she drew upon his strength to stabilize herself. Then, with an obvious pang of regret and reluctance, she pulled away from James, leaving him in his current state.

Ezeudo moved his consciousness to the sleeping man. James was still weak. He seemed to be doing better, but his recovery was taking longer than anyone had hoped.

Withdrawing his mind, Ezeudo took Samantha's arm as she stood up straight. "Thank you. I am no specialist in healing. Crystal is our best, and even she is not a master. The true healers are among the rarest of all thaumaturges. Destruction is far easier."

For a second, it looked like she might cry, but she swallowed a lump in her throat, brushed back her long hair, and got herself under control. "I don't know that we're going to make it. Last week, we lost our strongest position. They overwhelmed *all of us at once.*"

Ezeudo walked with her back into the sitting room, where Hugh still sat and read. Without looking up, Hugh mentioned, "I will take over the next round of healing this evening. I've been idle all day, and I'm sure Crystal has had other things to spend her energy on."

They thanked him and sat down on the couch.

Ezeudo wanted to say something, but it was difficult to find the right words in English. He was relatively fluent in it but less so than in his native tongue or French, which he had spoken while living in Geneva.

After a moment, he went with, "It is not over yet, Samantha. James is improving slowly, but he *is* improving. And their victory at James' house has perhaps made them overconfident. It may take longer for this conflict to end than we wanted, but the end is not yet here."

Hugh nodded. "Agreed."

From the kitchen, LeBlanc called, "Agreed."

Samantha sat back and breathed in deeply. "It's for the best that you all are less emotional than I am, I guess. I only hope you're right."

CHAPTER FOUR

Kera was in desperate need of fresh air and exercise. In a way, she reflected, it might have been good that their flight had been canceled since it gave her an excuse to tramp around her parents' expansive yard. Otherwise, she would have been cooped up first in a car, then on a bench at the airport, and finally in a seat on the plane, forced to sit still all day long. Barring the usual mad rush to the correct terminal between layovers, of course.

"Hey," Chris called. "Slow down. You said you wanted to go for a *walk*, not a jog."

She had increased her pace to a fast trot. Chris was not exaggerating much. "Fine." She sighed and reduced her speed to a brisk amble. Once Chris caught up with her, he was able to keep pace easily enough. She'd had a head start on him was all, and he was distracted by his phone.

Kera inquired, "Any luck? I'm guessing no since I kinda suspect we're not the only ones who got screwed over."

He exhaled, his breath coming out in tandem with a ragged sound of disgust, and shook his head. He clicked the phone's screen off and dropped it into his pocket. "Nope. The two times I've gotten through, I got an automatic message followed by five or six solid minutes of elevator music and 'we appreciate your call' stuff. Every other attempt, all I'm getting is a beeping sound. The phone lines must be jammed with endless numbers of people thinking *they're* the only ones who got screwed over."

"Yeah," Kera muttered, "probably. I checked the website, and it was the same type of shit. Sent them an email, which I'll be lucky to get a reply to two days from now. There's a banner message about how everyone is SOL thanks to that goddamn volcano."

She glanced at the sky. It was a cloudy day, and somehow it did look darker and hazier than normal. Furthermore, there was an odd smell in the air. She could not specifically recall an incident within her own short lifetime of an eruption throwing off weather patterns all over the globe, but she knew they had happened in the past.

She launched a lazy, absent-minded kick at a clump of sod that had worked loose from the rest of the lawn. "Just our luck. It'll probably be at *least* a full day before they have so much as an update on when we *might* be able to reschedule."

Chris rolled his shoulders and quipped, "Well, hey, you have a nice house. Your parents are pretty okay, for the most part. And if all else fails, we can cram a bunch of day trips into whatever extra time we have to spend here, justifying them by saying that we don't want to impose on them because they probably don't want us underfoot. That sort of thing."

Kera chortled. "Yeah, you may be right. I don't like the thought of leaving Lia and Steph holding the bag by themselves back home, though. Ugh. In the time we're wasting figuring this crap out, we would be halfway back to Cali if we drove."

Chris tapped his lips. "I mean, we *could* consider renting a car. A cross-country road trip would be interesting, but it would also take a long-ass time and potentially be pretty expensive."

Before they could discuss it further, Mr. MacDonagh appeared around the corner of the house and put a hand beside his mouth. "Hey!" he called. "Lunch is served. Come and get it."

For fun, Kera shouted back, "What are we having? We reserve the right to refuse service if the quality of the cuisine isn't up to our standards."

Her dad responded, "Hell if I know. There's no way to find out except by coming in to inspect it yourselves. If it should come to pass that lunch fails your exalted expectations, we can negotiate terms from there. Your mother was the one who made it, not me."

Chris laughed. "Do you two always talk to each other like this?"

"Sometimes." She grabbed his arm. "Come on. I was so busy being pissed off that I forgot how hungry I am. Mom isn't a big eater, though, so she might have skimped on the sustenance."

Fortunately, the meal turned out to be perfectly sufficient, consisting of club sandwiches and a nice pasta salad with plenty of veggies and dressing.

"Ah," Kera said, nodding with approval. "It would appear that the help has not disappointed us. My compliments."

Mrs. MacDonagh squinted at her. "Kera, don't talk to me that way, even if you're joking. I could have had the *actual* help prepare the meals, you know, but I gave them the weekend off specifically so I could cook for you myself before you head home. On that note, were you able to get through to the airport?"

As the four of them sat down in the dining room with their food, Chris repeated to the elder MacDonaghs what he had reported to Kera five minutes ago.

Kera's dad shook his head. "Typical. Well, volcanic eruptions aren't exactly common, but it's always *something*, I swear. If it wasn't a volcano, it would be a plague of zombies, a hail of toads, an alien invasion, or something like that."

"So," her mom extrapolated, "does that mean you'll be staying until you can book a flight? I hope you're not planning to *drive* across the continent. Yes, road trips can be fun, but there's an awful lot that can go wrong. Especially in," she lowered her voice to a portentous hush, "*Flyover Country.*"

Kera winced. "Mom, you do realize that that's sort of like how the British aristocracy used to talk about Ireland, right?" Her family was mostly of Irish descent, so the choice of example was not a coincidence.

"Oh, don't be silly," Mrs. MacDonagh shot back, though she didn't bother to respond to the criticism. "Anyway, I'm glad you're enjoying your lunch. I have to run out on a couple of errands, though. I'll be back in time for dinner. Please think long and hard about how you're going to deal with the present situation and let me know. Take care."

With that, she took her leave. Kera was of two minds. By now, she had spent enough time in her mother's presence that being free of her came as a mild relief. On the other hand, her mother had gone out of her way to make a tasty and hand-prepared meal just for the sake of doing something nice for her.

Families are weird, she thought. *I wonder if there's any other form of human organization that can breed the same simultaneous intensity of both love and annoyance. K-Pop fandom, maybe? Shit.*

Chris snapped her out of her ruminations with a suggestion. "Hey, I thought of something. We could take a train. Might be faster and cheaper than driving, and we wouldn't have to wait around for the sky gods to cooperate with modern aeronautical technology."

Kera looked up and saw her dad, who was still munching on the remainder of a sandwich, raise his eyebrows. "That might work," he agreed. "I haven't taken a train in years, so I can't offer much advice on how the system works now, but it's worth looking into. You'd be able to have a nice romantic cross-country trip, minus the hassle of driving yourselves."

"Right." Chris straightened a little, perhaps with pride that Kera's father seemed to approve of him. "I've never seen most of Flyover Country. It ought to be an adventure."

Kera smiled. "I keep forgetting that some people are actually *from* California, originally. Well, when I first went from here to there, I drove myself. Most of the way, I took what used to be Route 66, which ran from Chicago to LA. It was illuminating, sometimes boring, and kind of fun. Honestly, though, a lot of the middle of the country is just small towns with a Walmart, a McDonald's, a couple diners and gift shops, a grain elevator or factory or something, and that's about it. People are mostly pretty nice as long as you don't act like a stuck-up prick and use some basic street smarts. The scenery is nice and variable."

Chris nodded. "California has so much landscape diversity that it's easy to get spoiled thinking that you don't really *need* to see other places. Well, besides Oregon."

"Right," Kera conceded. "Nothing quite like the Great Plains, though. Oh, and what's really weird is when you come to a city that never shows up in movies but is, like, surprisingly big. I had no idea how massive Oklahoma City was. I thought it would be a small town. Nope. Skyscrapers. Smaller than LA or New York, but still."

Mr. MacDonagh, following along with the convo, was rubbing his chin in thought. "I'm not sure if there's a rail line that goes along what was formerly known as Route 66, but, again, it's worth checking on. There are some others that go through the mountains in Colorado and such if I recall. Plenty of interesting stuff out there."

Kera smiled. "I think we've made our decision. Well, unless it turns out there aren't any trains available either. But if there *are*, then I vote yes."

Chris forked pasta salad into his mouth and said around it, "Seconded."

They spent a moment finishing their meal before Kera's father added, "Your mom will probably worry about railway accidents based on some freak disaster that occurred fifty years ago, or she'll try to pressure you into taking whatever the 'best' option is, but I don't think she'll be too upset. Don't wait too long to try to find routes and tickets, though."

"We won't," Kera replied. "Chris is on it, or he will be momentarily, I'm sure. He's good at stuff like that. He's been a huge help with the agency so far, especially with all the boring research stuff that I hate. He and Lia handle most of that side of things."

Her dad nodded, though something in his demeanor had changed. He was suddenly a bit more similar to his wife. "I wasn't sure if Chris was an employee of the agency. If that's the case— and don't take this the wrong way, either of you—keep in mind that things don't always work out between men and women and that personal matters and business are best kept separate. *Capice?*"

Kera didn't like the implication of what he'd said, but she tried to remind herself that he was probably offering "general" wisdom rather than forecasting that their relationship would fail. "Yeah, I get it."

Chris didn't look overly pleased either, but Mr. MacDonagh pressed on to other subjects before they could dwell on it. "Anyway, it sounds like you're doing the smart thing in delegating tasks to the people who can handle them best. Still, you've been somewhat vague about the whole operation. So, Kera, what exactly is it that *you* do if not research? And since detective work, as I understand it, *is* mostly research, why did you pick this particular field?"

Willing herself not to scowl, Kera tried to think of a good response. Generally, she got along better with her father than with her mother, but sometimes, he could be just as much of a pain in the ass. However, he usually asked questions out of a combination of curiosity and concern, and that was all. The element of judgment that underlay most of her mom's questions was mercifully absent.

It irritated her that both of them couldn't just trust her and be done with it, though.

"I do whatever *else* needs to be done," she stated. "That's all. Someone has to do it. Look at the crap that keeps happening in the world. I'm not going to leave it for other people to deal with. It isn't right."

She surprised herself by springing up from her chair and walking out of the dining room. As she stomped down the back hall, she could faintly hear the two men conversing.

"Don't worry," Mr. MacDonagh commented. "As you've probably learned by now, she gets like that sometimes. Stay here. I'll go talk to her."

Chris replied, "You're the expert. Though yeah, I learn more all the time."

Kera scowled. She didn't want anyone to talk to her. She couldn't put her finger on why she was suddenly so agitated since her father hadn't been abrasive or anything. It was something else, something that went way beyond her petty family drama.

Though she knew that her dad would succeed in tracking her down within the next minute, she nevertheless continued her trot to the rear of the house and out the back door onto the lawn. The sky looked a shade or two darker. Birds were singing, though.

Mr. MacDonagh approached at a steady pace, his footfalls gentle despite his size. "Kera, dear," he began in a mild and neutral tone of voice, "what's wrong?"

Again, she was certain he simply wanted to ascertain the situation and then adapt to it, offering good-natured suggestions along the way. It was how he ran his businesses: staying informed of everything that was going on, avoiding dropping the hammer of blame on anyone unless strictly necessary, and constantly adjusting things as needed to maximize the overall performance of the organization. It seemed to work well.

Kera exhaled and looked down at the grass. Her confession was inevitable, but she made a show of delaying it by a couple seconds before she spoke.

"It's not you," she elaborated. "It's not Mom, either. Or Chris. He's great. It was our first case. It ended up being, um, how do I put this? Really surprising, and not in a good way. I didn't want to tell you because I thought you'd freak out. Well, Mom, anyway. It wasn't very...pleasant. I'm still dealing with it, I guess."

He didn't respond right away in case she had more to say. When she kept quiet, he said, "Mmm, I see." He was still behind her, and she continued looking at the ground, but in her mind's eye, she could see him adjusting his glasses and imagine the look of concern on his face. "You chose a business that isn't always going to *be* pleasant. You've never been one to take the easy path. Doesn't mean I don't care about your feelings, of course. But a private detective in a major city won't have the luxury of doing nothing but finding lost kittens."

"Yeah," she admitted. "I knew that going in. I was, uh, *partially* prepared. I might be a rich girl, but I've been around the block a few times, and I'm not sheltered. Still, we thought it was *only* an art theft. It wasn't. It ended up," she hesitated and took a deep breath, "also being a murder case."

Her father approached another couple of steps. "Well, that does sound unpleasant, as you put it. If you want to talk about it, you can. If not, then I understand that, too."

Kera was torn. She felt as though wangsting about her feelings would be a waste of time. Her dad had better things to do than stand there and listen to her complain about a case she had inflicted on herself, essentially.

But he *wanted* to help, and sharing the pain that had built up within her might lighten the burden she had to carry into whatever the next case ended up being.

"It's pretty fucked-up," she murmured. "The art thief was also a serial killer. Not a very prolific one, but still, she was nuts. I spent a little too much time trying to get into her headspace, and that's not a place I wanted to be. Plus, we were trying to help the police on the side, and we ended up seeing one of the bodies. It was frickin' awful. We weren't expecting anything like that when we took on the case. We figured it was only about a painting, and that was all."

Mr. MacDonagh came up beside her and laid a hand on her shoulder. "You said you solved the case," he pointed out.

"Yeah." Kera swallowed and rubbed her nose. "We did. We cornered her, and she, um, killed herself. We were able to deliver the evidence to the cops, so they managed to wrap it all up, so we stopped her from murdering anyone else. God, it was creepy, though. She..." Kera paused. "She was trying to copy the Black Dahlia murder if you've heard of that."

She had almost said that the Alchemist *was* the killer of Elizabeth Smart, which was true, but most people weren't ready for that information. It raised too many questions as to how the same person was able to commit crimes seventy-five years apart. The Alchemist, if only in a limited capacity, had possessed the gift, or enough of it, anyway, to extend her lifespan.

Kera was willing to confess to the ugly side of her chosen profession, but telling her dad about the existence of magic was still a bridge too far.

"Oh, dear." The man sighed. "You know, I think I saw a news sidebar about that. No idea my little girl was involved. I can't help worrying. I'm proud of you for putting a stop to it, but if you decide you don't want to deal with things like that again, no one will think less of you."

She turned her head, facing him for the first time during the conversation. "I don't really *want* to, but I can't walk away. I'm one of the people who can make a difference and put a stop to things like that. I proved as much when we caught her. Like, how can I potentially *let* innocent people suffer when my efforts might be the only thing standing in the way?"

Her dad adjusted his glasses. "Sweetheart," he began, and there was nothing patronizing in the way he said it, "all the problems in the world aren't yours to solve. Bad things will always happen.

Don't get me wrong, I love your good heart. There's nothing wrong with wanting to do what you can to help, but don't let all this consume you. I know you worry about getting roped into a conversation with your mother when you phone home, but seriously, if you ever need to talk, call me. I'll find a way to make time for you."

Kera let out a short cough to cover the single sob that escaped her throat and wiped away the moisture that had begun to form at the corners of her eyes. "Okay. I will. Thanks, Dad."

They hugged.

"And," she added, "next time, I'll try to get a case that's less goddamn disturbing."

CHAPTER FIVE

When every last thing of value had been collected and shipped off to the coven's growing treasure trove, and when the surviving members of the assault force had recovered, Anezka ordered them to raze the mansion to the ground.

Vassily, the tall, gaunt-faced warlock who had commanded the rear strike team and who sat beside Anezka on the Orthodoxy's elder leadership board, was the only one to dare voice a complaint or objection.

"It seems a pity," he opined. "A fine house, old by American standards, which gives it somewhat more grace and class than is typical of this country. Have we considered instead taking it over to use as our chief headquarters in the eastern United States? Occupying it ourselves would be a lingering insult to the council."

The two of them stood on the front lawn, watching the estate as the last of the witches who had lodged within filed out. Overhead, the sky was shrouded with dim, sooty clouds. A volcano had erupted in Iceland, and its effects were being felt all across the Northern Hemisphere.

"No," Anezka snapped. "Burn it. Leave no plank of wood unconsumed and no stone nor brick standing atop another. Should they try to return to this place, they must have no hope of ever resuming their old ways or position. We will find another place to lodge ourselves."

As Vassily responded with a grim nod and a raspy set of instructions to the lesser troops, Anezka reflected upon the miserable old church she had seized and converted in Los Angeles. Too many senior and powerful witches grew overfond of luxury and were unwilling to work their way up from the bottom. Anezka held such people in contempt.

The church in California was being restored as they spoke and would be splendid in time. Residing someplace humble did not trouble her. Her authority was not vested in buildings but in herself and in the awesome and terrible aura of power that surrounded her. She was the grandmistress of the world's most powerful coven no matter where she went, slept, or stood.

Her views formed part of her loathing for the council. Like many Americans, they were fat, lazy, soft, and complacent. Their wealth was probably less than that of the Orthodoxy, yet they chose to rule the continent from a virtual palace one of their younger members had inherited via the accomplishments of his forebears.

Anezka smirked as her followers spread out in a circle to commence the destruction of the ridiculous edifice. The Americans liked to pontificate about "hard work" and "individual accomplishment," yet their magical elite resembled the Western European aristocracy at its worst. She prided herself, meanwhile, on having risen to her position from the lowliest of Ukrainian peasant stock.

And over a coven composed largely of Russians, no less. Of course, it pleased her to promote people of other nationalities to high positions when she could, though ultimately such matters were decided by merit and utility. She did not play favorites; she awarded good to the good and bad to the bad.

"Now," she commanded, extending two black-nailed fingers.

In unison, the witches launched streams of fire and lightning at the mansion, creating a conflagration that possibly rivaled that of the recent volcanic event. Others summoned Wind Shields that contained the blaze while also disassembling the walls, furniture, and other fixtures. Casters who specialized in kinetic spells targeted large objects with projections of pure force that shattered them, which were further annihilated by the heat and wind and chaos.

One minute later, the Lovecraft estate, the seat of the North American Council's shattered power, had ceased to exist. It might as well have been struck by an atomic bomb. Even the cellars were ravaged, having been hollowed out by fire and then buried by collapsing detritus.

Anezka took a step back and breathed out through her nose. "Good." She turned around and beckoned. "Let us depart."

Once the battle had been won, she had dispatched a handful of her more persuasive subordinates to place compulsion spells on the various members of a transportation company that had sent a bevy of trucks to cart off the council's valuables. One tractor-trailer had arrived at the edge of the estate's grounds.

The various low-ranking soldiers climbed into the back. There was enough room for all of them, barely. For the lieutenants and elders, a fleet of cars and vans awaited.

Anezka took the passenger seat in one of the vans. Her ride would be more comfortable than that of the novices but hardly luxurious. In the driver's seat beside her sat a younger witch named Sergeyeva who had demonstrated an especial talent for scrying and reconnaissance.

"Grandmistress," she opened, "it is a pleasure to have you ride alongside me. You had asked me to find a suitable location for us to gather. I have prepared a hotel in Poughkeepsie," she struggled to pronounce the name, "which is not terribly far from here. It should serve us for the time being."

Anezka adjusted her hair, maintaining the chilly and aloof demeanor she generally used with lower-to-middle-ranking members. "Yes, good. Is there any sign of the surviving council yet?"

Sergeyeva turned the key to start the engine, and there was an obvious cooling of her aura, an influx of fear and tension. "No, madam. Well, yes, but so far, we cannot determine which trails are legitimate. They created false ones leading off in all directions to deceive us. One is clearly useless and has been stricken from the map, but the others require further investigation."

Anezka's nails drummed on the armrest of her seat as the fleet worked its way to the estate's private street, then rejoined the public road system of New York state.

"I take it we have people working on this?"

The younger witch replied in the affirmative, and Anezka nodded. If by some chance one of her subordinates was responsible for a major failure of attention or diligence, they would be punished, of course. But she herself had given the order for the assault team to remain at the mansion rather than immediately pursuing their foes.

If she were to attempt to fob off the responsibility on a lieutenant, it might make her look weak or petty. Instead, she would assume most of the blame while shrugging it off and focusing on what to do next.

Which was finding the survivors and terminating their lives. Most of the coven's resources would have to be dedicated to the job. A small contingent ought to be sufficient, meanwhile, for beginning to exercise authority over the minor local witches scattered across the continent.

Two hours later, all of the important leadership—their senior council, as well as a smattering of upper-middle managers and captains and highly-trained specialists—had convened in a conference room at the hotel Sergeyeva had commandeered.

They cloaked the room from physical intrusion, muffled all sound, and blocked it from any attempts at scrying. Then they passed around glasses as Anezka opened a bottle of expensive vodka, pouring herself two fingers' worth before handing it to Vassily to her right.

"We have won, for now," she announced, raising the glass. "Let us celebrate, but with the understanding that our work is far from done. The blow we dealt to the council has destroyed their legitimacy. As long as they continue to live, they will appear weak and incompetent by contrast with us, but they must not continue to live much longer. Crushing them utterly is our goal."

Words of assent went around the table as the others quaffed their drinks. Then Anezka opened the discussion to the others, allowing them to contribute their opinions and unique knowledge. Some had access to channels of information that others did not.

Vassily explained, "We have been observing the council for a long time, what with our spies having infiltrated the United States months before we made our initial incursion into Los Angeles during the ill-fated expedition to capture that rogue witch."

Anezka's hands curled into claws on the table's surface. "I do not enjoy being reminded of that, but Vassily is correct to bring it up. We not only failed to either recruit or destroy that girl—Kera, I believe—but we also lost Pavla. She was our finest tracker, and her services would be more useful than ever now."

Two of the captains chimed in with halfhearted reports that Pavla, too, had effectively disappeared. Anezka waved them off. If the Orthodoxy were to prioritize the matter, they could succeed quickly enough, but for the time being, the council was a more pressing problem.

Vassily continued his summary. "Our nemeses were, of

course, concentrated in this region. All of their primary residences were located within perhaps a four hours' drive of the Lovecraft estate. We have checked all of them, including the ruins of Diaz's villa; the council has fled to none. They are not entirely stupid. Wherever they have gone, it is somewhere less obvious. Two of them seem to have connections to the West Coast."

Anezka added, "And the LeBlanc woman is from New Orleans. If she and the others can escape there, finding them will become extremely difficult. There is magic in that place that we don't understand. The strange cultural stew that has formed there over the last three centuries has French roots but is otherwise too far removed from the European tradition for us to penetrate."

A captain reported, "We have two people watching New Orleans. More would be better if we can spare them, but if LeBlanc were to return there, it would likely create ripples that we would notice."

"Yes," Anezka agreed. "We should form an impenetrable wall around that city. Every other possible point of egress from the Eastern Seaboard must be blocked as well. We do not have the personnel to watch each individual road, and it would be unwise to spread our forces too thin, but surely we possess the power and the creativity to prevent them from escaping."

The icy undertone of threat had crept into her voice, and no one failed to notice.

Anezka raised her hand and gestured toward the senior council's newest member. "Milena. Thank you for leaving behind your work. How fresh is the blood in the fountain? We will need extra augmentation for the work ahead."

Milena, a petite and beautiful woman with short light-brown hair and pale gray eyes, was unperturbed by the question. "It will need to be replenished by tomorrow evening, Grandmistress."

"Do so," Anezka said. "The enhancements must be distributed

to every member of the coven before we fan out to begin the hunt. As we have all heard, flights are grounded by the eruption, so conventional air travel is not an option. Magical flight may be used as a last resort. Avoid it if other options are available."

No one protested. Witchcraft had unlocked the secrets of flight long before the Wright brothers, but it was a difficult and risky business.

Milena suggested, "Trains might be a good option. The United States does not rely upon them as much as some nations, but there is a functioning rail system that would allow several of us to spread across much of the country in little time."

Anezka didn't hesitate to approve the notion, but she allowed the others to discuss the merits and demerits of it. Their main problem was, of course, the bald fact that they had no real idea where the council was. So far, anyway. Sergeyeva and her team might be able to narrow it down in another day or two.

After another half-hour of debate, it was decided that approximately half of their overall personnel would remain in the Northeast. They would use all available intelligence to form a noose and gradually tighten it with the goal of both cutting the council off from escape and flushing them out if they were trying to hide.

The remaining half of their forces would disperse throughout the rest of the US as well as select locations in southeastern Canada and northern Mexico, just to be safe. The focus, though, would be on two particular locations. New Orleans was one.

"The other logical choice," Anezka concluded, "is Los Angeles. Josiah Kane seems to have lived there some decades ago, and Lovecraft and LeBlanc visited the place shortly before we arrived ourselves. Milena, you will go to LA with a small but elite group. Take the fountain with you. Yes, you might have to make do without a proper sacrificial table, but the fountain is the important thing."

Milena covered her surprise with a mask of stoicism. "Yes, Anezka." She had not expected to be deployed into the field, but she was not one to complain, let alone fail. "What exactly is my mission?"

A faint sly smile stretched Anezka's lips. "Find and kill that girl Kera, the rogue witch Pavla failed to acquire for us. She has far more power than most of your subjects, so sacrificing *her* would provide us with a tremendous boost in our efforts against the council. Further, she is a continued thorn in our side and could potentially become a rallying point for fringe casters who might seek to resist us. Oh, also, if you should stumble upon Pavla, kill her, or capture her to send back to us. That is a secondary priority, however."

Milena bowed her head in deference. "Of course, madam. We still have the notes as to Kera's location and activities?"

"Yes," said the grandmistress. "I will make them available to you shortly. Do not underestimate the girl. She overcame Pavla *and* Olina, though Olina barely counts in the great scheme of things. However, it has been months since that occurred. Kera may well have let her guard down. If she has forgotten us, she will learn that we have *not* forgotten her."

Anezka was glad she had thought of sacrificing Kera at the last instant. By tying the coven's revenge against the girl to their war against the Orthodoxy, she avoided appearing as though she were trying to save face by succeeding at the smaller task of finishing Kera off while success at the larger goal of overcoming the council yet eluded them.

Of course, Milena would be greatly inconvenienced by having to drag a fountain onto a train, but she would undoubtedly find a way to manage. There were reasons why Anezka had promoted her to so high a rank.

"Now," Anezka went on, "let us consider a psychic broadcast of today's earlier events, something obvious enough that the council will know that we *want* them to know. A repetitious image of the Lovecraft house being destroyed, combined with the death curse striking Zacharia McConnell."

Vassily asked, "Shall it be framed as a message or as a nightmare?"

"Nightmare," Anezka declared. "The more traumatic and humiliating, the better."

CHAPTER SIX

There was something odd, Kera decided, about an above-ground train station. She had taken the subway several times in New York City. It was practically an institution there, one which had a curious grungy, screeching, claustrophobic charm to it that contributed to the legendary misery, anger, bitterness, and generalized hatred of life all true New Yorkers shared.

But regular trains that ran on tracks under the open sky rather than beneath the streets of cities were something with which she had no experience. It was easy to forget that they existed in an age where everyone used planes or cars—or motorcycles, in Kera's case. Or for those who were truly desperate, buses.

"Kera," Mrs. MacDonagh began. Her voice had *that* tone to it, so her daughter braced herself for the worst. "Did the two of you rent a *private* compartment? It could be extremely awkward if you had to share sleeping quarters with total strangers while crammed into a small metal box, you know. Not to mention dangerous. You never know what sorts of people will—"

"Yes," Kera interrupted her. "We're rich, remember? We paid the extra out-the-ass amount to get our own room."

Chris added, "Though if she needs extra space, I can always get out and jog alongside the train for a while."

For some reason, Mrs. MacDonagh found that hilarious, and she waved a hand at Chris while cracking up. "Oh, isn't that gallant of you!"

Mr. MacDonagh added, "That was a Dad Joke, you realize. Clearly he is a man after my own heart."

Kera blushed but smiled. "It was nice visiting you guys, honestly, and being home again. Well, LA is my home now, and I don't plan on changing that, but you know what I mean."

Around them, there was a murmur that became a bustle as the crowd all moved toward the edge of the platform. Their train was approaching.

Kera's mom approached her daughter and hugged and kissed her. "It was wonderful having you back, sweetie. I know I ask too many questions, but I get curious about what you're up to. I only want the best for you, of course, but you seem to be doing well enough without me. You're growing into a lovely young woman and taking care of yourself. And I'm glad that you seem to have good taste in men."

"Thanks," said Chris.

Kera pretended to glare at him, then looked at her mom again. "Well, it's nice to know you're, um, proud of me. I'll do my best to keep up the good work."

"Remember," the older woman added, "these days, it's considered preferable for women to be established in their careers before they worry about marriage and children, but since you're doing a fine job of establishing yourself, well, there's no reason to delay things excessively. I'll be happy to come out to California for your wedding and first baby shower."

Kera's jaw dropped as half the goodwill they'd established evaporated in an instant. "Mom! What the hell?"

Fortunately, Chris was busy saying goodbye to her dad.

"Well," Chris began, shaking the older man's hand, "as Kera

already said, it's been fun. I'll do my best to take care of her, but sometimes it's more like letting her take care of herself and then helping her clean up afterward."

Mr. MacDonagh chuckled. "I know *exactly* what you mean."

"Good," Chris sighed with exaggerated relief, "since I was afraid that joke might have been a bridge too far. You seem pretty down to earth for a millionaire. No offense, but I was half-expecting one of those *Social Register*, WASP-Establishment-type guys you see in old movies."

Mr. MacDonagh quipped, rolling his eyes, "You mean my father. Well, we're Irish so not technically WASPs, but close enough. Anyway, have a great trip, and best of luck with your new career as my daughter's hired minion."

"Thanks." Chris nodded.

The train came to a stop and he was first to board, while Kera lingered behind for a moment to say her final goodbyes. She embraced her dad, who hugged her back as tightly as he could without injuring her spine.

Speaking into her ear, he said, "Remember, don't be afraid to call me if you need to. I always have your back."

"Literally." Kera grunted, and he relaxed his grip a notch or two.

"And be safe," he added. "You're pretty smart, but it doesn't hurt to remind you not to do stupid things anyway. You were always a bit of a daredevil."

Kera smiled. "Oh, you have no idea."

Kera fell in line with the others, and with her parents waving behind her, she stepped aboard the train. It seemed more spacious on the inside than it had looked from without, though the thick press of human bodies took up much of the elbow room.

Crap, she thought. *I shouldn't have let Chris go on ahead without me. I'll never find him again. I guess a lot of other people had the same brilliant idea we did after everyone's flights got grounded by that stupid volcano. Iceland will pay for this, mark my words.*

Two people in uniform, a man and a woman, appeared and began asking for and checking everyone's tickets. Kera fumbled hers out of her pocket, waiting with as much patience as she could muster for the female usher to work her way through the human mass and look at the slip, nod, and point her in the right direction.

Kera squeezed past her and found Chris waiting for her near the door to the next car, holding his bags. "Well, hello there," he greeted her. "Our lodgings are in the next one over, I guess."

Shrugging, she agreed, "Yeah, last one in line, isn't it? That means we won't have to worry about people trying to blunder through our room to get from one end of the damn train to the other. The perks of being willing and able to pay for premium, I guess."

They crossed to the rearmost car, noting with approval that moving between sections was safe, with the gap being narrow and well-protected by various additions. Beyond was a narrow hallway on one side of the car. The rest was taken up by what appeared to be a single chamber.

"Huzzah," said Chris. "Best room in the house."

They unlocked the doors and stepped in, marveling at the relative spaciousness that awaited. Not that it was big, but it was far less cramped than Kera had feared it might be. There were two single-sized beds with room between them to maneuver and get dressed—maybe even enough for limited exercise and martial arts drills, Kera thought—and what appeared to be a private toilet in a stall in the far corner.

Gesturing toward it, Kera sighed. "Well, *that's* a relief. I feel sorry for all the poor bastards who have to use the communal facilities, though. Oh, well."

They began unpacking, noting that the decor in the cabin was, though minimal, cozy and fresh-smelling and perfectly adequate for a couple of days' travel.

Chris observed with a barely perceptible sly look, "You know, it feels like we have something resembling privacy in here."

It was debatable how much privacy they had. The walls weren't very well soundproofed, though once the train started picking up speed, it would probably make enough baseline ambient noise to drown out the passengers' activities. And it helped that they were separate from the rest of the train.

Still...

"For now," Kera said, "let's just focus on getting settled in and adjusting to the, erm, coming trip. Oh, and I figure you can have the bed with the window since you haven't been on a cross-country trek like this before, whereas I have. Well, across different states, mostly."

Chuckling, Chris stretched out on the bed in question and looked through the glass. "So far, I see a train station."

Kera threw her pillow at him. "No shit. And I'll need that back eventually."

Chris, having caught it, clutched it to himself and rolled over away from her as though protecting and coddling it. "No," he protested. "And remember, you can't cast spells on me to get your way. You'll have to take it by physical force alone."

Reclining on her own bed, Kera pointed out, "That can be arranged if absolutely necessary. Hmm." She gazed at the ceiling, her thoughts wandering. "I know you're not supposed to think about work while you're on vacation, but I keep wondering how Lia is holding up. I might break down and text her this evening."

"It's up to you." Chris rolled back toward her and tossed the pillow at her face. She caught it one-handed in midair. "She might appreciate the gesture."

"Yeah." Kera half-scowled. "She's probably been working

nonstop this whole time, though I told her to only do what she had to to call it a reasonable workweek."

Farther down the train, the bustle of people finishing the boarding process began to die down. According to the time, they would be setting off momentarily.

The thought of Lia working made Kera remember something: the book.

She reached into one of her bags and pulled it out. It was still wrapped in the brown paper since she didn't want anyone to see it on the off-chance it fell out or the authorities demanded the privilege of checking her bags to see that she wasn't carrying a bomb or something. She unwrapped it, gazed at the cover, and opened it to the table of contents.

Sitting back down on her bed, Kera absentmindedly said, "Well, I'll be reading up on such enlightening subjects as brutal murders, morbid sacrificial rituals, ancient blood rites, and sundry forms of dark and forbidden magic. How are *you* planning to relax, lover boy?"

Chris had pulled out his laptop, opened it, and plugged it into an outlet so as not to run down the battery. "I've spent some time reading up on hacking techniques and will be practicing a few of them. Don't worry, nothing that's going to get us in trouble. Simply learning and poking around is still in the, um, gray area of legality...mostly."

"In other words," Kera surmised, "it's legal as long as you don't get caught doing something stupid or that pisses off an important person since in that case, the prosecutor would make it seem sufficiently illegal to ensure you get charged with the other stuff. Got it."

Chris frowned but nodded. "Yeah, more or less. Anyway, we'll need some way of acquiring information about what's going on in greater LA once we get home and start taking cases again. And," he added, shaking his head with disappointment, "it's not like the police allow the general public to browse their databases, unfortunately."

"Weird," Kera agreed. She turned her eyes to the Introduction, which lay across from a photograph of a stone altar covered with rusty stains, and shuddered.

———

The cab driver stated, "Here we are, ladies. You'll make it as long as you hustle. Stay safe out there."

Milena smiled into his rearview mirror. "Thank you. We appreciate your driving so swiftly and coming on short notice. I am sure your profession is very busy right now."

Her companions Hana and Daniela kept silent but put on similarly cheerful faces as they climbed out of the backseat to the left and right.

The driver chortled. He was trying to be good-natured, but in Milena's opinion, he came across as smarmy. "Not a problem. Don't want you getting the wrong impression of America, y'know?"

"I do know." Milena unbuckled her seat belt and climbed out to the left alongside Daniela. Then, leaning toward the driver and making a small gesture with her hand that he probably failed to notice, she added, "We won't forget this, but it is forgivable if you forget us."

The man blinked and stared vacantly into space, as he would continue to do for the next three or four minutes. By that point, the three charming ladies from Eastern Europe would be well out of sight, and his memory of their presence, what they looked like, and where they were going would be blank. He would not even be able to say for sure how he had arrived at the train station.

Each of Milena's assistants carried a single bag. They had

brought with them only the minimum of what was needed for their journey, resolving to rent or steal anything else.

Milena was not as lucky. She had to unload a large and bulky case mounted on a portable dolly from the trunk of the vehicle while the driver continued to drool and gaze into the void. Daniela helped her get it on the ground and then dragged it behind her as the three made their way toward the platform where their train was pulling up.

In Russian, Daniela grumbled, "You would think we could have spared *someone* to predict an event as obvious as a volcanic eruption. Anezka is obsessed with the American council and neglecting her usual duties."

Hana concurred. "I might have noticed it myself if I had not been ordered to perform surveillance of the roads. But, we will manage."

Milena nodded, her only response to either of them. Everyone was mildly annoyed at being unable to simply fly, but no one was stupid enough to protest Anezka's dictates. And at least, Milena felt, she had been able to pick good people for the job.

Hana was half-Russian and half-Japanese, her appearance favoring the latter, with straight black hair in a bob. She came from the island of Sakhalin, which had changed hands between the two countries several times over the course of the last two centuries. She was even smaller than Milena and specialized in scrying, divination, and astral projection. The gossip within the Orthodoxy spoke of her as being sullen and boring, but when she was given a task, she tended to accomplish it without complaining or arguing. She was exactly the sort of person Milena preferred to work with.

Daniela, meanwhile, was a tall and athletic Macedonian with curly dark-brown hair she usually wore pinned back by a barrette. Milena found her to be loud, obnoxious, and overly emotional, but she was an excellent fighter both with magic and without. As such, she was useful as a bodyguard and even more efficacious when a mission required violence of a more proactive nature.

They went through the usual channels en route to the train, noting how crowded the platform was. Theirs had been the last three tickets available, and securing them in the same cabin had required a certain amount of magical finagling. Other customers had to be *discouraged* from trying to purchase tickets at the same time. And the transportation company had to be *persuaded* to rearrange a few other passengers to accommodate them.

"Last call," one of the ushers shouted in a thick New York accent. "All aboard!" Five seconds later, an intercom repeated the announcement in a more genteel manner.

The three witches pressed against the back of the gradually shrinking crowd that had formed before the train's main doors. All had their tickets at the ready, with Milena handling the ones for both herself and Daniela so the latter could focus on manhandling her luggage.

Milena glanced at her companions. "I do not sense anything strange so far. Do either of you?"

Daniela just grunted. Hana spent a moment rolling her eyes before she responded. "It is difficult to say. There is a sense that magic that's not ours may be present, but it seems faint or diffused. Nothing that screams for attention, but perhaps..." Her voice trailed off.

"Yes," Milena replied, "of course. Remain alert, and observe everyone closely. This train station seems to have become one of the most popular routes of egress from the New York area. Certainly, it is unlikely that we would be so lucky as to meet one of the council members on board during our ride, but it is not impossible. And we were given explicit permission to seize any good opportunities that might manifest."

Daniela laughed, a low, unpleasant sound. "If we could kill one of the council members on your little device there and get their *input* to the fountain, that would help with everything else."

"Indeed," Milena agreed.

She wished Daniela would not speak openly of such things when they were in public, but it was doubtful that any of the people around them understood Russian. Besides, the platform was noisy, and they were all using low-level amplification spells that would allow them to hear one another while speaking in a soft whisper.

Hana piped up with, "The large-scale search, the scrying magic. A thaumaturgist of the council would be more than adequate for the power we will require."

Milena allowed herself to titter softly. "Yes, their blood would be far more valuable than that of a mundane person or one with only a light touch of the gift. And I am sure Anezka would enjoy it if we could report back to her that we had used the council's own strength against the rest of them. The one we sacrificed would contribute to finding the others."

It was a slim hope, but she liked the thought of it. Such a feat would earn her a great deal of respect within the Orthodoxy and all but ensure she would advance to Anezka's right hand in due time.

It would require another rather gruesome act of bloodletting, of course. As the trio stepped onto the train, Milena reflected that some people seemed to enjoy killing. She did not, but neither did it particularly bother her. She was a professional, and she had a job to do.

CHAPTER SEVEN

At long last, a day had come when there was nothing for any of the survivors to do—nothing except meet and discuss what to do next. Their enemies had not yet found them, but time was undoubtedly running out. It was so obvious to all of them as to make stating it aloud redundant.

Everyone was present except James. While the rest of the council and Ezeudo sat around Samantha's dining room table, he continued to languish in the guest bed.

Samantha sighed. "I wish we didn't have to leave him out of this discussion." Everyone was still in the process of finding their seats and getting comfortable, so it was an offhand remark and not part of the official proceedings. "But at least he is still alive."

Crystal added, "And recovering, however slowly. He was on the brink of death. And his will does not seem to have contributed much. I think part of him feels as though he deserves his fate, and he blames himself for all of this having happened. If his body does not heal well enough on its own, we will have to work on his mind and spirit."

Samantha's face grew tight as though she were wincing in pain. "I thought I had been doing that. I've tried everything, but perhaps I'm not doing it right. Someone else should try, maybe LeBlanc or Lauren."

Both the women she had indicated gave nods of acknowledgment but did not respond. The council, or what remained of it, had settled in and was prepared for their formal discussion to commence.

Lady Mary Carter Mitchell took the lead, as she often did when no one else leapt up for the task. It was customary for their host to act as the master of ceremonies, but Samantha did not seem up to it.

"Ladies and gentlemen, fellow thaumaturgists," she began. "We all know why we are here. There is little point in bothering with the formalities since we have been living under the same roof for so long now, but for the sake of decorum, we shall do so. We are still civilized. We are still the North American Council of Thaumaturges, the rightful authorities over the domain and usage of magic on this continent."

The others set their jaws and threw back their shoulders a little, hearing the truth. They sat up straighter, and the day did not seem quite as dismal as it had.

Rufus added his two cents. "What you say is correct, but our position right now does not reflect it. The Orthodoxy can rightly say that they defeated us in battle and drove us out of the place that came closest to functioning as our official headquarters. They are, without any doubt, using those facts for propaganda purposes as we speak. We look weak and illegitimate. To the masses, it often does not matter who the true authority is as long as the pretenders are seen to be occupying the formal positions of power."

Greeted with an array of scowls, Rufus clarified, "I do not mean to be a doomsayer or impinge upon Lady Mitchell's efforts to boost morale, only to draw attention to an important issue. That is, we will need a major victory if the minor covens are to view our restoration as a viable cause."

Amanda snorted. "The Orthodoxy doesn't care what anyone thinks of them beyond fearing their power. We are not trying to win a popularity contest, Rufus, we're trying to win a war. It will be decided by force, not by the 'appearance of legitimacy' or some such abstraction."

Hugh pointed out, "Since we are spending so much time on the run, which takes a lot out of us and requires expenditures of magic beyond what we would use in the comfort of our own homes, it might be wise to look into ways to augment our power temporarily. Or create a store for ourselves that may be drawn upon in emergencies. There are ways of doing that, of course."

Though it had occurred to half of them briefly, the other members all nodded and considered it. When Hugh spoke, he usually had something worthwhile to say.

"Yes," Amanda confirmed. "We cannot get too lazy or remain in the mindset that this is a mere inconvenience that will pass. Things are *not* just going to go back to normal any day now. Normality is gone for good unless we restore it by force. We might consider fighting fire with fire if need be, or more precisely, fighting blood magic with blood magic."

To Amanda's total lack of surprise, the others tensed, and the mood in the room grew colder and somehow darker.

LeBlanc cleared her throat. "That is best avoided, Amanda. There is a myriad of other ways of storing and augmenting energy. It is true that blood magic is immensely powerful, but given how ugly and dangerous it is, I would not use it except as an absolute last resort. For us to be known as willing to employ it would hurt our reputation with other casters, and they might view us as no better than the Orthodoxy. It could also draw extra scrutiny from the general public."

"Agreed," said Hugh. "I had something rather more mundane in mind, I'm afraid."

Amanda glowered but did not protest.

Samantha jumped in. "Potions are my specialty, so I could

begin work on an elixir. Perhaps keep a full cauldron of it here for large-scale use, as well as giving each of you a bottle or two to keep on your person at all times."

Waving her hand, Mary said, "Do so then, Samantha, and thank you. Amanda, everyone appreciates your commitment and values your input, but we mustn't go off the proverbial deep end, particularly not while our position is still so precarious. Along similar lines, Crystal, we might employ your namesake."

"Ah, yes," Ms. Green responded. "I have a small collection of channeling crystals, but they were buried beneath my home, which might well have been ransacked by now. Eventually, I will check, but for now, I might be able to make more." She sighed. "In between my other responsibilities."

To that, Mary added, "My background with living things, plants, means I can handle healing magic fairly well, too. I will take care of James while you are busy with other things."

Closing her eyes, Crystal nodded in relief.

LeBlanc had one more thing to add. "There may be still other methods like rare and valuable thaumaturgic artifacts. We can discuss the specifics in more detail later, but suffice it to say that such things do exist. I am unfamiliar with the location of any in this region, however. Were we to bear toward my homeland in Louisiana, I could seek out such objects."

Mary agreed that this was something to think about, and no one had an objection to making the idea Plan B.

The others went on to raise further points about ways in which they could maximize their limited remaining advantages and reposition themselves to strike back at their foes, though without undertaking a massive retaliation until they recovered their collective strength.

Mary raised her hand, fingers splayed, in an authoritative gesture indicating that she was retaking the proverbial floor and wished to address everyone and redirect the conversation.

"All of you," she declared, "have raised good points, and

everyone has been doing all they can since we were driven from James' estate. We definitely must focus on what we can do to directly defeat the Orthodoxy, but the public relations side of things cannot be ignored, either. Being able to sway the lesser covens into helping us could prove decisive."

Ezeudo spoke up. "Yes, that would show that it is not only about you wishing to retain your power and position, but that they have a stake in the outcome of this conflict too. They could help in the fighting, as well as convincing other magicians that you still have supporters."

Rufus smiled. "Precisely. Some power makes itself felt in a direct and obvious fashion, but there is also that power which resides only where people *think* it resides."

LeBlanc sighed at that. "Damian would be the first to agree with that statement since illusion was his specialty…but lamenting his absence and Zacharia's will do us no good. Nonetheless, what Rufus speaks of has less to do with outright magic than the fundamentals of human psychology and social behavior. The lesser covens should be a matter of both concern and priority."

"Yes," stated Mary. "And on that note, what were we able to learn about the presence of any other casters in our immediate area and what their feelings and actions have been thus far? There are only so many on the Eastern Seaboard, and all of them were disappointingly reluctant to aid us before. But the situation has changed."

Those of the council who had been scouting for potential allies had already delivered most of their findings to other members individually, so the group had a fairly good idea of what to expect. But until now, they had not formally summarized it all and therefore could not yet take informed action.

Josiah Kane and Crystal Green had been foremost among those who had gone out on "diplomatic missions," though Crystal had to keep returning to the house to aid in healing James.

Spending much time in the field would have exhausted her beyond all usefulness.

Josiah spoke first. "Well, they're skittish for the most part. Pick your animal analogy. Frightened rabbit. Deer in the headlights. Ostrich sticking its head in the sand. Any of the above would be accurate. I tracked down a few of them and managed to sidle up while they were out in public so as to dissuade them from using magic to escape or do anything else foolish."

Mary asked, "Why would they want to escape from you?" She knew the answer, but hearing it stated aloud would be helpful.

Josiah chuckled. "Implying I'm not as intimidating as I used to be, are you?"

Mary waited, unspeaking. She knew the others thought her humorless, but right now, she *cared* too much to be concerned about such things. Her concern for her friends and the general public ran far too deep for her to think about much else these days.

"Well," Josiah continued, "the impression I got is that they understood we were now wanted fugitives, you see. We are people they do not wish to be seen associating with. By voting to stay out of 'our' feud and assuming it was not their own, they signaled that they have no desire to bring the Orthodoxy's wrath down on their own heads. A young man I encountered at a farmer's market near Scranton clearly saw me, tried to pretend he hadn't, and attempted to leave. I cut him off, but his reaction was, in a way, encouraging."

Ezeudo blinked. "How is that encouraging?"

"Because," Josiah explained, "it means that he wanted to be able to say if anyone asked that he never saw a damn thing. He did not want to turn me in. He did not sound the alarm in the hope of receiving a reward from the people who have declared themselves his new masters."

Ezeudo gave a slow nod. "Ah, yes. It makes sense now." He felt foolish. In the past, he had observed such things in places riven by political conflicts. With all the magic flying around, it was too easy to forget that people were still people, regardless of any talent they might have for thaumaturgy or witchcraft. Magic in itself did not change human nature.

Amanda remarked, "That is only encouraging insofar as it is not the worst-case scenario. They are still cowards unless they agree to fight with us. If they're trying to avoid the conflict altogether, they're merely useless rather than actively harmful. You said you cut him off, Josiah. What then? Did you make our case to him or not?"

"In a fashion. I told him I recognized him, that I knew he'd heard what had happened, and that much of what he had heard was likely exaggerated or outright false. I informed him that we were in hiding and he had not seen the last of us. The council is far from finished, though we might need help soon. Then I let him go. After I placed a tracking spell on him, of course."

"Of course," Mary acceded. "Why the coyness, though? Was it to gauge his reaction?"

Josiah replied in the affirmative. "I had no way of knowing for certain that he hadn't been compromised, and since his powers were not great, he had no way of knowing I wasn't an illusion or someone imitating me who was testing him for disloyalty to the Orthodoxy, you see? There's a very conspiratorial and paranoid atmosphere out there."

Everyone was stone-faced. The destruction of the Lovecraft estate had obviously sent huge ripples throughout the magical scene across the continent.

"So," Kane concluded, "I scried him further and saw and heard what he did, which was nothing at first. He went home and tried to pretend nothing had happened, but later that night, he spoke to two friends within his coven and reported what he had seen. No one did anything. They were all nervous and hesitant. They are waiting for further signs before they take so much as the slightest action."

Rufus remarked, "Neutrality, then, but they might be moved toward supporting us with the proper motivation. Overcoming their intense fear is probably the biggest challenge."

"Fear," Amanda pointed out, "has a way of inspiring people toward other emotions such as anger. Perhaps we might seek to influence things in *that* direction."

Mary ran a finger absentmindedly along the edge of the table. She missed her houseplants, and it pained her to think that the Orthodoxy had probably found and killed every last one of them.

"Yes, you might be right in this case," she proclaimed. "It would be useful for the minor covens to know *exactly* how the Orthodoxy has behaved since their arrival. They should know that Damian Diaz was attacked at his own home, his villa was destroyed, and he himself brutalized before having his throat slashed."

Her hands trembled at the memory.

"They should know," she continued, "that the Orthodoxy brought a small army to James' house, offering no option of surrender and sacrificing some of their own people for the sake of destroying us. That they grievously wounded half of our number before finally felling Zacharia McConnell with a cursed wound, incapable of being healed, a spell so dark and vicious that it had all but vanished from the repertoires of the world's magic users."

Amanda could scarcely sit still.

"And," Mary extrapolated, "they should know that the Orthodoxy leveled James' beautiful estate, passed down through generations, as a final insult. And how even now they hunt us to kill us all. The members of the lesser covens can expect little better from them. They will be serfs at best or snuffed out of existence if the Orthodoxy sees no particular use for them."

Ezeudo frowned. He disliked the undercurrent of hatred in Mary's voice, though he understood it.

Lady Mitchell concluded, "Finally, as an appeal to sympathy, we can mention that James was wounded and has still not recovered. It would be risky; if our enemies intercept the message, they will know we are down another member and therefore weaker, but it might help sway the locals to our cause. I do not want James to die any more than anyone else. I would prefer to lose *none* of you."

Ezeudo raised a hand. "Perhaps it would be useful for me to be the one to speak about James? If we send out a message, having me involved might reduce the perception that this is only about your power struggle. I am, relatively speaking, a newcomer, an outsider. They might trust me as being less biased."

"Good idea," LeBlanc praised him. "I second that."

Samantha was next to agree, followed by Hugh. Everyone else soon joined in.

Mary gave them all a grim smile. "It is settled, then. We shall magically broadcast our statement, our account of events, so the minor casters of the eastern US will all see and hear it. The Orthodoxy will probably intercept it, but that is a risk we must take. They will find us soon, regardless. Let us prepare the spell immediately and send it tonight."

They rose from their chairs, relocating to the living room, where the greater space would make it easier for them all to perform the gestures associated with channeling.

As they walked out, Samantha quipped, "You know, this is the sort of thing James would have suggested we do. Develop a *marketing campaign*. That was his specialty."

LeBlanc put a hand on her arm. "He will make it. James is tougher than he looks, you know."

CHAPTER EIGHT

Kera could scarcely believe how much time had passed. She thought it had been perhaps an hour when it had been nearly three. Those things often happened when she became engrossed in reading something that aroused her interest.

Chris looked up from his laptop and squinted at her, though the subtle twinkle in his eyes and the faint twist at his mouth betrayed his true intentions. "You having a good time over there? Your brain isn't being demonically possessed by the evil spirits trapped within the book since antediluvian eons before recorded history or something?"

Blinking and snapping out of her trance-like state, Kera snapped her head toward him. "I'm fine, and to be honest, this book is pretty damn interesting. I mean, yes, a lot of it is grim and morbid and gory, but it's a hell of a treasure trove of obscure knowledge. No wonder the Kims recommended it. They're not the type to get suckered in by fluffy pop literature or bullshit trends."

Her boyfriend set his laptop aside and turned his whole body toward her. He clearly needed a break from the dry code-finagling and number-crunching of his chosen activities. "Sounds about right. They're solid. Even I miss them, so I'm guessing you do, too."

Kera smiled. "Yes, but there have been times when I was busy or they were busy and we didn't see each other for a couple weeks and it was no big deal, so I'm not too worried about it. Still, it's a different situation when they're, like, two thousand miles away. At least back in LA, I can hop on Zee and ride over to see them whenever I want to. Being back East, that's less of an option."

"It won't be long," Chris pointed out. "Especially if you keep reading that thing. By the way, I've been observing the scenery— they say you should give your eyes a break from staring at a screen every twenty minutes or so by looking out a window—but so far, things don't look too different from upstate New York. Still nice, but I have yet to see anything *new.*"

Kera yawned and stretched. She wasn't tired, merely disoriented as a result of her total absorption in the book.

"Well, give it time. Once we get into the Midwest, it will be fairly boring, to be honest, but that part of the country still has its charms. There isn't much on the Great Plains, but the sheer emptiness and openness are kind of cool. Also, about the eye thing, who is this mysterious 'they' to whom you're referring?"

Chris shrugged. "Oh, I don't know. The experts? I heard that somewhere. Yes, I know, you should always do your own research instead of blindly believing water-cooler gossip or clickbait headlines."

"Exactly," Kera confirmed, cracking her neck. "We're computer scientists, as per our education, and that has the word 'science' in the name. We, like, have a reputation to uphold here."

Chris laughed. "Something like that. The experts have a way of turning out to be wrong five minutes later, don't they?"

"Yup." Kera fingered the collar of her light riding jacket. "That's why I always tested spells and magical implements that I read about or heard about before using them. Well, usually.

Sometimes time constraints meant I had to wing it, like that time I invented a spell to trace Pauline's headquarters on the fly so I could plunge straight into the place and deal with whatever weapons and defenses they had with no foreknowledge or preparation."

Chris stared at her.

She coughed. "But it's generally better to do your own experimentation beforehand. Yeah, of course. Like, for example," she fingered the lining of her jacket and flapped it for him to see, "with this thing. Did I ever tell you about it?"

Chris scratched his head. "Um, no, I don't think so. It's a nice jacket, though?"

Kera opened it and showed him the interior. "See these little bumps? They're pieces of silver and iron that I sewed into it. The Kims helped me make it. Silver and iron tend to block the flow of magic. Oh, and for good measure, I sprayed the lining with silver nitrate. And the inside of my bike helmet, but I don't have that with me, so water under the bridge."

Nodding, he asked, "Okay, that's cool, but why would you want to *block* magic? Wait, you mean, like, as protection from other people's spells?"

"Yes," she confirmed. "Not only attacks and curses, but also from scrying or other forms of detection. When the Duo came looking for me—that's what I call those two thaumaturgists who ended up taking away the Kims' powers if you remember them— I'm pretty sure they were tracking me based on flare-ups of magic they could sense whenever I cast a spell. Well, this thing shields me so other casters can't notice." She grimaced. "Though it does make doing any casting of my own a lot harder. I've been finding ways to work around it, but it's more for when I don't plan on using a lot of magic. Like now, for example."

Chris had pulled a bottle of water out of his pack and unscrewed the cap. "Nice," he quipped and took a swig. "That's clever. Plus, I'm sure it's a good workout, lugging all that extra metal around every time you need to throw a 'light' jacket on. You're turning into a real biker after all."

She folded her arms over her chest. "I was *always* a real biker, thank you very much. But yeah, it's pretty cool. You're right, however. I should have *studded* the jacket with silver-iron alloy instead of sewing little chunks and plates inside it. Studs would look badass, and I don't think Motorcycle Man was ever reported to wear them, so it might help dispel the rumors if I had a different getup."

"There you go." Chris stretched his arms. "I wonder if they serve coffee on this train? We should have prioritized that kind of information before spending money on the tickets. I'll check shortly. Anyway, I need to get back to doing homework here."

Kera brushed her hair behind her ears. "Sure, try to get rid of me. I should return to doing the same thing. All our talk of experimentation has me curious if I should, um, shall we say, test out some of the magic in this book. Nothing serious or scary, but just one of the minor spells they describe that uses only a single drop of my blood. It might provide valuable insight into how this stuff works."

Chris' face swiveled back toward her with alarming speed, and his eyes were wide. "Er, I'm going to vote no. You have to draw the line somewhere. Scientific experiments usually have to get approved by an ethics board, don't they? In this case, the board consists of me. We regret to inform you that we have decided to reject your proposal due to humanitarian and safety concerns."

Kera muttered as she turned her eyes back to the tome, "You're no fun. You're also probably right."

The two of them drifted back to their respective studies.

Kera had gotten to the nastiest part of the book, which talked about specific methods of murder to be employed upon human sacrificial victims. Though the detailed accounts of obscure and potentially useful knowledge continued to entrance her, she found her skin crawling despite herself. Dread nearly stopped her from continuing to turn the pages.

Somehow, I know, I just know *I'm going to find the exact shit the Alchemist did somewhere in this book. It's inevitable. The info in here seems to be legitimate, and we concluded that she was practicing a variety of blood magic that actually worked. How else could you explain that she was at least ninety years old, maybe a hundred or more, but looked forty at most?*

Whatever the reasons or methods, the results were horrific and awful, and I don't fucking want to be reminded of them. But my duties are more important than my wants.

Toward the end of the chapter on killing techniques, she thought of something else. Pulling out her cell phone, she checked for messages or missed calls—none—and then brought up her conversation thread with Lia.

I'm sure Lia will be thrilled, Kera thought with a sardonic half-smirk, *to be sucked back into focusing on stuff like this, but she has her duties as well. She knows what she signed up for, right?*

She sent Lia a text asking her to look at some photographs from a book. Then Kera took pictures of the most important passages, describing how victims could be killed to employ their blood or life essence in various rituals and sent them to her friend. She concluded with a final message apologizing for the grotesquerie but explaining her hypothesis.

It was, Kera elaborated, possible the Black Dahlia murder was not the only unsolved slaying to have been the product of blood rites. Perhaps there were police files all over the world filled with the horrible end results of sacrificial magic, but no one had figured that out? She asked Lia to investigate any still-open cases in which the deceased had been mutilated in ways similar to what the book described.

Kera exhaled and hit Send. "Sorry, Lia," she said to herself.

Chris looked up. "Whuh?"

After Kera summed up her thoughts and told him what she

had done, he shrugged. "You might be on to something, honestly. And on that appetizing note, I'm going to go pester someone about how the dining system works and see if I can bring some food and coffee back for both of us. If that doesn't work, feel free to join me in dining out, I guess."

"Okay." She smiled and watched him leave.

Once he was gone, she plunged her hands into her pack, looking for the object she required—a small pocketknife.

She mumbled, "I knew I should have put it into its own little side pocket or something instead of allowing it to get jumbled in with all this other crap. Wait, there it is."

Kera pulled it out and unfolded the blade, which was only two inches long, thus keeping it safely under the threshold of what was legally considered a "weapon." She stared at the surface, the edge, and the point.

Her gut roiled. She had been injured on many occasions and liked to think she'd been a trooper through all of them. Dumb stuff had happened to her when roughhousing as a kid. A horribly painful sprained ankle when she was a teenager in cheerleading, as well as a couple of pulled muscles and cracked ribs from karate.

Not to mention all the abuse her body had been through since she had begun her career as a vigilante and then a detective. She didn't *enjoy* pain or the helpless feeling of being laid up and unable to function at full effectiveness, but she was able to get through it.

And yet, something about the thought of intentionally hurting *herself*, of sticking a knife into her own body...

"Humanitarian and ethics concerns," she whispered, echoing Chris. "Well, here goes."

Kera stabbed herself in the pad of her left thumb. The point only sank in a fraction of an inch, but it was enough to release a fat drop of glistening crimson blood. Her breath hissed as she inhaled between clenched teeth.

"Son of a bitch! *Ow!* It's different when the adrenaline isn't flowing. Like, this was barely a pinprick, but somehow it's worse than when I got beaten, stabbed, and shot half to death in the streets."

She flipped to a section describing a minor introductory spell in which any amount of blood, even a single droplet, could be used to bolster one's ability to channel the universe's divine and arcane forces. It was, she realized, the opposite of the spells that drew upon one's magical strength to augment the body. Of course, the incantation assumed the caster would be using blood that belonged to someone else.

As she prepared to cast the spell, she noticed her thumb continuing to bleed and winced at the sting.

"This is embarrassing as hell," she admitted to herself, "and I'm clearly too much of a wimp to do this often. Blood magic is a one-time thing."

Lia let out a long, rattling sigh and rested her forehead on her hand. Her long black hair spilled over her knuckles and brushed the surface of her desk. She should have expected Kera to come up with a request like this out of nowhere and right before she and Chris returned to LA.

Although Kera had given her a spare key and free access to the converted warehouse if she needed it, Lia had chosen to remain at home. The small house in a residential neighborhood in eastern Long Beach had functioned as her "nest egg" during her period of working for the late Pauline Testrevosky, as well as her safe house in case things went pear-shaped. Which they had.

She had housed Sven and Johnny here as well when the former was sick for nearly a month after being captured and abused by the coven known as the Orthodoxy and while the latter was making the transition to honest work. She was growing attached to the place.

Still, it was too far from downtown LA, where Kera, her new boss, lived and worked. Moving north might be necessary, and the sooner, the better.

To give her mind a short respite, she sent Johnny a text message asking how he was doing, and how Sven was doing, and if they had seen or heard anything the agency might find useful or interesting. They were trying to stay as far from the seamy side of life and the criminal underworld as they could, but their knowledge, skills, and contacts nonetheless made them useful as informants.

And she still cared about both of them. She hoped they did well in their new lives.

Lia blinked and turned back to her computer. She'd forwarded the stuff from Kera to herself to be able to examine it on a larger screen.

The scans, photos, and screenshots Kera had sent were not pleasant. She was relatively well-inured to brutality by now but did not think it was possible to become completely desensitized. The crime scene photos of Luis Domingo, the initial murder victim during their previous case, had disturbed her tremendously.

And now this. They had all agreed, Kera not least, to move away from work that involved or dealt with violence and the ugliest side of life. None of them had the stomach for it or a particular desire to get themselves killed.

Again, she looked at the images, which depicted human sacrifice and the accouterments of black magic it required in all its hideous forms. She would now get to see more of those, potentially, by browsing through the charnel house of old unsolved murder cases.

"I thought," Lia declared to the empty house and found herself desiring a cup of extra-strong coffee, "that when I got away from organized crime as a profession, my life and work would become *less* gruesome."

———

Milena's eyes flew open.

She had been resting, not exactly sleeping but sitting on her bed in the train car, leaning against the wall and meditating. As Hana had observed earlier, there was *something* strange around them or nearby, but it had been hard to identify in any detail.

And now it had flared up. Looking at Hana, she saw that the other witch had noticed it, too.

Daniela was the dullest and least perceptive of the three. For all her talents in certain areas, she was usually the last to pick up on subtle cues from the environment. She was, however, attentive enough to notice that something had captured the interest of her companions.

"What is it?" she asked, sitting up. She had been lying in the ground-floor bunk and tapping on her smart tablet. Her curly hair was disheveled, and her mouth was slack. She had removed her blouse and was wearing a sports bra beneath it. She looked like a slovenly American girl, in Milena's opinion.

Milena held up a hand to indicate Daniela should not disturb her. "Magic. Hana, can you identify it?"

Hana's eyes narrowed and her nostrils flared. Her gaze was vacant since her mind was searching far and wide and was not focused on anything in front of her. "It came from someone on the train," she stated. "It is still the same distance from us as it was a moment ago, so it was not someone we passed on the ground. Toward the other end. Toward the back."

That had been Milena's suspicion as well, but her perceptual and scrying abilities were not quite as advanced as her assistant's were. "Yes. I thought so. It had the flavor and texture of great power, yet none of the volume or brightness. A cloaked or suppressed spell?"

Hana did not answer until nearly a minute had passed, with the other two witches waiting in breathless silence and Daniela beginning to fidget in her impatience.

"Yes," Hana said, then, "I believe so. It was not a fluke. It might be one of the rare persons with great potential but no training or direction, but I think not. No, it seems we are on board this train with another like us."

Daniela's face lit up, and excitement practically oozed from her pores. "A council member? Milena, maybe you *were* on to something. Haha! To think we would have been that lucky."

Milena wanted to join in her comrade's enthusiasm, but it was too early to leap to any conclusions. "We do not yet know that it's anyone from the council. Still, if another witch is aboard, we can sacrifice them right here. It will take a smooth operation and some management of the other passengers, of course, but the Orthodoxy could be reaping the benefits of another infusion of blood as soon as tonight."

She looked at the massive, ungainly suitcase that held the fountain-altar. Certain spells had been necessary to protect its functionality while dragging it around in such an awkward fashion.

Hana came out of her near-trance. "Whoever it is, they are powerful."

Milena smiled and reflexively patted her pant leg, feeling the hidden straight razor she kept there. "Good."

CHAPTER NINE

Chris had been the first to fall asleep, sometime around ten-thirty at night. Kera lay awake, staring at the ceiling of their shared compartment.

He's still on his old nine-to-five sleep schedule, isn't he? I guess that's how it was for him for years, working his office job, and insofar as he's going to be one of the "day crew" at MacDonagh Investigations, it's probably for the best that he keeps it up. Still, it would be nice if the two of us were awake at the same time more often.

She rolled over on her side, briefly annoyed with herself for giving Chris the "window seat," but then dismissed the ungenerous notion. She closed her eyes, losing herself in random mental imagery rather than relying on external stimulation.

It's been hard for me to adjust to this new schedule myself. Granted, I'll still be the "night person" of the agency, but things will work out better if I can start hitting the hay by two a.m. or so instead of four or five like I did when I was working as a bartender. Not to mention prowling the streets the rest of the night after I got out of work.

But over the course of their vacation, she had been passing out around midnight as a result of adapting to Chris', and indeed everyone else's, schedule. At present, the prospect of getting through a train ride that would last over three full days petrified her.

She lost track of time shortly before she fell asleep. Though she was not aware of it, the hour was eleven-forty.

An indeterminate period of time later, Kera awoke in shock and alarm. The train was crashing.

"What?" she blurted, coherence not having fully returned. "What the hell? Dammit!" She rubbed her eyes, looked around, and clung to her bed as the train rumbled and jostled and metal screeched and groaned.

Their compartment was still dark, and sunlight was not yet streaming through the window. Chris had awoken more slowly than she had, but he was conscious, and he too was holding on to the mattress with white-knuckled hands.

"Did we crash?" he wondered aloud.

Kera could feel the train slowing down. Whatever had happened, they hadn't collided with anything powerful enough to bring them to an immediate halt or knock them off the tracks. In fact, she was starting to doubt that it had been a crash.

"I'm not sure," she said. "Maybe an internal problem. Doesn't seem quite as bad now, but definitely not good. What time is it?"

Chris, blinking and grimacing, began fishing around for his phone. "I think we broke down, like maybe the train ran over a discarded sofa and got too much pillow-stuffing in its engine or God knows what. And, uh, it's too early is what it is." He found the device and woke it up. "Four-twelve in the a.m. Around your usual bedtime, isn't it? Were you asleep?"

As the noise and chaos abated and the train ground to an uneasy halt, Kera told her boyfriend, "Yeah, I guess I was. I'm not sure when I passed out. Sometime after eleven, I think. Anyway, it doesn't seem like we're all about to die. Look out the window, though, and make sure we're not being bombed by China or something."

He did. "No bombs, just trees and such. I'm voting for mundane mechanical failure."

Kera stood up. "Probably. Let's go find out for sure, though. Well, *I'm* going to. If you want to stay behind, you can."

Chris was climbing to his feet. "Let me answer the call of nature here real quick and maybe splash some water on my face, then I'll make up my mind. Don't go too far, okay?"

"I won't." Stretching her limbs as she moved, Kera threw open the door to their cabin and stepped out, intending to cross the cars and head toward the center of the train, if not the front, until she found someone who knew what the hell was going on.

After the mechanical noises died down, other sounds began to replace them. People were emerging from their beds and chattering and shuffling around. When she crossed into the next compartment, Kera was not surprised to encounter a group of five people standing near the juncture between two cabins in their nightclothes and interrogating one another as to what had happened.

"Hey," a man asked, noticing Kera and turning toward her. "You okay? Did you see what happened back there?"

She shook her head. "No. I probably know as much as you do, maybe less, since it sounds like you guys are confused as well. I don't think we crashed into anything. Probably a mechanical failure?"

An old woman grunted and nodded. "Yes, makes sense. But it sounded like something got *damaged*, didn't it? I wonder how? These trains are supposed to be extremely safe and modern. This one wasn't built too long ago. It's not as though it's falling apart from age."

Kera was about to step out of the train when a message came over the intercom.

"Attention all passengers," it began. "This is the conductor. Sorry to disturb you, but we're having technical difficulties and had to stop the train. Nothing to be alarmed about so far, though we might be delayed a few hours. We've already called Maintenance. We're halfway between two stops, however, so it could be a little while. If you'd like to get off, the attendants will see to your needs."

Nodding, Kera got off. For now.

They were in a rural area, not far from the empty parking lot of what looked like an abandoned gas station on a side road somewhere in the hills of Pennsylvania. It was still dark out, but Kera could sense that pre-dawn would be arriving fairly soon. She had stayed up late enough for long enough to get a feel for the lifespan of the night's darkness, although the length of day versus night was different at more northerly latitudes than in Southern California.

About a dozen passengers had joined her in vacating the train, and by talking to them briefly, she gathered that they were concerned with what might happen if something collapsed or blew up.

"Although," a young bearded guy commented, "it doesn't seem like it was *that* bad. Hopefully."

Chris poked his head out a minute later, and Kera repeated what the others had said after confirming he had heard the intercom announcement.

"Mkay, then," he drawled. "I'm going to go investigate if all the appliances are still working."

Two attendants came out to address the small crowd.

"Okay," one of them began. "You all heard what the conductor said. It seems that there was a freak mechanical failure of a major engine part. We're not sure which one yet, but it seems bizarre since the engine on this train was just replaced about six months ago. Also, the guy who was watching for stuff like this claims he was wide awake, but he doesn't remember seeing the gauge go into the danger zone, so he probably fell asleep and doesn't want to admit it. But who knows?"

Kera rubbed her lips with the back of her hand. "That's odd," she muttered.

Her thoughts began to race, and she wondered if her imagination was overstimulated these days. The horrific ordeals she had dealt with in the recent case, and her previous vigilante endeavors, and that creepy, gory book... They were all making her paranoid.

Making it too easy to see black magic where none existed. Probably.

The attendants went on to explain that since the electricity was still on and the toilets and such still worked, the passengers were welcome to wait aboard until the train was up and running again, or if they chose, they could independently secure rides to the next station down the line, at which point the railroad would find them a seat on another train going the same way—at no additional charge, of course—or allow them to wait for the current one to arrive.

Other people had begun to filter out onto the empty ground that surrounded the tracks, some of them grumbling and complaining. Kera slipped away to examine the engine in case anything interesting suggested itself.

I can't help it. I'm a detective. I see a problem, I want to look into all the details.

Since she could not see into the interior of the machinery, there were no visual cues to go on, but something felt "off." It was difficult to put her finger on it.

Further, as she wandered back toward the main doors, she overheard the assistant conductor, the man who had supposedly fallen asleep on the job, protesting that he had no memory of being drowsy and didn't know what had happened or how or why.

Like taking out a sentry before you attack a base's power supply, Kera thought. *I mean, maybe not. Maybe the guy truly did pass out and screw up. But it seems unlikely, doesn't it?*

There was something else as well, Kera concluded. Something which went beyond mere intellectual reasoning, to a lower and deeper level of consciousness. It went beyond hunches and intuition. It went all the way to the roots of mammalian perception, which are the five senses.

Something *smelled* wrong.

She wasn't certain if it was a purely olfactory sensation or if the thaumaturgical aspect of her expanded mind simply interpreted it as "smell," but either way, the effect was the same. As an animal smells a dangerous creature upwind, so too could Kera tell beyond any doubt that dark, malevolent magic was at work.

Ever since she had, on a whim, purchased a copy of *How to Be a Badass Witch* and begun her study of thaumaturgy, Kera had found that her ability to perceive subtle things gradually increased over time. This was not only as a direct part of her studies but as a passive side effect.

And firsthand experience was the best teacher. She had begun to recognize the signature of hostile and destructive spells around the time she found herself fighting against Pavla, though given Pavla's mixed feelings, the effect had been muted.

When Kera went up against the Alchemist, she began to notice that especially evil forms of magic had a noticeable stink to them. Now, on the train she and Chris were relying upon to get them home, the odor (though faint) was too familiar for comfort.

"All right," she said to herself since the attendant was out of earshot. "I'll stay. Whatever the hell happened here, it's not something I should run away from. And I doubt anyone else here is qualified to deal with it."

A man brushing past her on his way away from the train glanced at her weirdly as though he'd overheard what she had said and was puzzled by it. She glanced up at him, but he was on the move and was looking forward once more.

Not him, she decided. *No magical aura at all, just a guy. Still, I need to get into the habit of not blurting things out loud when I'm in cramped-ass public quarters like this. I've been spending too much time alone or with a small group of friends in my apartment or at my parents' huge house.*

She looked at the milling crowd, trying to identify an aura, a suspicious-looking individual, or anything else that might help her guess who the culprit was. So far, there was nothing.

I know jack shit about who this caster is. Come to think of it, it might not be a caster at all. Like, do we know for certain there aren't mercenaries, hitmen, or others who don't get hired by covens to perform tasks with the aid of single-use magic spells that anyone can handle? That's a scary thought.

But if it isn't a mundane person wielding borrowed magic, it could be anyone or anything. I don't have a way of knowing if they're a novice, someone middling like me, or someone who's a goddamn master thaumaturge and would transform me into a greasy stain on the carpet with a flick of their hand if I tried to challenge them.

She frowned. *Fuck.*

Chris came up. He had his hand behind his back and was obviously concealing something. "It's true," he reported. "The toilet facilities *do* still work, and so does the coffee machine in the dining area. Since we were talking about proper scientific procedure and stuff yesterday, I thought you'd appreciate evidence rather than just taking my word for it."

He brought his hands out from behind his back, now holding two biodegradable paper cups filled with steaming hot coffee. "One is for you. Terribly sorry, but I'll be keeping the other one for my own purposes."

"Thanks, Chris." She took the cup he had in his left hand, which appeared to be the slightly darker of the two, since she preferred only the bare minimum of cream and no sugar, whereas he liked his a bit lighter and sweeter. She took a sip. "I'm heading back inside."

He raised his eyebrows. "On the train, you mean? So you've decided to stay?"

"Yeah." She glanced around again and expanded her mind to once more troll for any signs of magic. "It's better to stick with a sure thing, in my opinion. Like yes, it will take them a few hours to repair the train, but afterward, at least everything will be the same. Who knows what will happen if we try to go someplace else? Other trains might get overcrowded, then we'd end up trying to hire an Uber to take us across multiple states or something stupid like that."

Chris laughed. "I bet some of the ride-sharing companies would allow stuff like that, but it does sound...inefficient. Well, if we're lucky, things will literally quiet down after the train gets moving again, and we can go to sleep early this evening. I had half a mind to try passing out here, but there will probably be too much commotion for that. Hence, the coffee."

Kera chuckled and drank more of the hot beverage. Both her and Chris' logic was sound enough, which saved her from having to divulge the true reason she wanted to hang around the train.

Though it was unlikely she could or should keep it from him indefinitely. He was her partner in more ways than one.

Soon, she thought. *I'll tell him after I know a little bit more about who's responsible for this. Don't want to jump the gun and make him worry unnecessarily.*

In unison, the two of them turned and began weaving their way back through the crowd—much of which was still uncertain as to which option to take—and reboarded the train. Kera could see a couple trucks heading toward them. It was probably someone with maintenance skills, so the repairs ought to begin soon.

"You know," Chris quipped, "this coffee is pretty damn good. I'm going to have to ask what kind it is. Probably expensive as hell since this is a premium train, but still."

Kera squeezed past a cluster of three women. "Yeah, it's not bad." She was distracted. Her jacket caught on a rail and was pulled most of the way open. Her hand quickly shot out, grabbed it, and pulled it free before closing it around her.

At that exact moment, she *felt* something in her mind. It was like the sensation of being watched, but slightly different. Whoever was looking at her or looking *for* her, they weren't using their eyes.

Her abdominal muscles tightened and a cold spurt of adrenaline went through her, perking up her alertness and making it clear that something important had just happened.

The witch, thaumaturge, or whoever it was who had attacked the train was seeking Kera in the same way she had been trying to seek them for the last five or ten minutes. They were trying to determine who she was, where she was, and probably how powerful she was.

It wasn't a magical amateur with an artifact or a scroll. Whoever they were, they were an adept, trying to sniff out Kera's aura or scry her. The temporary hole in her defenses caused by her jacket being pulled open had made her vulnerable for a second.

Oh, crap. She moved on as though nothing had happened, and the sensation ended as quickly as it had begun. The feeling of being observed vanished once her jacket was safely closed around her body again.

This person being on the same train isn't likely to be a coincidence. They're looking for me specifically. I wonder if it's someone from that council or whoever, the people the Duo represented? Or the Orthodoxy? Or some random weirdo who was friends with the Alchemist? Ugh. No way to know yet.

When they reached their cabin again, Kera realized that her plan to wait to talk to Chris was going to have to be tossed in the proverbial trash.

"So," he began, none the wiser about what had disturbed her so much, "it looks like—"

She interrupted him. "Chris, I'm sorry, but this is serious."

He blinked. "Did I put too much creamer in your coffee?"

"No." She sighed. "I mean, there's something going on here, on this train. This wasn't a natural crash. Now, I know you're going to protest and get all worried, but I want you to please do what I say because this is important. I want you to leave. Head back out and find a ride to a different station. You can meet me somewhere else, like at a stop farther down the rail line, even if it takes a day or so for us to be reunited."

She gave him the set-jaw look combined with the calm but intense stare she always used when she was trying to make a point or convince him of something.

He was silent at first, his brow furrowed. "The bad guys found us again, did they? Something like that? Although I'm not sure who you mean."

"I'm not sure who either," she admitted, "but yes, that's the gist of it. Someone used magic to stop the train. They deliberately created a disruption in the hope of drawing me out and seeing how I reacted. I don't think they know who I am or where I am, or how to identify me, yet. The jacket helps."

She fingered its lapel, allowing herself a brief and morbid thought about how badly things would have gone if she hadn't had it. Then she pushed the notion from her mind. Focusing on what-ifs and worst-case scenarios was a pointless endeavor.

Chris grimaced. "That sucks. It's exactly what both of us *didn't* want or need to deal with. Are you sure they're here because of you? The world is full of weird coincidences."

Kera shrugged. "Maybe they weren't looking for me to begin with, but they noticed my aura once we set off on the train, and now they're doing scans and scrying to figure things out and isolate me. Look, a train isn't a good place to be cornered in. By the same token, if we both head off into the wider world, there's more of a chance that this person could cause damage or harm to the general public, and I can't allow that. They and I are both boxed in and can keep it between us."

He took a step closer to her. "Well, I'm with you. You'd probably benefit from my help, and I'll be glad to do anything I can."

She wanted to hug him for that, but she couldn't afford to get sentimental. She shook her head. "No, I'm sorry, Chris. I'm not sure I can keep you safe. There's too many unusual variables, too many things that can go wrong, and we don't have the elbow room here for me to keep you at a secure distance if things get ugly."

"Oh, I know," he agreed, and she could tell he wasn't going to give up without a fight of his own. "But as you may recall, I have the charm you made for me, not to mention there are the charms we got from Pavla, remember? That offers me some protection. I'm not helpless against magic. And I believe in your ability to be my knight in shining armor if need be, even if that's kind of embarrassing for a man, I guess."

Kera pursed her lips. "I don't want to risk it. I'd rather have you out of threat range altogether, at least until I can figure out what we're dealing with, if not resolve the situation."

Chris took hold of one of her hands and squeezed it, and she couldn't bring herself to stop him.

"Hey," he began. "When we started going out again, we made a deal. We agreed that I am part of your life, I stay by your side, and you keep me in the loop and let me help you. Call me crazy, but I feel like you are beholden to that agreement. I worry about you, Kera, and I would never want to lose you. I'm not just leaving you here on your own to face down something you don't even recognize yet."

Her jaw clenched, her lips trembled, and her eyes narrowed.

Son of a bitch, her brain raged. *I make a reasonable request based on my concern for his safety, and he hits me with his guilt-tripping lawyer-loophole shit. If I brute-force him into leaving the train, we'll have to have a dozen "talks" about it later until our relationship is back on track again. Ugh. I can't believe he's doing this to me.*

She took a long, slow, deep breath. "Chris," she stated, in a calm but steely tone, "I am going to leave the choice up to you, but I want you to hear my logic and not just treat this as some abstract thing about 'trust' or whatever. It's about life and limb, okay? If you stay, you might split my focus. I might freeze up or something, trying to protect you while I'm trying to deal with our mysterious stowaway, and end up failing at both."

He considered it for a moment, nodding slowly. "That's a good point. Then again, if you send me off and uncover this person, they might slip away when you're not paying attention. You wouldn't be able to protect me *that* way either, so..."

Kera raised her hands, which had balled into fists. "Oh, I hate you. Men! So goddamn difficult."

"We try," Chris said and kissed her on the cheek.

CHAPTER TEN

Ezeudo realized that what he felt now—the mindset into which he had slipped, the gear into which he had shifted—was familiar to him. It was not something he had expected to encounter in America, but life was strange.

It was the sense of being hunted, of being an outlaw, someone who did not belong here. He had to keep his head down and his voice low as he moved around and tried to survive and escape. The sort of thing that had happened again and again when he had visited warzones and found that his diplomatic or charitable endeavors had gone sour, and he and his companions would be treated as no different from enemy combatants by whatever gang of thugs now controlled the local territory.

Especially since, now that they had crossed into the relative backcountry of West Virginia, they were once again moving on foot.

"This," Samantha said, her voice growing thick with indignation and concern, "is *not* a good idea. James can barely walk, and we don't have a proper way of carrying him that doesn't involve draining us of our magic over time. If *they* were to ambush us, we would not be at full strength as a fighting force."

Mary Mitchell didn't look at her but frowned. "Unfortunately, you might be right, Samantha. For James' sake, we need to stop moving soon and find a defensible place to hole up until further notice."

Ezeudo, hearing her say that, loosened up with relief. Samantha's complaint was what they had all been thinking ever since they had ditched their vehicles at the Pennsylvania state line.

About a day and a half ago, they had commenced their plan to abandon Samantha's house and go back on the run. Though there weren't any specific indicators that the Orthodoxy was about to strike, everyone knew their enemies had not been idle and would find them soon.

Thus, Hugh Buchanan, the most boring and normal-looking of their group, had gone to rent three cars for them, convincing the agency to send people to drive the other two back to Amanda's house. Naturally, he had cloaked the vehicles before leaving and had also memory-wiped the employees so as to leave no paper trail for the Orthodoxy to follow should they wise up to the scheme.

Then they had loaded James into the backseat of one car, carefully strapping him in place and covering him with a blanket, with the rest of them crowding into the remaining seats. In unison, they had driven off.

Samantha had seemed sad to leave the house behind. She had grown attached to it, and their foes would almost certainly raze the place to the ground if they found it. However, it had served its purpose as a temporary safe haven.

Josiah Kane asked, "How is James? Will he make it to the next town?"

They were all mildly surprised when James himself answered the question. "I think so," he mumbled, his voice thick and ragged as though he were short of breath and his mouth was gummed up. "How much farther is it?"

Mary replied, "Less than a mile. We will be there soon. I

checked in advance in case we needed to stop this evening, and there is a hotel there that should be reasonably safe. It's an old-fashioned place in a three-story building, and it should not be difficult to secure lodgings for all of us on the top floor. That will provide a measure of security. And as it's an obscure little place, it is not as though we are going anywhere obvious that the Orthodoxy might think to check."

Samantha shut her eyes and nodded. She was helping James along with an arm around his waist and his head resting on her shoulder, though he was larger than she was. It was taking its toll, and others had offered to share the burden, but she had insisted on being the one to help James walk as long as she could.

"Good," she stated. "We all need a rest and James in particular."

James, who kept slipping in and out of full consciousness, gave a weak, dry chuckle. "I would rather...go on the offensive...but I'm not in...any shape for that. Sorry."

Amanda grumbled, "We would all like to take the fight to them and stop running like hunted animals, but we don't even know where they all are. They outnumber us by a substantial factor, and they've probably spread out by now, trying to encircle us."

"Well," said LeBlanc, "that has the advantage of diluting their effectiveness. If we should encounter a small party of their troops, we might well be able to defeat them quickly enough to escape before the rest of their forces can arrive as backup."

Josiah twirled his cane. Though he usually walked with it, he did not *need* it. "Indeed. They're not as mighty as they like to think. If they were, we would already have been destroyed to the last man or woman. Of course, the lack of significant response from the lesser coven members is concerning. I'm not sure if it's because no one dared to respond or bothered to respond, or if it's due to the Orthodoxy blocking any channels by which they *could* reply once they analyzed the frequency we used to send the message."

LeBlanc's face was grave, but she had remained serene, all things considered. "We should not invest too much of our hope in others coming to our rescue. Particularly not in this part of the country, where the Orthodoxy has concentrated the majority of their forces. It is effectively an occupied territory now. Elsewhere, their presence might be weaker, and we might have the opportunity to acquire certain things which could tip the scales in our favor."

Crystal Green said, "If you're referring to this mysterious relic you mentioned a couple days ago, then I hope you're right. The channeling crystals I constructed were a rush job, too crude to be of more than minimal effectiveness despite my best efforts. They'll give us an edge, but only a slight one."

The conversation died as the party continued its procession down the side of the road. They were cloaked, so no one would notice them, and if they did, they would regard them as unimportant and forget about them a moment thereafter. Individuals who were especially astute and observant might be more of a problem, but that was a bridge that could be crossed when they came to it, so to speak.

Ezeudo smiled. Thanks to magic, his odds were probably better than the ones he'd had in other countries during his past misadventures. A dozen ragged individuals stumbling down a road would have drawn great suspicion in some places and under some circumstances. Not so when spells were available to deflect all attention.

Samantha stumbled, and Ezeudo, who was closest to her and James, moved in. "Here. Let me, please."

He reached out and took James under the arms, helping him back into a slow, uneasy walk and allowing the shorter man to lean against him. Samantha looked like she wanted to protest but didn't. She was exhausted and could no longer deny it.

Mary glanced back at them, and her face was drawn with concern. "We are almost there. Only a little farther. We won't do this again and will plan to have vehicles available wherever we go. At least until James is better. The fact that he can walk and speak again is a good sign."

Samantha pointed out, "Putting him through this much strain might worsen his condition."

They all knew that, but James hadn't complained, and they didn't have any choice.

Cars drove past now and again. The road they walked down was a state highway, but not a very well-traveled one, and West Virginia was an out-of-the-way state. Quintessentially Appalachian, Ezeudo thought, based on what he knew of the region. It was beautiful but not a major hub of commerce or technological development.

Rufus asked, "Might we have been better off heading due west through Pennsylvania? The so-called Pennsylvania Dutch might have lent a *hexenmeister* or two to help us. They were among the covens more friendly to our goals."

"Not friendly enough to actually help," Hugh observed. "Besides, as the most direct route away from James' estate, it would be the most obvious region where the Orthodoxy would expect to look for us."

Sighing, Rufus agreed, "I suppose. How much do they truly know about us? Our origins and connections, I mean. Do they have enough information to be able to guess where we might flee?"

LeBlanc knew what he was insinuating. "They might. After all, I have never bothered to try to hide my identity as a Creole or my roots in New Orleans. Then again, they might assume we are heading to the West Coast instead. Or simply trying to hide somewhere in the heartland until we can rally resistance against them. Any of those are viable options."

Crystal said, "Look. The lights of the town."

It was true; they were coming to the edge of full civilization. For the last couple of miles, there had been nothing but wooded hills, sporadic houses, and the occasional gas station or drive-through restaurant.

"All right," Mary announced. "Everyone has done well in getting this far, and I think we can spend a few days here if we're careful and lucky. We must come up with further plans, though, and we need to get James back to health. It is imperative. I will do as much as I can. Crystal, Samantha, your energies are better spent elsewhere."

Ezeudo was glad to hear that. He had previously gotten the impression that Mary was a somewhat humorless and authoritarian individual—James had complained about her often enough —but she had proven to be one of the most conscientious of them in a crisis, and her legitimate love for the others was obvious.

"I hope," Ezeudo announced for the sake of having something encouraging to say, "that there is good food to be found here. I've heard that many small towns in America have excellent restaurants if you look for them."

Hugh chuckled. "We'll have to find out, and the sooner, the better. It's been a long day, hasn't it?"

The thought of rest and a meal cheered them all up. However, weighing on them heavily and lodged in the backs of all their minds was the silence from the lesser covens.

They were on their own.

Kera and Chris had spent the last hour languishing in their private quarters at the rear of the train, still mildly annoyed with one another. Kera was irked that Chris had more or less forced her to accept his continued presence despite the danger.

He, she suspected, disliked that the argument had happened

after how happy they had been together lately and how much they had both enjoyed the vacation.

Still, at least they both had tasks to distract them. Chris, now that the coffee had taken effect and begun to perk him up and compensate for his lack of sufficient sleep, had plunged back into his hacking exercises with a surprising degree of zeal. Kera almost forgot he was there.

For her part, Kera was searching with her mind, slowly, carefully, and with as much depth and thoroughness as she could muster.

There was undoubtedly a magical presence amongst the passengers on the train, but it was unlike anything she'd seen before. It was amorphous, shifting, and faint and did not announce itself as being attached to any particular person or place.

She began to wonder if she had been mistaken in her earlier conclusions.

Maybe, she pondered, *there isn't a caster on the train. Like, maybe someone marked the train in advance, and they're casting spells on us remotely from some other location. That would require a lot of skill and knowledge, which is scary as hell to contemplate, but it can be done. And it would arguably make more sense than trying to figure out how one person could create an aura that feels like a cloud of thin mist over the whole damn train, which keeps dissipating and then reforming in different places.*

Her ruminations were interrupted when the conductor again came over the intercom to update everyone on the situation.

"Okay, attention please, all remaining passengers."

He paused, and Chris and Kera perked up, looking at the ceiling and waiting. It occurred to Kera that she didn't know where the speaker was, which again set her mind into paranoid speculations that she tried to ignore.

"The repairs on the engine are done," the man stated. "It was only one small part, which had somehow melted without doing much damage to the rest of the engine. A freak incident, and I'm sure the investigation into how it happened will be fascinating. But, uh, anyway, we will be setting off again in about five minutes. If anyone is still outside the train and plans to ride the rest of the way, please return ASAP. If you have a friend or family member who is off somewhere, please text them and ask them to come back right now."

Kera hoped no one would accidentally be left behind, though she doubted it. About a quarter of the passengers had made up their minds to leave, and the rest seemed to have settled in and were simply waiting to get rolling again.

"So," the conductor went on, "if anyone you were with went on ahead to wait for you, inform them that we'll be at the next station in approximately one hour and fifteen minutes. Again, any alternative arrangements you've made will be taken care of by the company, free of charge. Without further ado, here's to a smooth ride that doesn't get derailed again by whatever the complete opposite of a miracle is."

Chris snickered. "I like this guy. He has a sense of humor. What's his name?"

Kera couldn't remember, but she found it oddly comforting that she wasn't the only one who realized how borderline impossible the mechanical failure had been. Then again, she kind of doubted the conductor had the slightest idea *why* the part had melted.

Kera did. It had been a spell, one she had become proficient in months ago, that concentrated heat on a particular point in space and intensified it to a set point, maintained there by the caster until released or canceled. She would be shocked if it was anything else.

Pavla taught me that spell, she recalled. *Damn, I miss her. Wait! She might have some insights on all this. Only problem is, how the hell do I contact her safely? She didn't leave me much to go on since she didn't want either of us leaving bread crumbs from one to the other that our various enemies could follow.*

She looked at her boyfriend, who was about to resume his adventures in the darker arts of computer science.

"Chris." She stretched her leg across the narrow aisle and prodded him with her foot. "Hey."

He looked up. "Yes, babe? You know, you can always call me if you need to talk. My phone is still on."

"Ha. Ha," she muttered. "Seriously, I had an idea. You said earlier that you still have that charm that Pavla made, right?"

He nodded. "Are you going to, like, try to use it to replicate its enchantment to protect us more?"

"No," she answered. "Though that's not a bad idea if it's even possible. I wanted to use it to try to track her down. I need to talk to her about something, and she might be the only one whose advice is really useful right now."

Chris looked uncertain, then he relaxed his face and shrugged. "You're the expert, or close enough to it. Be careful, though. A while back, you said something about, um, what was it? How that coven Pavla was in might be watching us? Trying to contact her by magic could clue them in as to where both of you are."

Goddammit, Chris. I thought women were supposed to be the ones who remembered everything someone said and used it against them later, usually at a highly inopportune time. You'll pay for this.

All she said aloud was, "Yeah, I did, but give me the damn thing anyway. I'll do this slowly and carefully. If I get any sense of someone watching, I'll abort the mission at once. You can be my spotter."

He nodded, then reached into his shirt and produced the little stone on a string. "If I get struck by lightning the instant I take this off, it's your fault," he pointed out.

"Dude," she snapped, "shut up. You've been on a roll as far as busting my balls ever since you woke up. I think you were spoiled by all the good nights' sleep you've been getting since you left your job, and now one night of sleep deprivation, and you're acting like this."

He exhaled, and his mouth turned sour with remorse. "Yeah, I'm sorry. It hasn't been a great day so far, though, and it's barely past dawn. Here." He handed her the charm.

Kera accepted it and instantly felt its power. It was cold and intimidating. It was, after all, enchanted for the purpose of negating spells rather than augmenting them, but only those meant to spy on him or harm him. It allowed benevolent magic to get through its net.

What concerned her at the moment was its connection to her former teacher—the friend who had betrayed her, only to come back to help her at the last minute.

Pavla, she thought. *If you're out there, I miss you. I think about you every other day. Maybe for only five seconds, but still, you're not forgotten. Where are you? How are you doing? They didn't catch you, did they?*

Kera allowed her thoughts and feelings about the Czech witch to unfurl naturally without trying to force them in any special direction yet. Part of this was for the sake of her own emotional stability, but it would also lay the groundwork for the spell she needed to cast. Reflecting on connections with someone was a prerequisite for magically locating them or sending them a psychic message.

Chris appeared to have drifted back into his hacking endeavors, but he kept one eye on his girlfriend. He didn't want to disturb her. The depth of concentration she required for magic was something he had learned about the hard way.

Kera stared at the wall and began to see the currents of magic that flowed across the country to the entire world. Her vision was no longer located in front of her eyes but deep within her mind.

Pavla. I need you. As she sent out her consciousness in search of her friend, she put a cloaking spell around it, barely aware of the subtle hand gestures or whispered incantations that went with it. She had never cast the spell in this fashion before, but it seemed to work.

See? she thought. *We can talk, and no one else will know or see or hear us. You'll be safe from the Orthodoxy, and so will I.*

To her surprise, in her mind's ear, she heard Pavla's voice responding to her.

Not for long, I am afraid. Kera, I have missed you, and I'm glad to hear from you, but things are growing bad for all of us. I had thought about contacting you myself to warn you.

Kera was dimly cognizant of the tension in her body and the growing feeling of acidic coldness. *Warn me about what? And are you okay? I won't ask where you are since I wouldn't want anyone else to know that if they can somehow listen in on us.*

There was a pause, during which Kera thought she saw swirling colors in a fog of astral power, as though Pavla's mind were gathering itself to decide how best to discuss things.

I am fine, the Czech reported, and Kera relaxed a little. *There is no guarantee that I will remain fine forever, but for the time being, I'm safe. America is a more dangerous place now, though. That is what I wanted to warn you about—the war.*

Kera felt a twinge of nausea, the natural outcome of sudden dread.

What war?

CHAPTER ELEVEN

Chris was now watching Kera closely without trying to hide it. His face was blank and neutral but intensely focused. He could tell something was wrong, but not wrong enough for him to need to intervene. He waited, cautious, and trusted his girlfriend to deal with whatever had disturbed her. She had gone to a place where he could not follow.

Kera was aware of him in a small portion of the back of her mind. Her eyes continued to work. But her mind was overwhelmingly fixated on her psychic conversation with Pavla.

What war? she asked again.

Pavla's voice, so oddly similar to her physical voice despite speaking through mental vibrations, replied at last.

The Orthodoxy, my former masters and compatriots, have launched an all-out campaign to annihilate another coven here on American soil. Since you have almost no involvement with the formal culture of magic, you would not be aware of the channels that would discuss such things.

Although Kera was pretty sure Pavla had not intended for the statement to chastise her, it was difficult not to take it that way regardless. She blushed, feeling stupid, like someone who swells with confidence after reading a book on a subject, only to make

113

an elementary error in a room full of people who have read twenty such books and written advanced peer-reviewed dissertations.

Sorry, said Kera.

Pavla's response was swift but gentle. *There is no need to be sorry. You have not done anything wrong. But it is true that you are... what is the expression about loops? Out of the loop, I believe. The magic users on this continent who are part of the formal coven system have talked about little else lately, but they speak quietly out of fear that the Orthodoxy might hear them. Although they are not the main focus of the campaign.*

Kera was well aware that the Orthodoxy was not to be trusted or trifled with, but she was curious as to their targets. *Who is the focus, then? Who are they trying to wipe out?*

They began, explained Pavla, *at the top. A coven calling themselves the North American Council of Thaumaturgy. They seem to be the largest, perhaps the oldest, and by far the most powerful and influential organization of magic users in your country, with authority also over Canada and Mexico. Virtually all of the other, smaller groups respect them or defer to them, and if I am not mistaken, they are the ones who tried to track you down before you met me.*

Kera felt a flash of cold anger like a rush of wind that makes one steel oneself and grow harsher in attitude. *Oh. Them. Yeah, if the Orthodoxy wants to stomp them out of existence, I guess it couldn't happen to a nicer group of people, could it? If they are who you say they are, their minions were the ones who robbed the Kims of their power before we restored it. Fuck them.*

Staring into the astral plane and somehow "seeing" their conversation take shape there, Kera observed the swirling colors that represented Pavla's consciousness contract and dim before resuming their usual hue. Her mind's ear registered it as a sigh of exasperation tinged with sadness, and she knew she'd said something stupid again.

Not that she cared. The bitterness over how the so-called

council had treated her friends and the knowledge that they would have done the same to her had never left Kera's heart.

Kera, Pavla retorted, *I am afraid you do not appreciate the gravity of this situation. You do not understand what it means. You have NO idea how brutal the Orthodoxy is in dealing with its rivals. If anything, we were gentle with you because Anezka wanted you to join us. She only ordered you killed after you refused. In a war with another coven, it is different. They will exterminate every member of the council, as well as anyone who has ever helped them and anyone who resists their rule in any way.*

Once more, Kera felt vaguely embarrassed. Her outburst had been childish. She did not want to admit it, but it was true.

And, Pavla went on, *conflicts of this sort are not merely to rebuke an enemy or for some members to claim scalps and trophies, they are territorial wars of domination. The Orthodoxy means to take out the council because North America, the whole continent, is the council's protectorate. If the Orthodoxy wins, they will claim everything for themselves, and you do not want them ruling over your homeland. I used to have excuses and justifications for their behavior, but no more. Trust me, they are cruel and tyrannical masters, and everyone will suffer if they achieve victory.*

While Kera processed all that her friend had said, Chris leaned closer. "Kera, is everything okay?" He asked it in a soft voice, not wanting to startle her.

She held up a hand without looking at him. "I'm fine," she whispered. The distraction was small, but her perception of the mind-link between herself and Pavla still seemed to fade for a second, and her heart thumped in fear at the thought of losing the connection. But as she focused again on her memories with the Czech witch, their time as both enemies and allies, her view of the swirling colors cleared.

Kera began, *That sounds bad, yeah. What I wanted to ask you about was if you, um, know about any witches taking a train ride from New York to LA by any chance. And now that you mention it, if that* might have anything to do with all this crap going on. *Ugh, I can't believe I was totally unaware of it. I feel stupid.*

Pavla spent a moment considering the question, and the multihued glow grew smaller and darker but paradoxically more intense.

Again, Pavla went on, *it is not your fault that you have not heard, but it's for the best that you know now. I will need to have a closer look to determine what you are asking about with this train. You think someone is on board who wishes you harm?*

Kera nodded, a pointless reflex given that her friend could not see her. *Yes. But first, what all has happened as far as these two covens fighting it out? Has the fighting started, and if so, who's winning?*

Around the periphery of the foggy astral mindscape, Kera began to see other things, distorted images like something from dreams or nightmares that she instantly knew were connected to her question.

Pavla declared. *The fighting began at least two weeks ago, perhaps longer. The Orthodoxy killed a man called Damian, a member of the council, then destroyed their headquarters. They have killed one more member for certain, and possibly one or two others. I believe there were a dozen council members originally. I am not sure how many the Orthodoxy has lost since I am no longer exactly welcome among them, but they probably sacrificed new recruits before risking their senior members. Still, Anezka and the other elder witches do not shy away from battle. For now, the rest of the American council is in hiding, but Anezka will find them, and every last one of them will die without help or tremendous luck.*

Kera felt her body groaning, and her mind responded likewise. *Oh, my God. Is anyone else getting involved in all this? Other casters? Normal people?*

Somewhat, Pavla elaborated. *Non-magical people are always kept in the dark about such matters, if possible. But there are people throughout the continent who have a small amount of power, not enough to be proper witches, but enough that gathering a mass of them could sway the conflict one way or another. The Orthodoxy is trying to intimidate them into inaction and seeks to rule them as vassals. The council sent out a couple of messages seeking to rally them to fight against the invaders. It seems they will do nothing so far. I have thought of intervening on the council's behalf myself. I do not know them, but somehow I hate the thought of the Orthodoxy ruling America the way it has ruled Eastern Europe and northern Asia. I don't want other young witches being deceived the way I was.*

Kera found it odd and poignant that Pavla would turn her back on her former comrades like that. The members of the Orthodoxy were terrible people, yes, but whatever had happened to change Pavla's mind had been even more of an epiphany than Kera had thought.

She herself had played a part in it. Their bond of friendship and the fallout from it was what had started the chain reaction that had led to Pavla's defection.

Pavla, Kera told her, *please don't do anything stupid and get your-self killed. It isn't really your fight, regardless of you wanting revenge. I can't control your decisions, though, and in the meantime, I value your advice. I know it might be risky for both of us, but can you reach out to my location and see if you can perceive any other witches nearby?*

When Pavla hesitated, Kera explained the unusual nature of the sensations she'd had while trying to pinpoint the source of the magic on the train and the suspicious melted engine part.

Not now, said the Czech. *I can do that for you, but not while we are speaking. It is not like putting you on hold on the phone. Please give me a little time, maybe half an hour, and then we will speak again. Don't do anything rash while you wait.*

Kera interjected, *One last thing, quick. Chris is here with me. I wanted him to get the hell out of here for his own safety since I don't know how much of a threat this person is, but of course he refused. And we have an agreement that I won't use compulsion magic on him or anything like that; it's a condition of our relationship. Can you think of a way to, well, make him do what I want?*

117

The colors flickered as though Pavla were laughing. *Use your natural feminine wiles if you must. Otherwise, it is his decision, not yours.*

Kera felt her eyes narrow. *Dammit, not you too! That's the same crap he told me, more or less.*

Well, Pavla countered, *would you wish to spend your life with someone who walked away from you when you were in danger?*

Trying to control her annoyance, Kera confessed, *I suppose not. But since I told him to walk away, it's not as though—*

Without warning, their connection vanished, and Kera found herself shuddering and blinking and staring at Chris' face.

"Uh… She could have warned me she was about to cancel the spell. It's like waking up too fast from a dream."

Chris crossed the space between them and sat next to her. "Well, you were off in the Phantom Zone or wherever, but the train started rolling again a few minutes ago. We're on our way back home. Anyhow, what did Pavla have to say? I'm guessing you got ahold of her."

"Oh, I succeeded." Kera pinched the bridge of her nose and shook her head. "It was nice to hear from her, but she didn't have much good news."

She summarized their conversation, minus the last part. Chris listened and nodded every minute or so.

"I see." He looked worried, almost frightened, but in a way that meant he appreciated the gravity of their circumstances. "That's bad, isn't it? Seems unlikely this curse on the train or whatever it was *isn't* related to the war between covens."

Kera decided to check her phone. "I hope not, but Pavla is going to get back to me shortly. Oh, hey, Lia replied. She's up early, isn't she? Especially by Pacific Time Zone standards. Hmm."

She read the series of text messages. According to Lia's research so far, there had been a few strings of murders throughout America that bore a disturbing resemblance to the human sacrifice techniques described in the book. The list included various older unsolved cases, but also two murders that had occurred within the last couple of weeks not far from where Kera and Chris had been. New York and Pennsylvania.

The slight nausea and the sensation of creeping dread were back.

Lia concluded by requesting they build a database that would allow them to search through crimes by murder method since the amount of information-parsing she had had to do was ridiculous and exhausting.

Kera typed her thanks, combined with a promise to look into the database thing.

"And...Send." She tapped the button, then put her phone to sleep.

Chris snapped his fingers. "I could build that for you. Her. Both of you. It would be useful for the whole agency, wouldn't it? Although if it's a *murder* database, I guess that means our plan to stick to nonviolent cases is being tossed out the window."

Ignoring the latter comment, Kera said, "That would be great. I'm sure Lia would appreciate it, also. She works too damn hard."

Chris shrugged. "No problem. Although, alas, I probably couldn't put it on my résumé."

Scowling, Kera prodded, "Oh, so you're planning to ditch my company and go work for the big leagues after a year or two, is that it?"

He chuckled. "I mean, only if I *have to*. I'd honestly rather stick around and help you reach the big leagues yourself."

She put an arm around his waist and kissed him. "I'm glad to hear that you still *sometimes* say the right thing at the right time."

They spent five or six minutes doing nothing but holding each other, allowing their mutual anxiety to dissipate in one another's warmth.

Then something inside Kera's mind opened up, demanding her full attention. "It's Pavla," she told him, pulling away.

Chris let her go but remained by her side.

Kera refocused her mind, and again the material world seemed to fade, replaced by the vague mists and obscure swirling lights. *Hello?*

Hello, Kera, said Pavla. *I see where you are, and I have looked around. Whoever is on the train with you, I can only say that yes, it is the aura of a person, or rather persons, and not a remote spell. There are at least two of them. I suspect they are from the Orthodoxy because the magic they are using feels familiar, though it is of a type I do not specialize in. I can tell you no more than that, however, without more information.*

Kera had expected the worst, and she was not disappointed. *I see. Actually, Lia, my business partner, just told me about two people being mutilated and murdered in the New York area, and it sounded similar to something I was reading about sacrificial magic. People being sliced up and drained of blood. Lovely stuff. Does that ring a bell?*

It suddenly looked as though the astral meeting place was coated with frost, and Kera shivered.

Yes, Pavla responded. *Yes, I see the connection now. Kera, I don't wish to alarm you, but you may be in terrible danger. The Orthodoxy sometimes employs sacrificial magic of that type when they wish to store and distribute magical power. It is a customary way to enhance their strength during battle or for a major ceremonial casting. A woman called Milena, who is a member of the Orthodoxy's highest council with Anezka, is an expert at that. I believe there are others who can perform it as well.*

Kera almost broke the psychic connection with her sudden urge to slap a palm to her face.

Fuck. You're telling me that's *who we ended up on a train with? This Milena chick, who uses people's blood to power the coven's goddamn war effort?*

Her friend seemingly regretted having spoken. *I cannot say for sure. It could be any high-ranking or powerful member. Perhaps Milena and one other, or it might be two or three people of upper-middle-*

specialist rank, much like the position I used to occupy in their hierar-chy. All I can say for sure is that you should leave. People who have the gift make better sacrifices than those who do not. Perhaps they were not looking for you to begin with, but they sensed your power and now wish to possess it. Be careful, Kera. I don't want to lose you. And I must go for now. We will talk again.

Kera tried to hold on to her and ask for more information, but once more, the Czech abruptly cut her off. She fell back on her bed, shaken and disoriented.

"Are you okay?" Chris laid a hand on her arm. "I'm here. Everything is fine."

Blinking and calming herself, Kera sat up. "Um. Yeah. I appre-ciate that you're trying to be reassuring, but based on what Pavla just said, you're wrong. Everything is pretty far from fine."

CHAPTER TWELVE

Things had been quiet on the train so far, but there was no reason for Kera to assume that they would remain that way. The Orthodoxy's minions were almost certainly still onboard. It was impossible to be certain, but a faint sensation of malign energy following her, combined with an intuition that they wanted to keep an eye on her, suggested that she was not the only magic user on board.

And they had set off again, with the train now speeding down the tracks, while Kera had been in the middle of her psychic "phone call" with Pavla. They had lost their chance to get off; there was no turning back.

Of course, there were other stops, and in theory, Kera could use magic or a bullshit story about having a medical emergency to get the train to stop elsewhere if it was strictly necessary, but she preferred not to. Had she and Chris slipped away while the train was broken down, it would have been easier to blend in with the other people who were already doing that.

But at this point, their leaving would look suspicious. The witches would take note and act accordingly.

"Dammit," Chris said, his fingers clicking on the keyboard on his laptop while his eyes stayed fixed on the screen. "I forgot how tedious and annoying databases are to make. I mean, it's not all that *difficult*, but it's, I dunno, unpleasant."

Kera was absorbed in some reading of her own. "Mm. I bet. Speaking of unpleasant, it sounds, based on what Lia is sending me, like my worst hunches were correct. Or if not entirely correct, then, at a minimum *likely*, and substantiated in part."

Chris stopped working and looked at her. "Oh? As in, the thing about unsolved murders?"

"Correct."

She had been reading up on cases involving various slayings, most of them suggested by Lia, and looking at photographs where she could find them. Then it was a matter of comparing the data to the stuff in the book on sacrificial magic.

She added, "I wish I was wrong. I mean, this stuff is grisly, and I thought I had enough of it after the Alchemist. But insofar as there *are* people out there performing human sacrifices to boost their own powers, someone has to put a stop to it."

Chris let out a gravelly sigh. "*Someone*, yeah. I wonder who?"

"Don't be all fatuous," she chided him. "Unless Pavla is way off, we have someone guilty of that exact type of crime on the train with us as we speak. It's not a thing to be taken lightly."

She shuddered. It had not occurred to her until she had perused the book how many ways the human body could be mutilated.

Chris set aside his laptop and leaned forward on his bed. "You know me. But I *am* taking it seriously. That's why I insisted on staying by your side, remember? So without further ado, what do you intend to do about it?"

Kera's mouth stretched across her face in a sour grimace. "Give me a second. I need to finish looking at this part. A plan is forming, but it'll take a minute or two for me to articulate it."

"Okay." He left her alone while she completed her reading.

When she was done, her mind, freed from focusing on one

thing while trying to think about another, switched to the task of how best to deal with the witches on the train.

Right, her mind began. *First of all, they're probably not right next door. I would guess they're somewhere on the other half of the train, maybe closer to the conductor and such. That would explain how easily they were able to fuck up the engine and put that poor assistant guy to sleep at just the right time.*

Second, we have to assume they know I'm here but haven't figured out my precise location. Or if they have, they're not in a hurry to come after me.

And third, it's possible they'll kill someone else as a sacrifice if they can't have me. I have to find a way to draw them out before they can do that without getting civilians caught in the crossfire.

Which is going to be an absolute bastard of a task on a goddamn train. We don't have the same amount of elbow room as when I had a whole half-empty city block to fight other witches in. And there's nowhere for anyone to flee if violence breaks out right next to them. Dammit.

She spent another moment collecting her thoughts, then told Chris everything that had occurred to her.

"Yeah," he concurred. "Those are all valid concerns. The problem is that we don't *know* much so far. If you ask me, our first priority needs to be reconnaissance. If you can figure out where they are before they figure out where *we* are, that gives us the advantage and will allow us to keep an eye on what they're up to."

Kera stood up and stretched her arms, then began pacing, her skin itching from a sudden sense of claustrophobia in the small compartment. "Yeah, well, they'll continue to cloak their magic, which will make it difficult to observe them, but there are other things we can do. Figure out which car or cabin they're in, then maybe set up remote-viewing spells like a security camera to see when and if anyone comes out."

"Good idea." He bristled with excitement, glad to be focusing on something other than databases. "And maybe leave a few traps for them in case they try anything. Not, like, explode-y stuff, but maybe subtle curses or tracking spells, as well as alarms that will let us know if they get too close."

Kera braced herself against her bed and placed her feet against the wall to stretch. "Yes, definitely. And it just occurred to me that in order to minimize the effects on other passengers, we might have to resort to old-fashioned melee combat if things get ugly, so don't mind me if I start practicing moves here. Ugh, I'm out of practice."

She went through a handful of basic karate drills and katas to the best of her ability in the limited space. She was sufficiently skilled and athletic that it being a week and a half since her last training session wasn't going to cripple her effectiveness, but it was long enough that she did not feel like she was in top form.

Chris remarked as he watched her, "It doesn't hurt to be prepared to kick some ass if you have to, but remember, finding out where they are ought to be our first priority. Don't get ahead of yourself."

Kera moved back and forth around the corner of her bed, launching kicks, punches, and knee strikes into the open spaces available to her. She wondered if she ought to practice in cramped quarters more often since it taught a set of skills one couldn't learn in more open areas.

"Yeah," she acknowledged. "In a minute. I'll go out alone. That way, I can do all the magic shit without you being at risk in case I, like, bump directly into them."

His face became grave, and she more or less knew what he was going to say, so she cut him off.

"Don't worry. I'll link us up mentally before I head out, so if anything weird happens, you'll feel it right away. You will know to come looking for me or call 911 or have them stop the train or something if it's particularly bad. But I doubt it will come to that."

Chris squinted uncertainly as he thought it over. "I suppose that makes sense and ought to be sufficient, but I can't help worrying. Then again, last time I went out to the dining car, there were still other passengers mingling around, not to mention they brought on some auxiliary engineers who are inspecting most of the train, presumably to figure out what the hell happened overnight. So with all that human traffic around, I don't think our friends will risk doing anything too nasty."

Kera began to clear her mind in preparation for the spells she would need to cast. "Yeah, probably."

Witches need to eat too, she recalled. *More than normal people in a lot of cases, so the dining car would be the place to lay most of the traps and recon spells. While I'm out there, I can keep scanning the crowd and the area to see if I can get a bead on which compartment they're in.*

Chris was spinning a pen in his fingers, and it occurred to her that if she were able to determine that things were sufficiently safe, she might be able to place enchantments on random objects and have him "accidentally" deposit them in different places around the train.

That would enable her to avoid spending too much magical energy—and thereby risking detection of her casting aura—at one time since the enchanting could be done after she returned to their cabin.

Kera took a deep breath and put on her silver- and iron-studded jacket to disguise what she was about to do from prying minds. "Okay, I'm going to test to see if our emotional link is working. Tell me if you get a sudden blast of, um, feelings." She raised her fingers to her temples, resting them against her head and allowing her eyes to glaze over as she focused her sight and attention first inward, then toward her lover.

Chris nodded. Five seconds later, he jerked in place, blinking and exclaiming, "Whoa! All this excitement must have gotten you riled up. Damn, girl. We definitely need to try that sometime in real life, when, um, things are a little more calm and relaxed, not to mention private."

Refocusing her eyes on the physical world, Kera saw Chris grinning at her with charmingly evil intent, and she couldn't help bursting out laughing. "Yeah, I'll think about it. I wanted to make sure I got your attention, and that seemed to do the trick."

"Oh, it did," he confirmed. "It did. I suppose if you need to use the link next time, though, it will be something that isn't as fun, like a stab of fear warning me of impending danger or blah blah blah." His smile faded. "Be careful. You know I'd be happy to come with you, but then again, I know you won't allow me to, so I guess it's pointless to mention it."

She leaned over and kissed him on the cheek. "Not pointless since I appreciate the gesture. It's always nice to hear that someone cares. But yes, you are completely correct in your prediction. I forbid you to follow me. If I get caught, I don't want them marking *both* of us."

He kissed her back, a quick peck on the lips. "Fair enough. But they might have seen us together earlier, you realize."

"Keyword, 'might,'" she pointed out. "We're not sure. If they haven't, I don't want to take the risk. Anyway, there's nothing suspicious about me going out to get food, so this ought to be easy, and I imagine everything will be fine. If they're planning to attack us, I doubt they would be stupid enough to do it in the middle of a crowded dining car. They would be more likely to either try it remotely by magic, in which case we both have charms and stuff protecting us, or to follow us after we get off the train."

Chris had to agree. "That's not a very pleasant thought either, is it? But we can burn that bridge when we come to it. Anyway, good luck, babe. If by some chance you do have to hit me with the warning signal, I'll, um, come to your rescue to the best of my ability. I can't cast spells, and I don't have my.357 Magnum with me either, but if I have to punch a witch in the face, I'll do it."

"I know you will." She flashed him a final smile. "Be back in a few minutes."

Turning away, she opened the door and stepped out into the narrow hall, then crossed into the next car.

Things were quiet so far. She could faintly hear people streaming movies or shows on mobile devices or having low conversations in nearby cabins, though the steady rustling hum of the train's movements muffled the bulk of the sounds. A slight chatter came from some people in the next compartment down as they left to head toward the dining car up ahead.

Kera suddenly thought of something and narrowed her eyes in annoyance at herself.

Damn. I should have laid a trap or alarm on the door to our room. Well, I can do that on my way back in. Might be safer that way, besides.

To the best of her recollection, the "food truck," as Chris had begun calling it, was eleven cars down from theirs out of the twenty-two the train possessed. It was the next compartment toward the front after the "foyer" car, which was right in the middle and was typically the one from whence the passengers disembarked or boarded at stations.

"Long way to go," she mumbled to herself, striding down the hall.

So far, she had not detected any obvious signs of magic that were fixed to a particular location. There was still the vague, cloudy sense of witchcraft in the air, but it was elusive, and she had no way of being sure if it would become clearer to her as she got closer to the culprits.

I bet they're in the front half past the dining car. Do I want to risk going all the way up to the front cab and sweeping the whole train, or should I only go halfway to get something to eat and call it good? That would be less chancy but it would also feel half-assed.

But if I can eliminate the prospect of our friends lurking anywhere in the back half, then that narrows it down enough for us to plan accordingly for the rest of the trip.

Between the third and fourth cars up from hers, noting the absence of other humans nearby, she paused to cast a spell.

Closing her eyes and resting against the wall as though she were tired or thinking in case someone saw her, she focused on the floor, the walls, the doors. Then she linked it mentally and magically to the specific feeling given off by the amorphous aura-cloud she had sensed hovering around the train. Whatever its true source was, if it came to this spot, she would know.

By itself, the spell would have made a sufficient warning, but Kera added another layer to it.

She thought about everything she had read about sacrificial magic, as well as all the stuff Lia had sent her and what Pavla had disclosed. Kera married it all to the idea of hostile intent.

If someone crossed the point where she stood meaning to perform dark magic of that sort, the alarm would announce itself three times louder and more intensely than if the witches were merely taking a harmless stroll.

A somewhat overweight woman crowded past Kera, ignoring her except insofar as she represented an obstacle to her progress. Kera stared at her back, trying to discern anything about her.

I don't think she's one of the Orthodoxy's. Way too American-looking, and she doesn't give off the slightest whiff of magic.

Then again, I probably don't either, provided I keep the jacket on and am careful. Do I? Shit. They might have similar protections.

There was only one way to find out.

Kera stepped through the transition into the next car. The woman who'd pushed past her was gone, but an engineer and another guy had removed a panel from the wall in the hall and were poking around, examining the wiring.

She approached them. "Hey, did they ever find out what caused the breakdown?"

Both men turned their heads to look at her. "Uh," the engineer began, "engine part failure, but we're still trying to figure out why that happened to begin with. There wasn't anything else wrong that could have caused it, so it seems like a freak accident so far. Right now, the theory is that it was caused by an electrical surge that got too close to the engine and electrocuted something through a crack in the insulation, but we don't really know to be honest."

She nodded. "Weird. Well, good luck."

Moving on, she found herself wondering, *Does the Orthodoxy have any male witches in their organization? Warlocks, I guess. Or just like, mercenary dudes who work for them. I don't recall meeting any around Pavla. Seems like magic is more common in women, but then again,* How to Be a Badass Witch *never said anything about sex or gender restrictions, not to mention there's the matter of Mr. Kim.*

She wished she had thought to ask Pavla about it when the chance presented itself, but she had been distracted. For now, she would have to assume the Orthodoxy's agents on the train were women, but it was by no means guaranteed.

Nothing happened as Kera progressed to the dining car. It was around five in the afternoon by now, and people were getting hungry for supper. As she crossed into the food truck from the foyer car, she counted no fewer than twenty-three passengers besides her, in addition to an attendant keeping watch over things and a cook bringing in a steaming pan to replace one on the buffet that had been emptied.

Realizing she needed to scope out the room better before casting her spells, Kera took out her phone and pretended to check a couple of things as she drifted around the periphery of the cabin. She repeated the charm she had laid between the third and fourth cars at the doorway between the dining room and the next compartment toward the front.

Next, she put her phone away and got in line, laying subtle spells on the food itself. She didn't want to inflict any harm on innocent people, so the only hexes she cast were those designed to inhibit magic and cause it to backfire. If they worked the way she hoped, the Orthodoxy's witches would end up ingesting something that disagreed with them in an unexpected fashion.

She smirked as she heaped a plate with as much sustenance as she could fit on it. *That'll teach 'em. Maybe they'll suspect something, but probably not. Since I distributed pieces of the curse throughout the whole array, it won't take effect until everything mixes together in their stomachs. Mwahaha.*

I just hope none of them are vegetarians or on a gluten-free diet.

As she laid the final piece of the spell on the dessert cart, Kera felt it again—the sense of someone looking at her, of an obscure power feeling around the edges of her suppressed aura.

Crap. They must be close, or I used too much magic at once, and it slipped between the cracks in the protection offered by my jacket.

Kera made sure not to flinch or look around too quickly. Still, as she made ready to depart the food truck, she did both a visual and a mental-thaumaturgic scan of her surroundings.

None of the other passengers, who all seemed like banal individuals and were mostly distracted by chattering with each other or focusing on their meals, gave off any signs of being witches. If by some chance any of them were her targets, their powers were cloaked exceedingly well.

Still, her nerves were beginning to fray. She knew she would be in peril if she hung around here too much longer, and she would rather eat in peace back in her room, anyway.

Kera took her food out of the dining car and made her way back toward the rearmost compartment. With two layers of security in addition to the hexed food, she felt pretty confident that her foes would not have an easy time getting to her.

I'm almost positive they're riding in the front half, and I bet they were on their way to the food truck right as I left. That means that they ought to eat the food I cursed before someone else finishes it off and ruins the spell.

When she was a bit more than halfway back to her and Chris' room, the alarm at the far end of the dining car went off.

Kera tensed and almost missed a step. The psychic wave it sent out was the lesser alarm, meaning that whoever had tripped it was on the move but was not coming toward her or anyone else with murderous or sacrificial intent. Nonetheless, it frightened her to know a deadly enemy was nearby, but not what they looked like or exactly where they lurked.

She rejoined Chris, who sat up on his bed the instant she came in.

"How'd it go?" he asked.

She told him everything, including the part about the warning signal a moment ago.

He rubbed his chin and nodded. "Yeah, interesting. The cursed food was a nice touch, heh. Hope they're ingesting mass quantities of it right now. And at least you seem confident that they aren't staying in one of the cabins close to us. That makes life easier. So, do you want me to head out and get some food as well to check on things?"

"Yes," she replied and flushed with guilt. "I don't want you risking yourself, but they probably don't know who you are, and you don't have an aura, so as long as you don't do anything really suspicious, you ought to be fine."

He raised a finger. "Plus, I have the charm, remember?"

She remembered. After eating half of her food, she placed further enchantments on a trio of objects—a pen, a nickel, and a paper coffee cup—that would activate low-level remote viewing and audio spells if any casters came too close to them.

"So," Kera explained, "just 'accidentally' drop those at a few points throughout the train. Ideally, if you can get past the dining car, drop one of them there. That way, we'll have advance warning if they head toward the middle of the train before we're about to get breakfast in the morning. And again, act casual."

Chris stood up and smiled. "Casual is my middle name, babe."

She squinted at him. "No, it isn't, but I don't think you ever told me what your middle name actually is, come to think of it."

CHAPTER THIRTEEN

Their night at the hotel had passed in relative peace, but the looming sense of danger had not gone away.

Mother LeBlanc emerged from the room she shared with Crystal Green and Amanda Moore. The informal conference they had agreed to would be beginning momentarily, and most of the other members were already in the living area of the largest room on the hotel's second floor. Samantha Martinez and Mary Mitchell were coming down the hall.

LeBlanc flagged them down. "How is James?" She wasn't sure which of them was handling healing duties for the evening, so the question was posed to both women equally.

Samantha frowned and seemed unsure of what to say, so Mary took the initiative. "He is somewhat better. The long walk worsened his condition after the improvements he had made, but not enough to put him back in critical condition. I would guess he'll be back to where he was with another day or two of rest."

LeBlanc nodded as they walked toward the meeting place. "Will he be in attendance? I'm guessing not, or he would likely be with you."

This time, Samantha was the one who answered her. "He's up. He said he'll join us in a few minutes if he's able, but we told him not to worry about it if he didn't feel up to moving around and talking."

They were right in front of the entrance to their destination when a door behind them opened. LeBlanc glanced over her shoulder and saw James shuffle out, so she waited.

A moment later, James was at her side. "Hi."

She looked him over. He had the appearance of a man who had undergone major surgery but had not had time for such trivial matters as a shower or a shave. He knew he presented a grimy and pathetic appearance, but he was trying to maintain his dignity.

"Good evening, James. I'm glad to see you're doing better. Shall we?" She offered him her arm.

He managed a wan smile and looped his arm around her elbow as they stepped into the living room of the double suite they had rented.

Everyone else was already there, waiting. There were nods and murmurs of encouragement at the sight of James, though half of them also furrowed their brows in worry about his marginal condition.

LeBlanc helped him sit down before she took her own place and waited for the discussion to begin. She assumed Mary would act as master of ceremonies, though she planned to do most of the talking today.

Lady Mitchell did not disappoint. "Good evening, everyone. We have come far, and for the time being, we are safe. Let us rejoice in the small victories we have won, but we need to discuss what to do next. Mother, I believe you had something you wanted to tell us or a suggestion to make?"

Mother LeBlanc raised her hands as all eyes turned to her. "Yes. We have thus far been unable to decide where we shall go from here. We cannot stay in West Virginia. It seems we've found a good hiding place for the time being, but our enemies will find us soon. We also have to assume they are considering the possibility of our flight to some other part of the country, or possibly to South America, Africa, Australia, or a similarly distant locale that is not under their control. Europe would be a poor idea, naturally, since that is where the Orthodoxy is strongest."

The other thaumaturgists nodded. What she had told them was a review, but it helped put their situation in perspective.

LeBlanc continued, "Allow me to make a firm proposal. I hinted at this before, but I now believe it is the best option that remains to us. I motion for this council to adjourn to my home city of New Orleans. I know it well, and they do not. It is a place with magical traditions that run deep and yet are unique. The Orthodoxy would not be familiar with our forms of thaumaturgy, witchcraft, and what is inaccurately called 'voodoo,' et cetera. We would have ways of protecting ourselves there that would not be open to us in any other spot on the planet."

Mary Mitchell rubbed a knuckle over her lips. "It makes a certain amount of sense, yes, but as I believe we discussed before, the Orthodoxy has likely obtained enough information about us to know that you hail from Louisiana. They may have anticipated us fleeing there and posted sentries, traps, or spies to alert them before we can get within a day's journey of the city."

Hugh made a low grumbling sound. "Sad but probably true. I feel like LeBlanc's idea is fundamentally good, but going there creates far more risk than if we decided to lay low in Pueblo, Colorado, or another random town that they would never suspect."

LeBlanc's face was set in her usual serene smile. She did not appear perturbed by her colleagues' remarks, though they were less than encouraging.

"I considered that," she retorted. "We are far from helpless, please recall. When we reach the Deep South, we can begin employing the necessary magic to scan for whatever traps the Orthodoxy may have laid, as well as cloaking and protecting ourselves. And if we keep our movements quiet the whole way there, they will not know for certain that NOLA is our destination. Thus, their forces will be spread across the country rather than entirely shifted to the bayou."

Rufus chuckled. "Yes, true. I suspect we were all cowed by our defeat in open battle at the Lovecraft estate, but we mustn't forget that pound for pound, any of us, individually, is more than a match for all but the strongest of them. As long as they cannot concentrate all their people against us directly, it is well within our power to overcome them. At least for long enough to take refuge in a city."

"True," said Mary. "But I must ask that we have a Plan B and Plan C in mind if something should go wrong. If, for example, we are ambushed by half of their troops at once somewhere along the way, which would weaken us beyond the point of all resistance as well as give away our intentions."

LeBlanc knew Mary was only playing devil's advocate for the sake of keeping them from failure. She had taken their humiliation, not to mention the loss of Damian and Zacharia, as hard as any of them.

"Of course," LeBlanc agreed. "But insofar as our Plan A *is* Plan A, we should invest the necessary planning and effort to see to it that it does not go awry except through the worst possible luck."

No one voiced any objections. The first to ask for further clarification of their specific goals, though, was Amanda Moore.

"Okay," she said. "You mentioned that friends of yours, as well as the unusual localized magical currents, can help hide us in New Orleans. But what then? Surely the idea isn't to simply hunker down and wait until the Orthodoxy decides to stop ruling the continent in our stead. Didn't you say something before about an artifact there that might be helpful to us in fighting back?"

Everyone had known going into the discussion that it would

be just a matter of time until Amanda brought up the subject of fighting. The rigors of their journey and the passage of time had taken only a tiny bit of the edge off her lingering anger.

LeBlanc neglected to respond immediately. She had to strike a delicate balance in discussing the matter and emphasize that what she sought in Louisiana was probably their best chance but she could not *promise* them anything.

"Perhaps," she stated. "It is a good prospect, but not a certainty. I must investigate it further and cannot do so until we arrive there. I reiterate that even if everything does not go in our favor, New Orleans will be a safer place to regroup than any other, and it might be the place where the tide turns. I can think of no better gamble, but we must keep in mind that *everything* is a gamble nowadays."

Amanda inhaled sharply through her nose. "Very well. I don't think we should flee any farther than NOLA, though. Sooner or later, we have to hit back, and I say we do it sooner rather than later."

The talk dragged on for another twenty minutes as they all voiced their concerns and tried to plan the exact sequence of actions they would undertake over the next forty-eight hours, complete with emergency backup plans. James contributed little, but he seemed well enough to follow what the others said if nothing else.

Toward the end, mere minutes before they wrapped things up, everyone went tense and cold as a psychic signal announced itself in all of their minds at once.

The room was as silent as an underground vault until Samantha asked in a whisper, "Who is that? They're using *our* signal."

It was quiet for another half a minute as each of the thaumaturgists, including Ezeudo and James, turned over what they had heard in their minds. Someone wished to speak to them, claiming to be locals who knew who they were and were on their side.

Josiah Kane pointed out, "It could be a trap. I don't think it is, but there is the possibility that the Orthodoxy has compromised someone among the lesser covens and is using them to get at us by broadcasting over our trusted astral frequency."

"Yes," said Mary, "that had occurred to me also. No one respond yet, please. Do your own scans of the surrounding area. We must find out who this person is, where they are, and if they're alone. If there is any significant reason to assume it is a trick, we mustn't reply, but if it seems safe to assume that they are legitimate, we should hear them out and perhaps invite them in."

Hugh Buchanan and Amanda looked uncertain but did not object. They all spent three or four minutes extending their minds over the surrounding region, searching for any trace of magic within ten or twelve miles in every direction from their hotel.

Finally, LeBlanc said, "There are two people who are making only the slightest effort to cloak or otherwise hide. I feel no trace of anyone else with the gift nearby. It is unlikely to be an ambush, but that does not eliminate the danger that they are compromised and waiting to send the Orthodoxy a text message once they uncover our precise location. We might not be in immediate danger, but there is a chance that they will put us on the path to trouble within the next several hours."

"Mm, yes," Hugh rumbled. "I agree. We might consider directing them to a location in town where we can read their intentions better and *then* meet them face to face if all seems well."

Mary closed her eyes. "Good idea. Everyone else, please collaborate on hiding me while I tell them to go to the feedlot on the other side of town. From there, we can determine if they are sincere or if we have to go on the run yet again tonight."

It took half an hour. The two minor witches, a man and a woman, agreed and stood awkwardly in front of the feedlot's fence. Watching them via a scrying spell, most of the council agreed they didn't seem excessively nervous, but it was hard to be sure. Similarly, Amanda, whose work with animals made her their expert on reading subtle feelings and intentions, could not detect any trace of duplicity or malevolence.

"All right," concluded Mary. "Let's bring them on board. Any objections?"

Hugh said, "None, but let us be prepared for fight or flight if by some chance our assessment was wrong."

They all agreed.

Since the town was small, it took only another few minutes for the pair to arrive at the hotel. The council had told the concierge/clerk with the aid of a suggestion spell to permit visitors but call them at once if anyone inquired. The phone rang, and Mary gave permission for the couple to ascend to the second floor.

Lady Mitchell hung up and glanced around. "Positions, everyone."

LeBlanc, Amanda, Josiah, and Ezeudo had been chosen to be the welcoming committee. The others stayed back to protect James and effect a retreat via the rear balcony into the nearby forest if need be.

Observing the approaching messengers via a remote-viewing spell that kept watch on the hallway by the stairs and the elevator on the first floor, LeBlanc saw no sign of suspicious activity. She took a deep breath and smiled as they came through the door.

"Welcome," she greeted them. "I'm Mother LeBlanc, and I believe I saw you two at the gathering of the covens we called some weeks ago, though I'm afraid we were never introduced."

The woman said, "Yes, my name's Mindy, and this is Dan. We wanted to say we're sorry. We should have supported you when we had the chance. Almost everyone in our coven feels the same

141

way. We want to do what we can to help, even if it's too little, too late. Maybe. Hopefully not."

Dan added, "We heard about what happened to Damian and Zacharia. The Orthodoxy is trying to scare everyone into line with nightmare imagery of what will happen if we cross them. We don't want people like that in charge."

LeBlanc exchanged glances with the other three, then looked at her guests again. "It's good to hear that some of you are finally coming to your senses."

A sense of cautious and hesitant peace had set in, combined with the certainty that it would not last. It reminded Kera of a typical morning before a workday that she knew would be long and difficult.

Chris tapped his fork on the edge of his plate, drawing a faint ringing sound from the impact of metal on ceramic. "Their breakfast spread is better than I was expecting," he remarked. "I'm also impressed that we get ceramic plates instead of paper or plastic ones. It's a nice touch."

Kera was deep into a platter of well-done bacon, just-right scrambled eggs, and a couple of nice fluffy biscuits. "Agreed," she said between mouthfuls. "Looks like they use the cheap kind of syrup for the hotcakes, which was why I didn't get any, but I mean, you can't have everything."

She was distracted, though. The hammer would fall fairly soon; it was inevitable. She only hoped that she and Chris hadn't missed anything important while they were asleep.

Chris continued to make attempts at conversation. He had gotten a good night's sleep and was oddly refreshed and animated this morning.

"You know," he went on, "it's weird that we haven't seen or heard anything from the witches yet, besides that minor ping you got when they went into the dining car yesterday evening. Do you think it alerted them that you were keeping watch on the place, so now they're avoiding it?"

Kera scowled at her eggs. "Of all the questions you could have asked, you had to go with *that* one. I don't have an answer to that, and my guess is only slightly better than yours. Like, I didn't notice anything that would suggest they knew what I did, but then again, they seem to have themselves well-cloaked. So it's tough to say. We're going to have to wait it out and see what they do next."

While she shoveled the remainder of the food into her mouth, Chris sat contemplatively over the bit that still lay on his plate. He sipped his coffee and gazed at the wall, his eyes vacant but oddly focused.

"Have you been gaming scenarios for what we should do, depending on what *they* do? I would have done more of that sort of thing myself, but I'm not a thaumaturge, so I'm not in as good a position as you are to work out the details."

Kera washed down the mass of biscuit and egg with a swig of her coffee, which she had left black. "Yes. Kinda. Give me another ten minutes to wake up and we'll go over some of that. Honestly, though, most of them are just variations on 'stay out of the way while I beat the shit out of these people, and keep other people out of the way too.' I'm getting tired of waiting for the other shoe to drop."

Chris nodded. "Well, if they follow us to LA, we can probably get away with delaying the fun stuff until then. That way, at least we're on our home turf instead of on this goddamn train."

Kera managed a chuckle at that. "Yeah…" Her voice trailed off, and her eyes were heavy with sadness as she looked over Chris' shoulder and out the window. "It's only a matter of time before I'm in a fight, though, and probably not an easy one. I wish…" She sighed. "I wish Pavla was here right now."

Eyebrows shooting upward, Chris refocused his eyes on his girlfriend's face. "Whoa. That bad, huh?"

"Yeah," she muttered again. "Makes me sound like one of those girls who can't make up their mind about anything, doesn't it? I mean, she *was* a friend. She did some pretty detestable shit due to her conflicted loyalties at first, but the part that was good was *genuinely* good. It was just mixed in with the bad."

"True," Chris affirmed. "Even when you were the most furious with her, I could tell you missed the good parts of your working relationship with her as a tutor, confidante, and so forth. I suppose it doesn't help that that was when I was being a bit standoffish over our trust issues, but we resolved those, didn't we?"

Kera nodded. "Yes. But it's not only a personal thing. With Pavla, I mean. She knows what she's doing. She would understand what's happening on this train and be in a better position to confront it than I am. Or you are, no offense. With her around, at least I wouldn't be on my own." She paused and blinked. "For the magical part, I mean. Again, no offense."

"None taken," he replied, finishing his coffee. "I might be a muggle, but I'm still here for you and will help however I can." He reached over and put his hand atop hers.

She blushed. "Thank you, Chris. I was seriously pissed when you wouldn't leave the other day after I asked you to. Like, I felt I was doing the right thing, and you kept giving me all this logical crap and disagreeing when I wasn't in the mood to argue, and just...ugh. But now that I've slept on it," she exhaled, "I appreciate you being here. And I'm glad you chose to stay with me."

He came over to her bed, sat next to her, and held her for a minute or two.

She enjoyed it and allowed herself to relax, but her mind could not help focusing on the tasks at hand.

"Hey," she mumbled as much to herself as to Chris. "I wonder if we could try having Lia and Stephanie look into this stuff back home? The Orthodoxy, I mean, and if they're still operating in Los Angeles. They obviously had a presence there before when they were after me, but now I'm thinking that they might have a 'permanent' base of operations for their war against this other coven."

Chris gave a low grunt. "Hm, yeah. That could be. Doesn't sound pleasant, though, if that's the case. And definitely a long stride away from our supposed goal of staying out of trouble and away from nasty, dangerous stuff."

"I know," she shot back. "But again, we might be the only ones qualified to stop them if that's the case. Besides, I don't want even more witches waiting for me when we get back. Let's run it by Lia and see what she says."

Chris set her free of his embrace and she snatched up her phone, then sent Lia a text asking her to trace the information that Pavla had left them and look for anything suspicious in the greater LA area that might point to an influx of magic users. *And if so*, Kera typed in conclusion, ***they should definitely be found and stopped. After I get back.*** Then she tapped the Send button and waited as Chris drifted back to his laptop.

Lia replied a minute and a half later, and Kera opened the message immediately.

> **I can check, but don't expect miracles since I'm not qualified to look for things that are hidden by magic. Still, we're building enough of a knowledge base that I might be able to turn up something. You'll hear from me before you return.**

Smiling, Kera put her phone away. "Lia is a heck of an employee."

It looked like Chris was about to say something by way of reply, but he stopped when he saw the look that took over Kera's face.

She stiffened as her eyes glazed over, entranced.

The witches on the train had tripped another of the spells, specifically the enchanted pen that was lying on the floor in the corridor past the dining car. She had set it up to begin a remote-viewing session as soon as their targets passed.

"It's them," she said. "And I can see them."

CHAPTER FOURTEEN

Milena's face burned bright red. She *hated* that she was unable to control her reaction, but on the occasion—the *rare* occasion— that she made a mistake of this magnitude, it was functionally impossible for her not to blush.

She was a professional, and professionals at her level weren't supposed to make mistakes.

Hana stepped past her in the hall. Her usually serene face was tight with alarm, and she was already extending her hands in the necessary gesture to disrupt or cancel the spell. Milena was capable of neutralizing it herself, but she was too distressed. Plus, she had to turn her face away. Not only out of embarrassment at having flushed to the color of a ripe strawberry but also so their hidden adversary wouldn't get too long a look at her features.

While Milena stood facing the wall, trying to calm herself, and Hana focused on the pen, Daniela did her part by blocking the two of them off from other passengers. The train was relatively quiet at this hour. Breakfast was mostly over, and people were returning to their cabins to relax, but there was an old couple passing by.

Daniela positioned herself so the old folks, much to their annoyance at her rudeness, were forced to go single-file around her. That conveniently kept them away from the other two witches.

In Russian, Hana said, "It is a crude spell, but strong. I have blocked it, but it will take a moment to defeat it altogether. This person, whoever they are, has a substantial amount of power, though their knowledge of how to use it is amateurish. Brute force rather than finesse, you might say."

Milena's hands were shaking with anger and humiliation, but by crossing her arms over her chest and clamping her fingers around her biceps, she was able to hide it. Her face was not as burning hot as it had been a minute ago; it must have been returning to its normal color.

"Yes, I had figured that out myself. Thank you, Hana." She was halfway sincere. Hana was doing what she was supposed to and serving her purpose well enough, but it irked Milena that she had to make such an obvious statement and draw attention to the fact that their opponent was of inferior skill.

Milena sniffed and turned around. The old couple was long gone. Aside from the passengers lodged in the cabins around them, they had the car to themselves.

"This," she opined, "is what I hate about untrained magic users. They do things that no sensible person would devise, thinking they can get away with it because of their ignorance of how sloppy they are."

Daniela let out a sharp, snorting laugh. "Well, it worked on us, didn't it?"

"Shut up, Daniela," Milena snapped. "You are not helping. Yes, it did work, but only for a matter of seconds. She, or he, might not even have known how to properly view us once the spell was triggered. At best, they received a glimpse of us, and that would have been from a low and awkward angle since they dropped the pen on the floor like an imbecile."

Still, Daniela was technically correct. There was a chance that the other witch knew what they looked like, whereas the three of them were still in the dark about who their secret adversary was. They had no idea if it was a man, a woman, old, young, or anything else. It could be virtually anyone on the train.

Hana's face strained itself with the amount of effort and magical energy she had to expend to shut down their rival's arcane "camera." It took only a few seconds, though. Once she'd ascertained the exact power level of the spell, the crudity of its technique made it relatively easy to disarm. The energies surrounding the pen dissipated and returned to the spiritual realm from whence they had come.

Milena nodded in approval as Hana turned back to the other two.

"So," Milena began, "we made an error by *overestimating* our target. We assumed she was on our level and fell for one of the simplest tricks in the proverbial book because it was so obvious that we did not assume she was stupid enough to try it."

She defaulted to referring to the mysterious person as "she" out of the common knowledge that witches were more commonly female, but it was no more than a placeholder until they could learn more.

Daniela, of course, could not leave well enough alone. "Actually, we fell for *two* simple tricks. Or wait, three. The tripwire spell last night, and also the thing with the spell being spread across all the food on the buffet. That one was pretty clever if you ask me. If we catch them, I'll make sure to send my regards while I'm breaking their jaw, arms, legs, and other body parts." She grinned and planted her right fist in the palm of her left hand.

"Yes," said Milena. "Feel free to do that when the time comes as long as you do not kill them or inflict too much damage on the important body zones. I must have a victim who is healthy and mostly intact, remember."

Daniela frowned but wasn't about to argue. For all her obnoxiousness, she was not an idiot and understood the importance of respecting the Orthodoxy's ironclad chain of command. Milena ranked higher than she did and had the final say.

Hana raised a hand to add her opinion as they continued down the hall toward the dining car. "We have learned several things that are of use to us, though. We know this witch is strong, which makes it perplexing that their aura is so hard to detect. They must have put special consideration into cloaking themselves and learned to do it to a higher level of sophistication than most other procedures."

"Perhaps," agreed Milena, "or she has an artifact that does the work for her. Maybe she accidentally stumbled onto the efficacy of silver or iron without grasping the implications for her casting abilities. We should keep an eye out for anyone wearing metal of any kind."

Daniela nodded. "Yeah. Noted."

They opened the door to the dining room. All three had been mentally scanning for tripwire spells similar to the one they had triggered yesterday, but it seemed their foe had not bothered to replace it after they disarmed it last night.

"Remember," Milena chided, "we are not to make the same mistakes twice. Hana, stay focused on anything that gives off an odor similar to the magic we have encountered so far. Daniela, keep your eyes on everyone who comes in. I will check the food before we eat."

They got in line, doing nothing to make themselves obvious or suspicious. There were only two people ahead of them at the buffet, the older couple who had squeezed past them a couple of minutes ago.

Much to Milena's annoyance, the staff was on the verge of closing down breakfast and had not bothered to replace the food with anything fresher, so they would likely have to use minor heating spells to heat their food up from lukewarm once they were back in their room.

She went first, examining and scanning every item of food as she passed it, including things she did not add to her plate, as well as all of the condiments, utensils, napkins, and other accessories.

Nothing, so far.

How adorable, she thought. *Our upstart thought that hitting us with a mediocre inhibition spell once would be enough to stop us from doing anything for the rest of the journey. She or he is making this whole business more difficult and irritating than it needs to be. I look forward to having the job done and over with so I can return to pursuits that are a better use of my valuable time and talents.*

But Anezka has spoken. I will do as instructed, no matter what.

Reminding herself of her duties and her reputation for reliability calmed Milena and brought her back up to the height of her mental powers. They had encountered a handful of minor setbacks, that was all. Flushing the hidden witch out was a foregone conclusion, regardless of how long it took.

After Milena had cleared the food, her companions filled their plates. None of them had realized at first that they had been hexed by last night's supper, and the aggravating process of waiting for the hex to weaken and then using what powers they could summon to accelerate the spell's decay had stopped them from accomplishing much last night. But they would not have the same problem again.

Daniela muttered, "Not many people here, but no one looks suspicious. Nobody wearing iron or silver unless it's hidden."

Milena nodded. As they moved away from the buffet, she looked at Hana, whose eyes were still vacant as her mind searched the whole of the train.

"I perceive," Hana stated, in a soft voice, "that what little of the witch's power isn't hidden is located that way." She gestured at the back of the train. "But that tells us nothing we did not already guess."

"Of course," said Milena. They were reasonably confident that their target was not staying in any of the cabins in the front half. "Let us return to our room. Another opportunity to deal with this...person will present itself soon. Of that, I have no doubt."

Once back in their quarters and able to reheat the food, she tried to relax. It was necessary to remain partially alert, but nothing suggested they needed to rush or panic.

Until Anezka contacted them.

All three froze, their forks poised in midair and their eyes bulging as the grandmistress' imposing and irresistible presence entered their minds. *Stop whatever you are doing,* her psychic voice commanded, *and check your email. I do not have time to explain everything to you directly. Follow the instructions therein and reply with your assessment before deleting everything.*

Then it was gone and the trio relaxed, feeling as though an ice storm had blown through them.

Milena wasted no time. She pulled out the tablet she had brought, fired it up, and went immediately to the encrypted email account that was only used for Orthodoxy business. A new message had arrived in her inbox four minutes ago.

Hana and Daniela moved closer, but Milena held up a hand, palm outward. "Please do not read over my shoulder. I will tell you what we are to do after I have read it."

They frowned but obeyed. Milena inhaled and opened the message.

Anezka's campaign against the North American Council was getting bogged down; things were not proceeding as swiftly as they ought. The surviving members had not yet been located, although various sweeps and recon missions had at least narrowed down the possibilities. Namely, they were all but certain the council had not fled anywhere north of the former Lovecraft estate.

That left the question of whether they were hiding somewhere for the longer term, fleeing due south, or moving southwest.

Milena paused for a moment to consider the data. Based on the remaining coven members, that meant the council probably intended to make for either New Orleans or the West Coast. If the latter, Milena might end up having to spearhead the operation against them.

She read on and discovered that Anezka's chief concerns were not quite what she'd expected.

Recent intel suggested the council was receiving limited aid from local covens. They had assumed the minor hedge witches were all cowed by the Orthodoxy's display of shock and awe.

Furthermore, surveillance of the American magic users' idle conversations revealed a rapidly growing resentment against the "brutal foreign occupiers." Milena had suspected something like this but had not dared to argue with Anezka too loudly. The grandmistress did not, in her view, fully grasp the importance Americans attached to the "legitimacy" of leadership. They did not worship pure power or victors who won by ruthless or underhanded means.

The Orthodoxy was beginning to worry that they might have to deal with a low-level but ongoing guerilla resistance against them if the conflict with the council was not resolved quickly. It was imperative that all available resources be turned toward finding and destroying them so as to remove a potential symbol for resistance against the Orthodoxy's supremacy on the continent.

Your particular talents, the email went on, *can be best employed in granting us the necessary power to perform a collective ritual that will unveil our enemies' location. Since they too are talented magicians, their cloaking abilities have confounded us so far. This must not continue. Sacrifice an individual who has enough of the gift to ensure that we receive sufficient extra strength.*

You have forty-eight hours to complete this task, but completing it within twenty-four hours would be better.

With that, the email concluded. Milena skimmed it a second

time to fix the details in her mind, then deleted it. She looked up and saw her companions waiting patiently for their briefing.

Milena cleared her throat. "I must perform a sacrifice by no later than tomorrow night," she stated. "It must be someone powerful so Anezka can complete the task of locating and crushing the council. That means that we are running out of time in which to spring the trap on our guest on this train."

Hana nodded, but she looked disturbed.

Daniela said, "Well, we were going to capture them and kill them anyway. Let's do it soon. Tonight?"

Milena stared at the two of them. Both witches were of sufficient magical strength that if necessary, either of them would be able to contribute an appropriate level of power to Anezka's ritual. The grandmistress would undoubtedly consider losing a mid-level member a worthwhile price to pay to defeat an adversary as important as the council.

"Agreed." Milena smiled to distract her subordinates from any suspicion about what she had just been thinking, though she suspected it had occurred to both of them already. Certainly to Hana. Daniela, being denser, might still be in the dark, but she was not a complete fool.

Hana raised her hand. "After everyone is sleeping, we will do a full sweep of the train, then? With your permission, of course." She seemed downright nervous now.

"Yes." Milena veiled her thoughts. "As you pointed out, the stowaway is powerful albeit unskilled. They will make an ideal sacrifice, and capturing them should be our first priority. If we succeed at that, it is unnecessary to consider any alternatives."

Hana relaxed if only a little. On the other hand, Daniela appeared to tense. It must have just occurred to her what the "alternatives" would entail.

Milena stood up. "So, let us begin planning how we will go about it so that there are no mistakes and things will go well for all of us."

It went without saying that the Orthodoxy's creed of serving the general good first and the individual second would be fulfilled, however. Milena had no illusions and no compunctions. She would do whatever she must.

CHAPTER FIFTEEN

"All right," Kera declared, putting her fists on her hips. "No more messing around. I'm tired of waiting for God knows what to happen while these chicks, or pricks, or whatever they are, lurk on the other half of the train playing their little games. If it's going to be a test to see who flinches first, then it might as well be one of us flinching from a *fight*. Not from sitting around and ruminating over what *might* happen."

Chris, who was still finishing off the plate of food he'd claimed as a late lunch, gave her one of his looks: serious, concerned, but willing to hear her out and open to the idea of helping with whatever she decided upon.

"Okay. So, what do you intend to do? Specifically."

She took a long relaxed yet deep breath. "Sweep the train," she told him. "Tonight."

He cocked an eyebrow. "You mean, like, *late* at night? After everyone has mostly passed out? That might be the best way to approach it."

"Smart man." She patted him on the head, which caused him to grin in a ridiculous fashion. It was difficult not to hug him.

"Yeah, that's what I was thinking. Like, around midnight or so. Maybe more like one in the morning."

Chris scratched his chin. "Ah, yes. The witching hour. That seems to be your favorite time for engaging in dangerous shenanigans."

Shrugging, Kera replied, "It's a good hour. Things will be dark and quiet, although if someone sees us snooping around, it will be marginally more suspicious than if we were doing it during the day. But it's far less likely that anyone *will* see us, and I can always hit someone with a persuasion or relaxation spell if they think I'm the one who sabotaged the engine and am preparing to do it again or some shit like that."

"Mkay." Chris stood up. "Good deal. I think there's a security guard on board, though, who might be patrolling or at least standing watch somewhere, so be prepared for that. Also, I'm guessing that they don't completely kill the lights in the hallways and non-residential cars; they're probably just dimmed. If we want total darkness to prowl around in, you might have to, well, actually sabotage something."

Kera drummed her fingers on her arm. "Damn. Yeah, that could make things more complicated, but we'll do what we can. I don't think killing the lights would be necessary anyway since what we're mainly doing is recon. We know there are three of them, all women. I got a halfway decent look at them before the remote-viewing spell failed. I saw the two smaller chicks' faces, the white brunette and the Asian-looking one. There was the third whose face I didn't see, but she was bigger and kind of buff, with curly hair. All we need to find out is which cabin they're in. Then we can 'quarantine' them, so to speak."

Chris glanced at his laptop. "Beats building that database, though I suppose I'll have to work on that until midnight, won't I?"

The hours crawled by. They had supper toward the end of the period when meals were being served and supplemented their food with strong coffee to ensure they were still awake when the time came to launch their mission.

At 12:23, they decided they were ready.

Kera observed, "The train seems quiet. I think virtually everyone is in bed by now. Well, asleep, since there aren't many places to be *other* than in bed."

"It's okay, babe," Chris assured her. "I knew what you meant. Anyway, am I coming with you up to the front of the train, or will I be standing guard somewhere in the middle?"

She considered it for a second. "Probably the latter, but let's see what's up." She made sure her jacket was on, then nodded at him, opened the door, and stepped out. Chris followed a couple of paces behind.

Nothing happened at first. In the fifth car, though, they encountered the security guard.

He noticed them immediately since Kera hadn't bothered to cloak them with magic. She wanted to save her stamina and also appear more natural.

The man nodded. "Evening. Where you headed this late?"

"Dining car," said Kera. "Yeah, it's late, but still."

Chris smiled. "They serve midnight snacks, don't they?"

The guard eyed them half-suspiciously, but all he did was rub his chin and say, "No, but there's usually a few dry things left out overnight. Stay out of trouble."

Kera waved as they moved past him. "We will, don't worry." She felt bad about telling the massive lie.

A couple of minutes later, they arrived in the food truck, which was mostly dark and empty of other passengers.

Chris whispered. "To be frank, a midnight snack *does* sound pretty good right about now, so I'll hang out here and eat, uh, saltine crackers or whatever else they left sitting out. Ping me with the emotional blast thing if anything goes wrong."

She nodded and put a hand on his shoulder, giving it a squeeze. "I will. Um, to make things clearer, though, let's decide on what different emotions mean. Since it usually helps to clarify that when speaking to a man."

"That's a cheap shot," he protested, "but probably true."

She went on, "If what you feel is me being afraid for myself, like physical panic, that means that I need help. On the other hand, if it's more like me being intensely worried about something, that indicates that things are getting out of control, and I'm afraid there's going to be collateral damage or we're all about to get in trouble. In that case, be prepared for damage control."

He agreed but wasn't sure what to do in that scenario.

Growing impatient, Kera grunted. "Whatever seems best. You're smart. I'm sure you can figure it out. And I want to get started here. I trust you, all right? Just be there to back me up, whatever happens."

He sighed, clearly disappointed by not having received a straighter answer. "So be it. I trust you, too. You've pulled through during events that were a lot more difficult and dangerous than this, after all. Good luck." He leaned over and kissed her.

She nuzzled him back. "Thanks. I'll be right back, probably."

Kera turned away, strode directly to the door that led from the dining car to the front half of the train, and opened it, stepping through and clearing her mind of any extraneous worries. As with fighting, things would work out far better if her brain wasn't congested with counterproductive nonsense. There was only the task before her, and she projected the calm confidence that she could adapt to any developments and handle herself accordingly.

With a gentle motion, she closed the door behind her. Then she set her expanded consciousness to work scanning the compartment.

It was difficult not to lapse into a trance-like state. She knew she would have to stay sharp to retain the usual functions of her physical senses and remain alert to what was going on around her. She spent a moment putting her normal modes of perception on autopilot, so to speak, and was then able to shift more mental energy toward her psychic-astral sight.

As she had expected, there were no obvious magical auras anywhere in the car. What was uncertain, though, was whether that was because the witches were elsewhere or they were well-cloaked.

I might have to peek into the rooms one by one if I can't sense their presence otherwise, Kera realized. *That means all kinds of spells to muffle sound, make myself as close to invisible as possible, manipulate locks, and so forth. And if those witches are still awake, or have any alarms set that might be triggered by magic, then even with my jacket on, I'd risk alerting them. Shit.*

After a moment of frustrated hesitation, she resolved to simply walk from car to car, scan each compartment, and see if anything notable turned up. If not, she could move on to taking more desperate measures.

The next car was the same as the first. Nothing of interest, although this one did contain an emergency exit to the outside of the train. She made a mental note to use it if she had to, though that could create complications of its own.

Partway into her assessment of the third compartment up from the food truck, though, something happened.

The indefinite cloud that drifted around the train, representing the power of the sorceresses onboard, seemed to coalesce, and as she had before, Kera felt the sense of someone *noticing* her and looking for her but not quite finding her. Her jacket, lined with anti-magical metals, continued to protect her from easy detection.

But someone was making an active effort to overcome it. And though she couldn't put a finger on why or how, she knew they were getting closer.

She perked up, hearing the faint sound of approaching footsteps.

Shit! I must have tripped a silent alarm, and now they're coming after me in person, aren't they?

Kera turned around, flung open the door she had come through, and dashed into the second car from the dining area. She slammed the portal behind her, heedless of the noise. She heard another sound at the same time: someone opening the door at the other end and coming in her direction.

Though she had shifted the bulk of her attention to immediate and physical matters, the magical portion of Kera's consciousness remained partly aware of the witches' auras focusing on her, growing stronger, and making less of an effort to hide. Having seen them remotely, it was easier to trace their thaumaturgic emanations to the source than it had been when they were anonymous.

Kera hurried down the hall. She stopped at the juncture next to the doorway leading out to the side of the train, debating whether to continue into the next car or slip outside and wait until the danger was past.

She probably had only a second or two until her pursuers came through the door behind her. She made an instant decision, reaching for the side door and performing three quick spells at once.

First, she encased several feet around her in a field that would muffle sound and inhibit electrical signals. If it worked correctly, it would silence not only the door but any alarm the train might have in place to warn the conductor if someone slipped outside while the vehicle was in motion.

Second, she telekinetically opened the door leading to the next car and shut it a second later, allowing it to bang closed loud enough for the witches to hear.

Third, she beamed an emotional signal to Chris, the one that indicated she was worried about collateral damage. It wasn't accurate, but if she warned him that *she* was in danger, he would probably rush to help her and risk ending up in the three women's crosshairs. By using the other signal, Kera could make sure he was alert and ready to figure something out without doing anything stupid.

Then she yanked open the emergency exit, instantly hearing and feeling the howl of the wind, and stepped out.

An alarm tried to go off, and Kera flinched at the loud keening, but it echoed within the magically enclosed space she had created before dying after the first cycle. The last thing she heard behind her as she closed the door again was footsteps and what sounded like people whispering in a foreign language, presumably Russian or some other Slavic tongue.

Kera clung to the metal ladder located right outside the door. Her eyes widened.

There wasn't much room. All that lay beyond the side door was a short, narrow ledge with a thigh-high rail to offer minimal protection and the rungs she now grasped, which led to the top of the train. Dark masses of land and trees sped by in a shadowy blur, moving far faster than the night sky and stars above, which seemed weirdly peaceful.

Shit, shit, shit, Kera rebuked herself. *I ought to have thought this out better. This isn't like a cargo train where it's designed for people to walk the whole length of the thing. It's a sleek passenger train, and no one is supposed to be out here, are they?*

She felt the witches getting closer. They were right outside the emergency exit door.

Kera grabbed the ladder with both hands and began climbing. The realization of how fast they were moving and the cold rush of the wind made it difficult, but she managed. Reaching the top, she lay flat, grasping the topmost rung and waiting.

The auras of her pursuers wavered, then expanded. She wondered if they were spreading out, each of them searching someplace different in their drive to find her.

A minute later, the door below opened.

Kera shut her eyes. A woman's voice barked something in Russian, and she knew she was fucked.

All right, then, she told herself, resigned to what had to come next. *It's go time. Bring it on, ladies.*

She opened her eyes and crawled forward, casting a spell to shield herself from attacks.

Below her, a tall, athletic woman with curly hair, the biggest of the three she had seen via Chris' enchanted pen, was looking up, snarling, and raising her hand. Her fingers crackled with electricity.

Kera tried to attack first, but she wasn't fast enough. A bolt of lightning leapt from the woman's hand to crash against Kera's shield. It didn't penetrate, but the electrical charge flowed into the metal below her.

Abandoning her attempt at a counterattack, Kera created a second shield that clung to her skin barely in time to avoid being fried, though she felt a painful static shock as the charge attacked her muscles. She gritted her teeth, concentrating and trying not to panic.

The surge of lightning had begun to affect the train. The lights in the windows below flickered, and it seemed for a second like the train slowed down. If anything had been seriously damaged, everyone on board would be awake and stomping around soon.

The witch looked frustrated. Before she could try something else, Kera extended her hand and unleashed a wave of freezing water. Predictably, the curly-haired woman managed to raise a shield, but a barely sufficient one. Sheets and stalagmites of ice rose around her, encasing and trapping her on the tiny narrow platform next to the door.

Kera laughed, but there wasn't time to hang around and gloat. Keeping low to the surface to minimize wind resistance, she crawled toward the next car to the rear. That was probably the direction the other witches had gone, but it was also where Chris was. She had to get to him.

The edge of the car was less than ten feet away. Reaching it, Kera stopped, wracking her brain for the best way to attempt something as stupid as crossing an open space while clinging to a fast-moving vehicle.

Well, my shield is blocking the wind, isn't it? And since I'm moving in the opposite direction the train is, the wind is at my back. Should be a piece of cake.

Sucking in a breath, she sprang up and jumped, casting a light augmentation charm on herself at the same instant.

The world, earth, sky, and train all became a blur of motion as she sailed over the narrow opening between compartments. Below her, someone shrieked in Russian, and flames rose as though someone had tried to throw a too-thick fireball through the gap.

Her shield blocked the heat, though, and she landed a good four feet onto the next car. Still, she almost fell off, and her heart throbbed angrily in her chest, trying to rise into her throat.

I may be a badass, but not enough of a badass to stay up here. I need to get back down inside the train. They know where I am, though. My only hope is—

Though she could barely hear over the rushing of air around her, voices and motion came from somewhere below. At the risk of expending too much energy on spells in too short a time, Kera scried on the car beneath her.

In her mind's eye, she saw the security guard marching forward with Chris right behind him. The guard opened the door between cars and was then face to face with two women—the smaller witches, one of whom had tried to burn Kera as she jumped.

She couldn't hear what was said, but she could guess that the guard wanted to know what the hell was going on.

Good man, Chris, she thought. *Unless they're ruthless enough to kill anyone who gets in their way. I don't think they'll risk it, though.*

She maintained the scrying as she crawled down the car. The witches argued with the guard for a moment longer as Chris meanwhile slipped away, moving more or less in unison with Kera toward the dining car. They would hopefully be reunited in a minute or less.

Then the witch who seemed to be the leader, the petite white brunette, waved her hand and the guard slumped against the wall, unconscious. She shoved him aside, and she and the Asian witch marched into the car. The taller one followed, looking wet, ruffled, and extremely pissed off.

Crap.

Kera scrambled forward. When she reached the edge of the dining car, she waited until Chris crossed into it below her—he didn't notice her right above him—and magically sealed the door, spending about half of her remaining strength to ensure the spell couldn't easily be undone.

She jumped across the gap and looked for a way to descend. There wasn't a rail, so, inhaling and hoping for the best, she clambered into the narrow gap between the cars. There wasn't much to hold onto, so she had to use a levitation spell to keep from falling and being chewed to pieces beneath the train.

I can't believe I'm doing this shit. She scoffed. *Oh, what fun if my parents found out about it.*

She squeezed into the space in front of the door to the dining car, flung open the door, and stepped in. Chris was halfway down the hall in front of her, and he spun around, startled, as she shut the door behind her.

"Whoa! It's you. Where the hell were you?"

She flapped a hand. "On top of the train. Fun times. Come on, we have to get back to our room. I sealed the door, but they'll be able to get through it with a little effort, I'm sure."

Glancing over her shoulder, Kera could see the dark silhouettes of the witches through the window, crowding against the door into the other car and presumably working to crack her magic and continue their pursuit.

She and Chris hurried into the dining area, pausing to make sure the Orthodoxy's agents hadn't gotten through yet, then moved on to the next car.

Kera sighed. "I think we lost them. They aren't playing around, though. Honestly, we might have to get off the damn train in the morning to avoid—"

Metal shrieked as the ceiling above them was ripped open, then a small, slender form plummeted to the floor between them.

Chris was knocked over, falling on his ass and then rolling. Kera, realizing she was a split-second away from identification, cast a glamour to obscure her features, followed by a shield. There was no time for anything else.

The petite brunette witch must have climbed or flown around, taking much the same route Kera had before making her entrance into the car from above. She raised her hands to attack before she even got a good look at her enemy.

Lights flashed, and Kera was knocked backward and lifted into the air to crash against the interior wall of one of the sleeping cabins. Her shield had protected her but barely. She raised her own hands and responded with a hybrid confusion and relaxation spell.

The witch, cursing in Russian, stumbled and raised her hands to her head, shaking it as though something was stuck in her hair. The spell had stunned her but not disabled her, as Kera had hoped.

"Not good," she muttered and rushed ahead to pick up Chris, who was still struggling to his feet. From around them came the rustlings of people in the sleeping cabins waking up from the racket.

Behind the lead witch, the other two were gaining, though the

Asian one stopped to magically repair the hole in the train's ceiling.

Kera hoisted Chris to his feet and they ran ahead, tearing through the doors to the next car. As they crossed, the brunette witch dashed after them.

Kera's gut clenched. She was starting to feel the fatigue despite the rush of adrenaline; all the magic she had used in the last five minutes had taken its toll. She would have to rely upon her body and her wits to get through this.

"Chris," she said, "grab that fire extinguisher and hide around that corner over there. I'm going to fight this bitch since she's not backing down, and I'm almost out of magic. If she gets past me, or if I start to retreat, jump out and, uh, either spray her or whack her with the can. Better yet, both."

He groaned. "Sure, whatever you say. We should probably call 911, you know. Where's the conductor? He hasn't noticed there's a gang fight going on? You'd think he would have stopped the train by now."

Kera turned back to face her approaching enemy.

The witch appeared again, seemingly from thin air, and struck Kera with a nasty net of electricity before she could defend herself.

Goddammit! She's fast. And was she invisible or something?

Kera's muscles convulsed; she was helpless as the woman approached.

"Surrender," she said in a pleasant, lilting voice tinged by a Slavic accent. "I do not wish to kill you unless I must. We only want to take you back for questioning. If you do not comply, I will hurt you very, very badly. Tell your friend not to interfere, either."

As the witch came closer, she kept one hand, fingers spread, aimed toward Kera with the obvious threat of another shock spell. Her other hand disappeared into her clothing and reemerged with what looked like a straight razor.

The pain faded and Kera found that she could move again, but she pretended to still be paralyzed. Her strength was almost spent, but something told her the petite Russian lady was lying through her teeth.

The witch continued, "Do not worry about witnesses. We will erase their memories. Simply do as I ask, and all will be well." Behind her, the other two were approaching.

Kera pounced. She drove her fist into the lead witch's face, shattering her nose. At the same moment, she stomped on her opponent's foot, then grabbed her wrist to throw her into the wall while wresting the razor from her grip. The witch cried out in pain, and her two cohorts stopped.

Before any of the Orthodoxy sorceresses realized what had happened, Kera had their leader pinned in front of her, the open razor at her throat.

"Back off," Kera told the other two, who stood poised in front of her. There was more noise from the cabins, and she tried not to quail at the thought of random civilians seeing the ugly scene. "Go back the way you came into the next car. Then I'll let her go."

The lead witch hissed something in Russian, and the bigger girl responded in the same language. Then she and the Asian witch backed away and slipped through the door to the next car.

The leader whispered through gritted teeth, "You will not get away with this. You are only making more trouble for everyone on this train. We will come again, you know, and next time, other people will be hurt."

The hand holding the blade trembled. *She can't come again if she isn't alive,* she realized. Then nausea almost overcame her. How could she even have thought that? She refused to execute an unarmed woman.

Instead, she lifted the razor away and kicked the witch in the rump, driving her forward to stumble and fall to the floor. "No," Kera said. "You try anything else, and next time I *won't* let you go. And if you hurt *anyone* on this train, you'll get your razor back after you fish it out of your own stomach. For now, I'm keeping it. Have a good rest of the night."

Disgusted, Kera turned and stormed away.

Chris rejoined her as they crossed into the next car. Their timing was good since they could hear the cabins opening behind them as the other passengers decided to investigate.

"Well," her boyfriend commented, "that didn't go as smoothly as it could have. Do we get arrested in the morning? Does nothing happen? Does the Orthodoxy just nuke the train with a meteor spell and be done with it?"

Kera didn't feel like ruminating about it. "I don't know. Hopefully, nothing. Let's get some goddamn sleep first, though."

CHAPTER SIXTEEN

Stephanie began, "Don't get me wrong, Lia. Nobody cares more about Kera and her safety than I do except her parents, I suppose, and maybe Chris. But I'm gonna be honest with you here."

She paused, and Lia, who was sitting across from her, had to admit she was curious to discover what her friend was building up to.

"It is *damn* nice," Steph concluded, "to have something to do again besides waiting tables, eating, and sleeping. With Kera and her man being gone so long, I was starting to wonder if this agency was ever going to get off the ground. Worried I might never be able to quit my job. Plus, I crave all the fun and excitement we have around here. Right?"

Lia rubbed her eyes. "Fun and excitement is part of it, yes, but there's also the tedious research and data-crunching, which, if *I'm* being honest, is the majority of what we'll be doing today. Still, it *will* be a change of pace from your usual work."

Steph pouted in momentary disappointment. "Oh. Damn. Well, yeah, better than nothing. What exactly are we trying to figure out? You said something about a safe house but didn't go into detail."

"Yes." Lia uncrossed and recrossed her legs, adjusting the hem of her skirt. She had spent so much time at home lately that despite her longstanding commitment to dressing like the professional she was, wearing a proper suit-dress ensemble for a workday in her own living room was beginning to feel rather silly. "Specifically, safe houses used by the Orthodoxy. You remember them, I'm sure. That's where the excitement comes into play."

Stephanie fell silent for a minute, and her jovial demeanor faded. "Oh, I see. Yeah, I remember them well. I wish Kera had told me more, but I guess she figures I still have a day job, and you're the one who works full-time for the agency. Are those witches after her again? Is it something to do with Pavla?"

Lia explained all she knew, everything Kera had told her. At the end, she added an extra piece of information, one which Kera was not yet aware of.

"Pavla contacted me last night. Well, I got an encrypted message from someone claiming to be Pavla. We have to hope it wasn't the Orthodoxy laying a trap, though that is a definite possibility. But something about the choice of words in the message and references to specific things only Pavla would know makes me think it was genuine."

Stephanie nodded. "Got it. Mind if I look it over? We also ought to run it by Kera if we can."

Lia pointed out, "Pavla explicitly requested that we not alarm Kera, but yes, you can read the message. You might recognize some of what she says better than I would, in fact. First, do you want coffee? There are also a couple of muffins on the counter if you're interested."

They each had a cup of coffee and split a muffin. Then they settled in at Lia's desk to read the email.

Steph chuckled as she perused it. "Yup, she remembers what we ate that night we celebrated after taking down El Peluquero. It's got to be her. Only way I can think of it wouldn't be is if the

Orthodoxy captured her and, ugh, tortured it out of her or read her mind or something."

Lia asked, "Is that possible? The mind-reading thing. You possess magic and I don't, so in this case, you're the expert."

"Yeah," said Steph. "Kinda. I can't do it myself yet, but between that book and what Kera was saying, there's a spell for almost everything. I guess we have to consider that it *could* be a trap."

Lia opened the drawer in her desk and checked to see that her compact .380 pistol was there, which it was. "We will prepare for that prospect to the best of our ability. If there's any significant suspicion, we'll disregard the request not to inform Kera."

"I agree." Stephanie leaned back in her seat. "Anyway, let's get to work."

Lia tried hacking into systems associated with places Kera had mentioned, while Steph, who had more magical experience but less tech-savviness, browsed news stories and other mundane pieces of information for anything that suggested it might be related to their situation.

An hour later, they had turned up nothing.

Lia sighed and sat, silent and frowning at the screen, as her mind turned over different ways of approaching the problem.

Stephanie did likewise until something occurred to her. "Could we try just, like, asking Pavla? She messaged us, so you can reply to it, right?"

Lia blinked. "Um, yes. Good point. Forest for the trees, I suppose."

She typed a brief response to the email from earlier, noting that if by some chance it *was* a trap, asking for extra information would push them into its jaws that much quicker. Still, she could not think of a better way to quickly gather more info that might be useful to Kera.

After sending the request, she and Steph went back to work, accomplishing little in the seven minutes it took for Pavla to reply.

"Damn," remarked Stephanie. "She's as punctual as ever."

Lia opened the message at once, then read it aloud.

"Okay, here's what she has to say: 'Our base of operations was a rundown church in the neighborhood where Kera, Stephanie, and I fought in that alley. Steph will remember. However, I do not know if they are still using the place. Often one location will be used first, then they will switch to another. Further, the Orthodoxy always establishes safe houses on the periphery of major cities. Check the outer suburbs in areas that are almost completely abandoned but where seemingly useless properties have suddenly been purchased by obscure buyers. Often a large house will be purchased in a neighborhood that has been cut off from other residential areas by industrial development. Especially note if a conversion from rubles to dollars is involved.'"

Steph nodded. "Makes sense, but not sure how much that narrows it down. People buy and sell random-ass properties around LA all the time."

Lia nodded in grim agreement, then continued reading the screen. "Next, she says, 'If a place seems likely, investigate it, but be careful. They will probably not have guards since they are putting almost all of their personnel toward the war against the council, but they are always booby-trapped, both conventionally and with magic. Some of the traps are quite simple, like curses that activate when someone steps over the threshold of a door and things like that, but be wary. If you are uncertain, you might need to wait for Kera rather than try to penetrate them yourselves. Stephanie may be able to disarm some of the magic traps. Good luck.'"

Both women sat back in their chairs, digesting the new information.

Steph quipped, "It's nice that I have her vote of confidence as far as dealing with the damn curses. However, I'm not on the same level as Kera yet, so I have to agree that we need to be sure what we're doing before we go barging in someplace. And first, we have to find one of these locations."

Surprisingly, Lia's face had twisted into a smirk of amusement.

"What Pavla said is enough to get us started," she observed. "And I gather these people do not think very highly of un-magical humans. Part of their power is based on the fact that most people don't know they exist and wouldn't believe it if they *did* know, and general secrecy, which allows them to operate without much scrutiny. I bet they've become sloppy over the years."

Stephanie laughed. "Could be."

Lia went on, "I think this might prove easier than Pavla suspects. The arrogant do not bother to close all the loopholes that should be closed. If I can say so, I'm exceedingly good at finding those who don't want to be found or who *think* they're smarter than everyone else is."

Ezeudo wandered to the window of his room, which looked down from the hotel's second floor at the parking lot. Their truck had arrived.

"Ah, good," he said to himself. "I am growing tired of this place, and LeBlanc has me curious about what awaits us in New Orleans." It was a city he had never seen—granted, he had never been to the US before—but had always wondered about since it had an interesting and mysterious international reputation.

But first, they had to get there. That meant a long, difficult, tortuous, and clandestine journey across more than a thousand miles of roads spanning hills and cities, countryside, and urban freeways.

Last night, they had, with the partial aid of Mindy and Dan, decided on the best route to get them to NOLA without arousing too much suspicion. The direct route, which was more or less due southwest from their current location in West Virginia, was out of the question.

A couple of members had briefly proposed that they instead drive due south along the Atlantic coast before bearing west toward Louisiana, but that too was discarded. The Orthodoxy seemed to suspect they would head either for NOLA or the West Coast, and fleeing south before they turned west would clue their enemies in to their plans.

Instead, they would drive directly west, not turning south until shortly before St. Louis. Then they would drive down to Memphis, assess the situation, and determine if a diversion or detour was needed before crossing Mississippi and finally reaching the Louisiana bayou and LeBlanc's hometown therein. They could feint westward if need be and then double back to their destination.

Since James had not improved from his marginally functional state, transporting him would be the hardest part. Hence, the moving truck.

Josiah Kane observed, speaking to no one in particular as Ezeudo went out into the hall, "The sheer simplicity of the plan is its brilliance. A vehicle of this sort will accommodate a bedridden man far more easily than almost any other."

Crystal Green commented, "Yes, true, but we'll have to keep him secured. If we have to stop suddenly, he could roll out of bed and crash into the other cargo. Someone will have to be with him at all times, and we might have to use an illusion to hide him in case we're stopped by the police and we have to open the back."

Mary Mitchell waved a hand. "Yes, those are valid concerns, but we can deal with them. Samantha and Rufus claim they have come up with a rigging system for keeping James secure during the ride, though they said it will be irksome getting him in and out of it each day and night."

Hugh Buchanan gave a dry, snorting chuckle. "Clever, but it

seems excessive if you ask me. Back in my day, we were able to transport sick men on bales of hay loaded into the backs of horse-drawn wagons that had no seatbelts, and yes, before you ask, those men survived. People were made of sterner stuff back then."

LeBlanc sighed. "I remember those days. While there isn't anything *wrong* with a certain measure of sternness, our modern conveniences really are quite nice and useful. We will take advantage of as many as we require to get to New Orleans in one piece."

By now, everyone had packed up the minimal belongings they had brought with them. Ezeudo had only a small suitcase's worth. Half of it was an extra set of clothes and some toiletries he'd carried from Samantha's house, and the rest consisted of vitamins, water, a first aid kit, and a small toolkit he had purchased this morning in town.

As a group, they descended the stairs to the first floor of the charming but somewhat rundown old hotel.

The clerk there stared at them with a vacant, relaxed expression, having been heavily enchanted the whole time they had lodged here. Ezeudo did not like the idea of using people as puppets, but all of them could well end up dead if even the slightest scrap of information about them were to make its way into the wrong hands. In any event, the man would be released from the spell once they were safely out of town.

Mindy and Dan had been the ones to rent the truck and drive it back. Mary had given them the money for it since they both came from relatively humble backgrounds.

The two of them jumped down from the vehicle as the council streamed out of the old building. Dan told them, "This should be big enough, and we didn't notice anyone following us."

Mindy added, "Hope everything will go well. We did what you said, using false names and all that. You say we're invisible right now? I felt a little magic, but not as much as I would have thought for a spell like that."

LeBlanc smiled at them, and Ezeudo realized the young couple probably wasn't aware of the full magnitude of the council's power.

"Yes," said LeBlanc. "This should serve us well, and no one more than two hundred feet away can see us. We also have our magical signatures well-dampened against tracking. If the Orthodoxy, particularly their stronger members, was focusing directly on our location, it wouldn't pass muster, but a casual scan of the region will not find us. And, of course, we are leaving now. Please keep a low profile yourselves. We would not want you to suffer any reprisals for having aided us."

Amanda approached Mindy and Dan and handed them a pair of small objects. "Charms," she explained, "made by Zacharia. She was talented at them. They'll protect you from both surveillance and attack. We can't thank you enough."

Everyone else joined in, giving the two witches their gratitude or shaking their hands. Not only had they procured the truck, but they had also used informal lines of communication with non-magical people in the state to ensure that no one would mention having seen a large party of weird people moving westward if anyone asked.

There was one question remaining, though, which was whether the party should split up or ride together. In addition to the large moving truck, they had also purchased a sedan and a van from the local dealership. A couple of suggestion spells had expedited the paperwork.

As the discussion resumed in earnest, Ezeudo watched in dismay. Four members—Amanda, Rufus, Josiah, and James during a moment of lucidity—had voted for splitting up. The rest favored staying together, but their majority was not large enough to overrule the objectors.

Ezeudo felt he finally had something to offer.

"Excuse me," he interjected, "but if I may, in my past experiences, it was always better to keep a group together. Yes, a larger party moves more slowly and requires coordination, and if you are discovered by hostile people, there is no backup, no other group that can carry on without you. But those disadvantages are smaller than the one great advantage, which is that there is no possibility of one group getting lost and having to waste great amounts of time trying to meet back up."

James was sleeping again, but the rest thought it over.

Amanda shrugged. "So be it. I hereby change my vote to staying together. If we're ambushed, now that I think about it, having all our people in one place will make us harder to defeat."

Grudgingly, Rufus and Josiah acceded to the majority.

Ezeudo closed his eyes. Not only was sticking together the wiser option, but he was impatient to get moving rather than linger and argue. The Orthodoxy was drawing closer with every minute wasted.

Mary announced, "All right, once James is secure, we can leave. How is that coming?"

Since they had designed the rig, Samantha and Rufus had taken it upon themselves to cart James, who was lying on a stretcher they had "borrowed" from the fire station, into the truck and begin the process of securing him.

"Five minutes," Samantha called.

"Ten," Rufus corrected her. "Or seven, at least."

Hugh chortled. "In my day, we could do it in *four*."

CHAPTER SEVENTEEN

Milena tried not to sneeze as her nose began bleeding again. Sneezing would only make things worse. She breathed in through her mouth, cleared her mind, and cast a light healing spell on herself, focused on her sinus cavity. The bleeding stopped, but she immediately became lightheaded from the magical expenditure involved, which interacted badly with her head injury.

She raged as her small hands curled into fists. "I am going to fucking *kill* that bitch."

Daniela, who had been quieter and more sheepish than usual since last night, looked up. "Well, that was always the plan, was it not?"

Hana added, "I am surprised you said that in English, Milena. Someone might overhear."

"Be quiet," Milena snapped in Russian. "We blanked the memories of everyone in this car. For all they know, I could be cursing at something in a video game. Now, go get me another cocktail. I keep having to heal my nose, so I can't risk wasting my healing spells on my tailbone. Ugh, how could this have happened?"

If she did not have an example to maintain in front of the lower-ranking witches, she might have cried. It wasn't only the pain, it was the embarrassment. Hana and Daniela had both seen the American witch disarm her, beat the shit out of her, and dismissively kick her to the floor.

Once again, they had overestimated their target. They had assumed she would stick to the use of magic rather than resort to the ultimate crudity of brute force. If it weren't for their orders to capture the young woman alive and then sacrifice her, Milena would have been happy to let Daniela beat her to death as a form of poetic justice.

Hana did as she was told, sliding off her bunk to head to the dining car and fetch another beverage for her superior. While waiting for her to return, Milena reflected on the amount of extra work they'd all had to do, scrambling to control the repercussions caused by their debacle of a sweep.

The memory wipes were only part of it. They'd also had to cast persuasion spells on the security guard, who was also suspicious as to why he had suddenly passed out in the middle of a conversation with Milena, the conductor, a couple of the engineers and handymen, and one of the cooks. They had needed to keep other people behind screens of illusions while they rushed to repair the parts of the train that had been damaged in the fight.

And all the while, Milena was working with a flattened nose and a bruised and possibly cracked tailbone. Healing spells had controlled it somewhat, but when the job was over, she would probably need mundane surgery to look normal again.

Focus, she told herself. *Focus on the importance of the job. That girl is a fool, a sentimental idiot. She's stronger and more wily than we expected, yes, but she has an obvious weak spot in that she could have killed me. She certainly should have. If that is how she wants to play, then we will fucking play.*

When I have her on the sacrificial table, she will not be the beneficiary of my usual clean and efficient technique. No, I will "accidentally" make a mistake or two and draw out the process of her death longer than strictly necessary. Such a pity when that happens.

She did not enjoy killing people. "Enjoyment" was not what she sought, but she would not tolerate insult and embarrassment. The girl had to pay.

After Hana returned with her cocktail and she'd drunk it, mellowing as the alcohol took effect, a new plan began to form.

They had brainstormed a few different things that morning in their brief stretches of downtime between cleaning up the general mess, but the problem of how to capture and kill their quarry was becoming intractable. Another direct assault presented too many risks. Waiting till the end of the train ride pushed them far too close to Anezka's deadline. They had already wasted one of the two days allotted to them.

They needed a way to put the American witch at a disadvantage and draw her into an *unfair* fight without time to prepare. Ideally, it should happen elsewhere than on this wretched train.

Milena's mind settled on a solution. It presented risks and what some people referred to as "ethical concerns," but it was unlikely to fail. Success in her profession was ultimately the only thing that mattered.

"Stand by," Milena told her cohorts. "I have arrived at the beginnings of a plan. I must think longer still, though, about how to implement it. Once I have a better idea, I will solicit your input. Soon."

Hana stared at her with the calm, clear look she often used to acknowledge that she had heard something but could think of nothing to say in response. Daniela gave her a nod and settled back into sullen, cantankerous boredom.

Ignoring both women for the time being, Milena's mind worked on the problem that loomed before them.

The logistics and timing would have to be perfect. They would need to execute the operation at precisely the right hour and minute in conjunction with both a lull in their enemy's likely activity and an appropriate stop on the train's route so that a quick egress would be a simple matter.

There was also the issue of finding a suitable subject. For that, Hana could be useful, given her talent for mentally scanning not only for magic but also for the personality auras of regular people who did not possess the gift.

Finally, Daniela would likely be the best one to carry out the selection. She was capable of responding with crude physical force if need be, and Milena and Hana could easily cover her tracks.

Milena said to herself, "It can be done."

She checked the train's itinerary on the railroad company's website. By now, they were well into the Great Plains, more than halfway across the United States and close to the Rocky Mountains. With fewer stops in the less populous regions of the interior West, they would make speedy progress toward their ultimate destination of Los Angeles.

But before they arrived in the City of Angels, there was to be another stop in Riverside. That wasn't far from a certain location the Orthodoxy had secured, one Milena had been involved in briefing the lower-ranking members about, in fact.

The train would be pausing at the station there in the early hours of the morning before dawn. Perfect.

Milena breathed in and out, relaxing and thinking about the inevitable success to come. She finally looked at her subordinates. "Hana, Daniela. Fate will be kind to us. Late at night, before the sun rises, we will spring the trap. This will coincide with our arrival in Riverside, California, near our safe house."

The two other witches perked up.

Milena continued, "Let us now discuss the details..."

Lia's posture abruptly straightened, her body growing tense and her eyes gleaming with excitement. "All right. We have a location."

Stephanie looked at her. "Oh, damn. Where?" She had been taking a short break. A bowl of half-eaten yogurt and a cup of half-drunk tea rested on her portion of the desk while her phone stared at the ceiling, unattended but not yet asleep.

Before she responded, Lia closed her eyes and inhaled through her nose. "It's in Jurupa Valley, over by Riverside. A bit of a drive but doable. Less than an hour if traffic isn't god-awful. We can make a day trip out of it. But," she frowned, "Pavla warned us that these places aren't generally left just sitting there. We'll have to contend with their defenses."

Already plotting how to approach it, Steph suggested, "Email Pavla again and tell her we're going in. What do we need to know? She can probably give us a rundown of what their defenses will be like."

Lia's vague scowl implied that she wasn't too keen on the idea of barging in on the place, but she nonetheless typed a message and sent it. Meanwhile, Stephanie fished around in her bag for her bootleg copy of *How to Be a Badass Witch* and began reviewing spells and charms that might help her.

As they waited, Lia turned to her friend. "I mailed Pavla, but frankly, I think it might be better for us to wait for Kera and Chris to get back before we rush into anything. That way, we will approach the situation while we're at full organizational strength. As a unit."

Steph countered as her eyes skimmed the spells for physical self-augmentation and improved luck, "We're not going to assault the place and take on the whole Orthodoxy. It's only a scouting mission. You and me make a pretty good unit. I figure you can stay here and keep doing research and stay in touch while I go scope the place out. That way, Kera will know what's up when she gets back."

Though she still didn't seem thrilled about the idea, Lia agreed.

Five minutes later, they heard back from Pavla. "Oh, this doesn't sound good." Lia sighed. "Magical traps are especially common, and they seem to prefer subtle ones that impair a person from being able to snoop more, not to mention scare them away, without causing obvious damage. Those are combined with mundane booby traps that can injure or kill a person while being made to look like an accident. That sounds like a bad combination."

"Yeah," Steph had to concede. "But it also sounds like they're mainly concerned about normal non-magical folks stumbling in. I've got an edge against all that."

Lia pointed out that Pavla's message went into more detail and printed it for Stephanie to take with her and review before she went in. Then she gave her the address, and they shared a quick hug.

"Be careful," said Lia. "I don't want anything to happen to you, not to mention Kera would kill me."

Steph separated from her and stood up. "True that. I'll check in every few minutes once I'm there." She brought a small dashboard camera with her, intending to turn it on to stream what happened upon arrival back to Lia.

She left the warehouse, got into her car, and hit the road. Traffic wasn't too bad, so she figured she could make it to her destination in fifty to fifty-five minutes.

Compared to LA or Long Beach, Jurupa Valley was a small town, though it had to some extent amalgamated with the generalized suburban sprawl that stretched across Southern California from Redlands and Moreno Valley in the Inland Empire to Thousand Oaks and San Clemente on the Pacific coast. Nonetheless, the address Lia had provided lay in a less-populated area close to the freeway but set away from other houses and businesses.

It was a medium-sized two-story house, probably built in the 1970s or 80s. It was surrounded on three sides by a seven-foot fence and had a mostly bare front yard of dust and gravel. Lots of privacy. It looked deserted.

Stephanie pulled her car up and parked on the side of the road, far enough away from the house that she could claim to be going somewhere else or scoping out the neighborhood real estate if she had to, but close enough that it wouldn't be a long sprint back to the vehicle if there was trouble.

"Okay," she murmured and did a brief re-read of the printed suggestions from Pavla.

Apparently, the Orthodoxy liked to set up falling-object traps that would either injure or kill an intruder or drive them unwittingly into other magical snares that would badly frighten or disorient them. The idea, the Czech explained, was to get rid of anyone who happened by without being too dramatic about it so as to avoid scrutiny from the neighbors or normal authorities.

Nodding, Stephanie cast two spells on herself: one to amplify her perception, reflexes, strength, and speed and the other to increase her overall luck so chancy and ambiguous situations were more likely to tip in her favor. For good measure, she spent a moment meditating and expanding her mind to gain better insight into where the magical traps might be located.

There was no more time to delay. Steph climbed out of the car and walked toward the house. No one seemed to be around.

As she strode across the desolate lot, her expanded senses picked a whiff of magic within the structure. It wasn't possible yet to discern what curses might lurk within or where they were, however.

She inhaled. "Here goes nothing."

When she mounted the porch nothing happened, so she put her hand on the front door and tried the knob. It wasn't locked.

She turned it all the way, pushed the door open, and stepped inside.

There was a small foyer area adjacent to a living room where a couple of pieces of furniture lay draped in dirty sheets. Everything was covered in dust. To her right, a staircase rose toward the second floor.

While advancing toward the stairs, Stephanie looked up. A large, heavy bucket perched on a stray beam along the ceiling was tottering.

"Shit!" she exclaimed and dived forward as the bucket fell. With her reflexes sped up, she avoided it handily. The bucket was filled with dry cement and hit the floor with a deafening crack, damaging the floorboards and kicking up clouds of gray particles.

As Steph moved away from it, she sensed the growing presence of hostile magic right behind her. Spinning, she saw nothing, but her mind was attacked by unreasoning fear.

It's probably a spell to scare me into doing something stupid, she surmised. *There's nothing here. Well, actually, there* are *things here, but it's all trickery and bullshit.*

Trying to ignore the inclination toward blind panic, she mounted the staircase. The fourth step collapsed under her feet.

She had half-expected something like that to happen and jumped upward, riding the half of the board that flipped upward before hopping onto the first landing. Then the second hex, which had been cloaked and obscured by the fear curse, triggered.

Stephanie gasped as a cascade of bright purplish-pink flashing lights erupted in front of her face.

Just a color-spray spell. It's harmless. It was probably trying to get me to blunder into whatever trap they have on the next set of stairs.

But as she turned around, carefully moving toward the steps, the lights didn't go away. Like fat magenta raindrops striking a sidewalk, they kept bursting in front of her face. Something was wrong.

The feeling of dread was back, now combined with an overpowering sense of being watched. The Orthodoxy's defenses were thicker and nastier than she had expected. There might be an alarm somewhere, too, which would tip them off that one of their sanctuaries had been invaded and cause them to defend the place with even worse things.

Fine. Time to abort the mission. It pained her, but Steph realized she couldn't scour the whole house without either backup or more planning and preparation.

She jumped over the hole in the staircase, landed on the first floor, and was back out the front door in seconds. As she slammed it behind her, her heart sank. The trap spell, which had at first seemed to merely be an evocation of unnatural colors in the outside world, was in truth a curse laid upon her own senses.

"Oh," Steph moaned, putting a hand to her face and rubbing her eyes. The bright magenta spots continued to bloom and blossom across her field of vision. They did not flag or fade. She saw them whether her eyes were open or shut. "Dammit. Damn, damn, damn. This is going to make it hard to drive and just about impossible to sleep."

Glancing around and ignoring the spots to the best of her ability, she determined that no one was pursuing her and no unfriendly vehicles were approaching. She jogged back to her car, started the engine, and pulled onto the road.

Things went well enough at first. The maroon bubbles were distracting, but by moving her head in one direction or the other, she could still see enough of what was in front of her to drive. But in time, it would drive her crazy.

Her mind raced, then wandered. *I wonder if they had hidden cameras at that place? Or some other magic trap, like a scrying spell or whatnot, that let them see what my car looked like and got a good look at my license plate.*

If that's the case, I might have to trade this thing in soon. It's getting old anyway.

Halfway back to Long Beach, after she had crossed the hills and was nearly to Anaheim, Stephanie found herself growing nauseated. The incessant movement of the blooming spots was giving her an unusual low-level motion sickness, and the winding road around the middle of the route and the extra elevation changes had made it worse.

Grudgingly, she pulled into a gas station. She could stand to refill her tank, but mostly it was simply an opportunity to stop and rest and recover.

Standing still and pumping gas helped, but the spots weren't going away.

Steph went to the bathroom in the gas station, where she took advantage of the extra privacy to dial Lia's number, hoping she would pick up quickly.

"C'mon, girl," she muttered, tapping her foot.

The phone clicked on the third ring. "Hello?" Lia's voice asked. "Stephanie. Are you okay?"

"Kinda," she replied. "I got out in one piece, only, um, how do I put this? I think I'm sick. Feeling a little weird, and it's hard to see. I can explain more later, but, um, let's say I picked up a bug while I was out there. I'm gonna need some treatment for it. Don't think it's contagious, though."

Lia was quiet for a few seconds. "Okay, can you make it back here? I can come get you if need be."

"Yeah, I think I'll manage. I found out some good stuff, though. Plenty to tell Kera. She'll have to be the one to deal with it in the end, I'm sure." Steph expanded her consciousness to scan for anyone in or near the restroom who might be listening to her conversation. No one seemed to be. Then again, her abilities along those lines were not as developed as Kera's were.

Lia responded, "That's great, but we'll need to, ah, get you healthy again too. Hurry back and call me again if you have any problems. I'll be here. Over and out."

"Bye," Steph said and hung up.

Before returning to her car, she splashed cold water on her face. It seemed to help a little. The neon bursts of color continued to torment her, but her other senses calmed and adapted to a small degree.

On the rest of the drive back to Lia's place, between dodging people driving like morons and navigating the general congestion, Stephanie wrestled with the fact that they were going to have to tell Kera everything. She wouldn't be happy.

"Mmhm," Steph grumbled to herself. "She's going to be all, like, 'Stephanie, why did you take that risk? You could have been killed. Shoulda waited for me to get back.' Blah blah blah. Like I don't have the same powers she does. Well, technically I don't, or at least not to the same degree, but I'm still one of the few people who can do magic. It's not as though I'm helpless."

Soon, she was back in Long Beach. As she pulled her car into the driveway, Lia came out the front door of her house and watched her, probably hoping to gain a modicum of advance knowledge as to what her mysterious affliction was.

When Steph climbed out, Lia said, "Well, I'm glad to see that nothing is *visibly* wrong with you. Come inside and tell me about it."

"Right, that's the plan." Stephanie rubbed her eyes again. There was no change in the intensity of the hex; the magenta spots tormented her every bit as viciously as they had an hour ago. "But let's agree on one thing until further notice."

They strode inside, and as Lia closed the door, she cocked an eyebrow and asked, "What?"

Steph grimaced. "Kera doesn't need to find out how we know about all the damn booby traps. We can just say a little bird told us."

Lia poured a cup of coffee for each of them. "It's worth a try, though I imagine it will be a futile effort to get her to believe that."

"I know," Steph admitted. "But she'll take the bad news better after she's distracted by dealing with all that shit herself. We can slip it in then."

Lia laughed. "Good idea."

CHAPTER EIGHTEEN

It was dark, and the train slept. Everyone except the security guard, who was still ruffled and confounded over what had happened the other night when he had lost consciousness for no apparent reason, slumbered in peace. They were oblivious to the plan about to be carried out by three of the passengers.

Milena glanced out the window of their compartment. They were traveling through northwestern Arizona and would be in Southern California presently, but there was time to carry out the operation, provided nothing went disastrously wrong. And if something *did* go that badly, then they might have to crash the train to cover their tracks.

There were always options. There was always a way to turn a situation to one's own advantage and snatch victory from the proverbial jaws of defeat.

The mesas on the plateau outside loomed like black monoliths against the barren yet majestic landscape, which was faintly illuminated by the glow of the moon and stars. The sky was a deep, dark blue speckled with bright nodes of silver.

She looked at Hana and Daniela, who were standing at attention. They were ready to move out.

Milena raised a finger. "Before we begin, let us review your orders and our overall priority of goals. It is highly unlikely that the American witch will anticipate what we have in mind or have any way of stopping it unless she has somehow been able to scry us, which is all but impossible. Nonetheless, recall what we are to do if the plan fails."

Hana spoke first. "Cloak ourselves, befuddle the passengers, leave the train, and float to safety." Her face was placid with the numbness of calculation.

"Then," Daniela finished, with a cruel twist of the mouth, "we seal them in, blow up the engine, and push the train off the tracks. Why don't we just do that anyway? It would make things simpler."

Milena frowned at her. "In the short term, yes. In the longer term, no, since we would have a great many deaths to account for, and a disaster on this level would be investigated thoroughly by the authorities. Oh, our tracks would be covered, but it would create unnecessary hassles. It is better to kill only the minimum number of people necessary to accomplish the goal. Not to mention, we would then have to quickly find a replacement sacrifice."

While Daniela scowled and grudgingly resigned herself to obedience and moderation, Milena's thoughts turned back to the ultimatum given to her by the grandmistress. They were running out of time. The Orthodoxy needed the empowerment Milena's talents could grant by the middle of the coming day.

Otherwise, their war against the council would drag out longer and might even face the prospect of actual *failure*. Anezka would be greatly displeased.

The trio spent two minutes reviewing all the steps in their Plan A, then placed their hands on one another's shoulders and got to work.

The first thing they needed to do could be done from the privacy of their cabin, which would make the night's labors far easier. The three witches linked minds and began sharing power amongst them, forming a circuit into which the divine powers of the universe flowed at their summons.

Hana had been maintaining a potent but relatively untaxing enchantment that dissipated their auras into a vague, misty presence, making them imperceptible to anyone but the strongest of witches and all but impossible to trace to a single individual except for those of extreme skill and long experience.

Now, they weaponized it. The magical cloud enveloped the whole train, growing denser and darker as more energy was channeled into it. It seeped into every crack and hovered around the face of every sleeping passenger.

"Sleep," Milena said. "Sleep until we arrive in Riverside. Sleep as though you had never slept in your life and were so tired that this alone was your chance to rest, a chance not to be missed, precious beyond all else to you. Sleep deeply, unable to be disturbed by sound, by motion, by touch, by smell, or by any sixth sense warning of danger."

The mist curled through the passengers' nostrils, mouths, and ears and worked its way into their brains. Their unconsciousness deepened to resemble a coma more than sleep.

There was only one point of resistance, and the three witches had no need to guess who it was: their foe, their rival, their soon-to-be sacrifice. The spell was not working against her as well as it should have.

But Milena had expected as much. "More power," she intoned, and the trio channeled extra energy and influence into their enchantment. The slight sense of alarm that had begun to rise from the girl's aura dampened, though, alas, still not into catatonia.

Milena had considered that if the spell did incapacitate the girl as well as everyone else, they could try kidnapping her. However, that created enormous opportunities for risk if the magic failed in even the slightest fashion. She had been right in deciding they should take an indirect approach.

The enchantment reached its end. The American sorceress was sleeping, albeit not as deeply as the others. Milena had no intention of getting close enough to her to wake her up, regardless.

She stated, "Let us move out." They lowered their hands, maintaining a partial mental link but ending the full conduit that allowed them to cast spells as a group.

It would be a journey down the train. The child they sought was in the first passenger car past the foyer compartment and slightly past the train's halfway point toward the rear.

Daniela led the way, ready to use brute force if necessary. Hana was in back, continuously scanning and focusing on enchantments. Milena stayed between them so she could direct either of them as required or help with whatever needed doing.

Aside from the continuous white noise of the train, everything was as silent as a crypt. Even the conductor slept, though the train would be fine without his guidance for a little while.

It was in the second to last compartment before the dining car that they happened upon the security guard. He had been walking a slow patrol when the sleep spell had hit and lay slumped in the hall, twisted against the wall. Milena had Daniela pick him up and haul him along with them, depositing him on a chair in the dining car so he could instead sleep in a sitting position with his head on the table.

The trio moved, shortly reaching the car they sought. Daniela and Hana stood on either side of the door leading into the sleeping compartment while Milena peered at it, twisted her hands, and whispered a few sharp words.

The door opened of its own accord. It didn't make much sound, but even if the family within *had* heard, they gave no indication. All three of them slept like the dead.

The father slept by himself on one bunk, while the mother

and daughter slept together on another. Milena stood aside and gestured. Daniela stepped in, hesitated a second, and then grabbed the little girl around the waist, pulling her free from the sleeping woman. The child didn't stir. She was about six years old, Milena estimated. Daniela put the girl over her shoulder and then returned to the hallway.

Milena replaced the covers around the mother, making it appear as though nothing had happened and the girl had never been there. Then she stepped out, closed the door, and went past her companions to the juncture of the current car and the next one toward the back.

So, my friend, she thought, fixing her mind on what she could recall of the American witch's aura, and allowing her anger to percolate, since you are more talented than we gave you credit for, you will surely have no difficulty receiving this message when the time is right. Will you? No, none whatsoever.

Hana and Daniela waited as their leader cast the spell, a delayed-action psychic missive which, once the rival witch passed by, would introduce itself into her mind with too much force and clarity to resist. However, it would not seem like a message specifically intended *for* her. It would have the appearance of a psychic echo, like a haunting, which their target would just so happen to perceive as evidence.

It would make it clear that because of her, Milena and her cohorts had no choice but to kidnap the child, and sacrifice her in the American witch's stead. Then, they would go to their safehouse in Jurupa Valley to perform the ritual.

And the American witch, who seemed to be a fearless and proactive sort of person, would charge to the rescue—at which point it would be over. On friendly turf, the Orthodoxy's agents would have a massive advantage, and the sacrifice could at last be completed.

Waving her hand to finish the spell, Milena turned and gestured for her subordinates to return to the foyer car. Once everyone was gathered there, Milena took over holding the unconscious child while Daniela gathered their bags from their room and brought them out.

This way, the instant the train arrived in Riverside, the three of them could stroll out and be gone while everyone else on the vehicle was still rousing themselves from their magically-enhanced slumber.

Milena smiled. "Excellent work," she said as much to herself as to the others. She looked at the little girl in her arms, who was pretty and harmless-looking. The child seemed to have an ever-so-faint touch of the gift of magic.

"Interesting," Milena commented. "If by some chance the American does *not* come after us, all is not lost."

Catherine Trammell awoke slowly, emerging from the fog of sleep with more difficulty than she would have expected. It was as though she had chased a half-bottle of booze with two or three sleeping pills and then, in the depths of her dreaming, forgotten where she was or how long it had been since the last time she was awake.

She groaned and yawned and stretched. Her vision was a blur, and the sounds of the train around her an insensate mass of noises. It took three or four seconds before she had the slightest idea of what was going on.

She was on the train to Los Angeles with her husband Aaron and their daughter Jessica, and Jessica had been sleeping next to her.

Catherine lowered her hands. The girl was nowhere to be seen. She came alert, her senses sharpening all at once, and sat upright in the bed, kicking off the covers and scanning the room. Aaron was still lying in his bunk but was beginning to stir.

She grabbed his shoulder and shook him. "Where's Jessica? She's not in here."

Aaron mumbled and opened his eyes. For him, too, it took a moment to regain full consciousness, though perhaps due to the urgency in his wife's voice, he came back more quickly than she had. "I don't know." He started to crawl out of bed, obviously concerned but struggling to regain functionality. "I was asleep. Did she go out to the bathroom? Dining car?"

Frowning, Catherine got out of bed and went to the door, still in her light pajama top and shorts, and opened it. "I'll go check the dining car and up front. You wait here to see if she comes back from the other direction."

It looked like he was going to insist that he go instead, but she didn't delay another second. She was out the door and down the hall by the time he reached the threshold.

"Jessica?" she called. "Jessica, it's your mother. Are you in the bathroom?" Their compartment had a tiny communal lavatory in the center of the car. Hearing no response, Catherine knocked on the door. Then she opened it, saw no one inside, and hastened toward the dining car.

As she stumbled down the hallway, it was clear that the train had come to a stop at what had to be one of the last stations before LA. A handful of passengers was milling about, all of them looking as zombified as she had felt before worry and adrenaline had kicked in to perk her up.

Catherine saw no one in the foyer aside from an engineer who was resting on a bench and seeming to only now be waking up. She went past him into the dining car.

"Jessica?" She got to a good vantage point for viewing the entire compartment and scanned it.

There were four other passengers standing there, looking confused about what they were doing. The security guard was dragging himself out of a chair at one of the little dining tables. A cook was rubbing his eyes and apologizing for being behind schedule. He didn't seem to understand what had happened. Last he recalled, he was wide awake.

No one else was present.

"Oh, Aaron, make sure you stay put," she muttered under her breath, worried that he might tramp toward the rear of the train and miss the girl, and she would get lost trying to find the right cabin on her way back.

Catherine proceeded to the front half of the train. Two minutes later, she had poked through every car and reached the conductor's seat at the front. She did not see Jessica, and no one else claimed to have seen her either.

A sick, desperate sensation of panic was rising through her stomach and into her chest, making her heart thump and her lungs heave. "We're on a train. There aren't many places she could have gone. They haven't even opened the doors yet. Have they? Are the emergency exits child-proofed?"

That did not even bear thinking about, and she tried not to sob.

Back in the dining car, she flagged down the security guard and told him what had happened, describing what Jessica looked like for good measure.

"I'll tell them to keep the doors closed until we find her," the man replied, hoisting his communication device.

Looking past him, Catherine saw that her husband had come into the dining car. "She's not anywhere in the back half of the train," he reported. "You didn't find her?"

Catherine's hands were shaking, and it took all of her strength not to scream, wail, or pound on the walls. "No," she growled.

CHAPTER NINETEEN

Kera froze, not caring that she was blocking Chris in the door between cars.

"Hey," he asked, his voice somewhere behind her. "Is everything okay?"

She didn't hear him. Less out of conscious choice and more out of a primitive instinct to lean on something, she stumbled forward and to the side and pressed her shoulder against the compartment wall, allowing it to support her as the awful vision that had detonated in her mind played out.

The witches from the front of the train. Under the cover of darkness and perhaps using spells to keep everyone else pacified, they had invaded the room of a family on this car, snatched a little girl right out of her mother's arms, and took her away. After the three women departed the room, it was hard to see what they had done next.

But Kera could feel and hear the gist of their intentions: to steal off the train before anyone else was up or realized the girl was missing. They wanted to get far away with their captive and would cloak their progress with magic.

However, a phrase seemed to bubble up out of the witches'

mental residues, and Kera was almost positive it was their destination: Jurupa Valley.

"Kera," Chris said, coming up beside her as another passenger came through behind him and squeezed past, "what's wrong? Talk to me, will you?"

She shuddered and blinked, and the vision was gone. Cold revulsion spread through her bloodstream, but anger followed it.

Her eyes snapped upward as another car or two down, she heard a woman sobbing and a man shouting something. It wasn't hard to guess who was making the racket.

"Chris," Kera told her boyfriend without looking at him, "get our stuff. We need to get off at this stop and start doing detective stuff *right away.* Trust me on this. I'm going to go talk to that couple. Meet me up there in a minute when you have our things, okay? I'll explain everything later."

She turned to look at him. His face was contorted with a mixture of worry, confusion, annoyance, and legitimate appreciation for how serious she had become. He knew full well that she could see and hear things he could not, so he wasn't fazed when she said something strange out of the blue.

"Okay," he replied in a soft voice. "Just promise me that whatever we need to do, we're going to be smart about it."

She gave him a kiss on the cheek. "I promise." Then she darted toward the crying woman.

Kera found a couple in their early or mid-thirties standing in the corner of the foyer car with various train officials standing around them: the conductor and one of the other engineers, as well as the security guard and one of the cooks. The woman was on the verge of hysteria, red-faced and teary-eyed.

The man wasn't much better. He struggled to stay calm and oscillated between shouting in frustrated anger and wanting to join his wife in sobbing in despair.

"What do you *mean,*" he demanded, his voice cracking, "all the passengers aren't accounted for yet? Are you trying to tell us that someone could have slipped off the train with our *daughter* before anyone even knew we had stopped? What the hell kind of shit is going on with this rail line?"

The assistant engineer put a hand over his eyes, muttering to himself, "This has been the worst trip *I've* ever seen, that's for damn sure."

The security guard tried to reassure the couple that he had made all the necessary phone calls. The railroad authorities had locked down the station and were sweeping the place and checking their security cameras. They were already in touch with the police, who would be putting out an Amber Alert as soon as they had a little more information.

Kera waited until the train's employees began to drift away before she approached the couple. "Excuse me."

The man raised a hand toward her without looking. "Not now."

"Pardon me," she went on, "but I'm a detective. You know, a private investigator. Yes, I know I look young, but I have several cases under my belt. I heard what happened, and I might be able to help find your daughter."

The man and the woman stopped their slow pacing and pivoted to look at her. She could see the intense pain and fear in their eyes, and her heart almost broke.

"Okay," the man responded. "Credentials?"

Kera produced her business card, glad she had brought some in her wallet. The man looked it over, then pulled out his phone. "Don't mind if I check to see if you're legit? No offense."

Kera shrugged. "That's fine. Can you tell me more about what happened? What your daughter looks like?"

The woman appeared to be Latina and the man was Caucasian with dark hair, so she doubted the girl was a blonde or a redhead. Otherwise, Kera had not been able to glean anything about the child from what she had overheard. Details about the girl's appearance had been fuzzy in her vision as well.

The woman was getting her crying under control. "My name is Catherine, and this is my husband Aaron Trammell," she stated. "Our daughter's name is Jessica. She's six years old, with straight dark-brown hair a little past her shoulders. She was wearing a pink sweater. She looks more like her father than like me. She...*oh, God!*"

Kera hesitantly put a hand on the woman's shoulder as she broke down again and waited for her to get herself back together. The father, Aaron, glared at her briefly, but then his expression softened.

Looking up from his phone, he declared, "All right, looks like you're a real company, though I'm not seeing much information about past cases you've been involved in. We can't afford to give you a down payment, but if you can bring our little girl back to us, then name your price. We'll figure out a way to pay it."

Kera was suddenly embarrassed, even ashamed. She was anxious to get out and begin searching for the child—mentioning that she was a detective had simply been a way to expedite the process and gain the couple's trust—and she hadn't thought about money.

"Umm," she began, "don't worry about it for now. I just want to help. I have people who work under me also. In fact," she turned her head as Chris came into the foyer car, lugging their crap, "here's my IT guy now. Hi, Chris. These are the Trammells, and I think they've hired us."

Aaron grunted. "Yes, we have. Now get out and find her. I'll keep your business card and give you a call as soon as I hear from the stuffed shirts around this station about the make and model of the culprits' getaway vehicle or anything like that."

Catherine added, "Thank you. Please, anything you can do!"

"I'm on it." Kera nodded at them, hoping her eyes conveyed that she meant it.

Rushing to Chris' side, she grabbed her half of the luggage. "Okay, we need to get a move on. I have an idea where to start."

They stepped out of the train and onto the platform, noting that guards and cops were milling around and looking everyone over.

Chris coughed. "Okay, great. Start what? I missed the part where someone explained to me what the hell is going on."

A police officer walked toward them. Kera inhaled and rapidly concocted a spell to dismiss suspicion from her and her boyfriend, casting it just as the man stood in front of them.

"Hi, Officer," she said. "We already spoke to the parents. We heard what happened. As you can see, we don't have the girl with us, and if you want to know anything else, talk to them. Catherine and Aaron Trammell."

The spell clearly worked since the cop just raised an eyebrow, said, "Oh, okay. Good," and walked away.

Kera exhaled in relief as they went on their way.

Chris pointed out, "If they talk to the parents, they'll know we were hired for this job, whatever it is. Actually, ugh. You referred to them as 'the parents' and mentioned 'the girl.' Don't tell me those witches snatched a *kid* off the train?"

"If you insist," Kera murmured. "Then I won't tell you that was *exactly* what they did."

Chris groaned as they left the platform and went to the terminal, which held desks and booths for renting cars. "Oh, that's fucking lovely. Well, it's good that we're on the case since the cops aren't going to be able to track people who can hide their passage with magic. Still, this wasn't how I wanted the tail end of our vacation to go. So, then, what's this piece of information you have about where to start?"

"Jurupa Valley." Kera chose a car rental company and headed toward their booth. "Not far. It was in a...vision I saw. Kind of like when the Duo—those thaumaturgists from the council, the ones who were probably behind the book—left me that message about how they wanted to train me or else, except that it didn't seem like the vision was meant for me. I was just a third-person observer."

Chris got ahead of her and blocked her. "Hold on. It might be a trap, you realize. Those three were trying to capture *you* earlier. It probably *was* meant for you, especially if they conveniently mentioned where they were taking the girl."

Kera's brain was still burning with the urgent need to track down their quarry and rescue the kid, so for a second, she contemplated shoving Chris aside, but then she stopped and sighed. "Yeah, that could be. But," she inhaled, "it doesn't make much difference. They can't be allowed to get away with this, so if you don't mind, step away."

Instead of moving to the side, Chris kept walking in the direction she had been going, staying ahead of her.

"You promised me we would be smart about this. We need a plan; we can't just charge right in. You'll need me, and it wouldn't hurt to talk to Lia and Stephanie first. If they're using the girl as bait, she probably isn't in *immediate* danger, right? She will be worse off if you get killed trying to rescue her than she will if we spend an extra fifteen minutes making sure you *don't* get killed and *do* rescue her."

Kera wasn't about to disagree, though she disliked the thought of delaying the search as long as that. "Yeah, I guess. Now let's rent a car. Or you can call Lia while I do that."

He took out his cell. "Agreed."

As soon as she'd heard the report, Anezka had left their new temporary headquarters behind, conscripting a random low-ranking witch who had experience with American cars and roads to act as a driver.

The other senior members were busy with other things, but Anezka was able to send them a message during the ride. They would be on standby, and those who could spare the time would come to her side at once. It would not take long for them to join her.

Having sent the texts, Anezka put away her phone, straightened her black hair, and folded her hands in her lap, looking straight ahead as the young woman in the driver's seat took them deeper into West Virginia.

"Grandmistress," the witch named Tatiana commented, "they will have gone by now. Shall I keep driving in the same direction, or do you want me to stop where they were sighted?"

Anezka raised a hand, not as a rebuke or to cast a spell but as a gesture of casual authority. "Go to the site I told you and stay there while I inspect the scene. I want to examine all the evidence they left so we can determine which direction they are headed. We might also need to wait for input from the other elders. If by some chance it is a trap, do not fear. I will deal with it."

Tatiana nodded and agreed, wisely choosing not to argue. Anezka appreciated that the girl was willing to ask intelligent questions, but everyone in the Orthodoxy needed to understand their place in the hierarchy and act accordingly.

And it was, Anezka felt, extremely unlikely that the council had laid a trap for them. The witches who had—finally!—picked up their trail had not come to any harm, and Anezka could sense their auras ahead. They were still there, watching over the scene.

Further, if the council meant to pick off high-ranking Orthodoxy members, they probably would not have guessed that Anezka would be willing to investigate matters like this herself with virtually no backup. Granted, they had all seen her personally lead the attack on the Lovecraft estate, but most powerful leaders were not as bold as she was.

Some had implied that she was reckless, yet their coven had flourished under her dominion. She scoffed at such petty criticisms.

Soon, they arrived in the little town of Barboursville in the far west of West Virginia, near the state's juncture with southern Ohio and eastern Kentucky. The psychic splatter the scouts had picked up—the careless magical residue that one of the council had left behind, probably by accident while in a hurry—was located on a back road off the interstate near the Guyandotte River, which flowed through the middle of the town.

It was a hilly, heavily wooded region, where primeval forests took over as soon as one was outside the immediate grasp of civilization. It reminded Anezka of the Carpathian region in western Ukraine.

The two scouts, a man and a woman, were standing guard when the car pulled up. Of course, they had diligently deployed magical barriers against the unwelcome eyes and ears of the locals. Once the vehicle was inside the cloaking dome, Anezka raised her hand again.

"Stop here," she instructed the driver. Tatiana brought the car to a halt and, remembering her earlier orders, waited while Anezka climbed out.

The grandmistress instantly began scanning the earth, the air, the atmospheric moisture, and the trees and bugs and human litter—anything that might have absorbed the slightest trace of magic.

Five seconds later, she had a fairly good assessment of what had happened here, but she nonetheless allowed the two scouts to approach her and give their reports.

"Grandmistress," they said in unison and gave shorts bows of their heads. The young woman continued, "We estimate they stopped here and something happened to frighten them or disturb them emotionally, so they hurried off."

The young man nodded. "Yes. It could have happened no more than three, perhaps four hours ago at most. Likely two to three. Unfortunately, they cleaned up after themselves well enough that we have not been able to determine where they went from here."

Anezka gave them a curt nod of acknowledgment, then stepped past them, extending her hands and letting her eyes glaze over as her consciousness expanded for nearly a square kilometer.

The river. Her subordinates were reasonably skilled, but they likely hadn't attempted to examine running water, which was usually anathema to any stable magical process. But Anezka knew better. Not everything in a river moved along with the water.

Her inner sight descended through the rushing, churning torrent, seeking out tree branches stuck against banks, large rocks submerged at the bottom, and living creatures hiding out in tiny grottoes that might have witnessed the council's error.

A moment later, she had it. A familiar aura-signature, the scent of Mother LeBlanc, and it smelled of *nostalgia*. Nostalgia and intentionality.

The waters of the Guyandotte wended their way into a larger river—the Ohio, if Anezka was not mistaken, based on her recollection of maps of the region. She was almost positive that the Ohio River, a long way to the west, joined the Mississippi. Then the Mississippi River flowed more or less due south until it emptied into the Gulf of Mexico just past LeBlanc's home city of New Orleans.

Anezka blinked once, and her eyes returned to normal. She turned back to the two scouts, who were trying not to disturb her while also looking diligent. They turned their attention toward the grandmistress as she strode in their direction.

"They are headed for New Orleans after all," Anezka stated. "And I suspect they mean to go west first, then south. Perhaps they think they will fool us or lose us by doing so instead of taking the more direct route. Perhaps this is all a diversion and they truly mean to head for the West Coast, but I doubt it."

The scouts were clearly burning with curiosity to hear more, but they obediently waited rather than try to rush their leader with stupid questions.

Anezka went on, "Remain here. Others of the elder council will arrive shortly to confer with us. No, I have changed my mind. You," she pointed at the male scout, "go ahead a short way and continue searching for traces of their passage. Anything that might help us determine if they are heading northwest or southwest, but certainly west. I have no doubt of it."

"Yes, Grandmistress," the man said. Wasting no time, he turned and jumped, floating across the river and vanishing into the trees.

Minutes later, a black car pulled up beside the one Anezka had ridden in and out stepped Vassily. As usual, he looked dour and gaunt-faced, but his eyes gleamed with excitement.

"Ah." He sighed. "I can smell them. They must have stopped here and experienced something *terrible*. Such a pity. It feels as though one of them almost died, or someone went mad or did something to threaten them all with discovery, then they all convened to try to snuff out the effects of it before hurrying away. They did a poor job of wiping this place clean of their tracks, however."

Anezka smiled. "Indeed. And as I was linked to Mother LeBlanc's mind for a short period, I can easily sense the residues of her thoughts and emotions atop those of the others. My reading suggests that they are fleeing west, intending then to turn south toward New Orleans."

"Excellent." Vassily came closer and he and Anezka walked toward the river, out of earshot of the young female scout as well as the drivers of their cars. Quietly, Vassily added, "It will still be difficult to track them. Alas that we no longer have Pavla to handle such things."

Her face hardened, and Anezka snapped, "I know that. It is useless to lament what has already happened. The loss of Pavla was an inconvenience, but not an insurmountable one. All we need is enough power to penetrate the council's cloak for a moment or two to glimpse their exact location and get some idea of their plans. Then we can move in and finish them off."

Looking away from her right-hand man, Anezka pulled out her phone and called Milena. While waiting for the other witch to answer, she examined the sky. It was about two hours past dawn here in the eastern part of the United States. Milena and the others on the train would be a few hours earlier, probably into the Pacific Time Zone by now.

Milena answered on the fourth ring. "Anezka, how good of you to call me. I would like to inform you that—"

Anezka interrupted, "How close are you to being able to perform the necessary sacrifice? We have made a crucial break-through and need the extra power to be delivered to us with all due haste. I was hoping to have it already, but I will allow you another, say, three hours at most. That puts us approximately at the original deadline, does it not? Usually you are not tardy with delivering the required results."

Milena audibly swallowed. "Yes, Grandmistress. I have obtained a suitable subject, a young child with a faint trace of the gift, and we are on our way by rented car to the safe house in California's Inland Empire region. We have left the train. I can perform a sacrifice of moderate potency at once if you prefer, but please allow me to suggest that we wait a short while longer for a still-better one. There is an American witch who would likely provide an enormous boon to us. I need only lure her to the safe house, and I feel confident in saying that she will be here soon."

Anezka paused; it annoyed her that Milena was being so vague. "This witch...might it be Kera MacDonagh by any chance? A slender young woman, early to middle twenties, with hair dyed black?"

"It, ah," Milena responded, "had occurred to me that it might be her, but we could not confirm that. I suspect it is. Even if it is someone else, however, her strength is substantial. Sacrificing her will be worth a short wait, I assure you. And once we have her, we can sacrifice the child as well for yet more benefit. Our coven will possess more than enough power to complete the task of locating the council."

Anezka stroked her chin. Child sacrifices were generally avoided since they caused more public outcry than killing adults, but there were ways of diverting the populace's attention from them. Under the circumstances, given the importance of locating LeBlanc at all costs, Anezka felt the choice was clear.

"Do it," she instructed Milena, "but do not hesitate too long. Kill the child first if Kera does not show up by the deadline. And assuming you are successful, as you almost always are, inform me immediately. I will begin the scrying ritual in two hours' time, and I can hold off releasing the spell for another hour thereafter. Remember, if by some chance both Kera and the child escape, select another subject *at once*."

She hung up. Milena understood what she meant by that, of course. She was not the sort to quail about moral questions when it came to her duties. Losing Hana or Daniela would be unfortunate, but the Orthodoxy could afford to spare them more easily than it could afford to let the council get away.

Anezka turned back to Vassily. "We need a proper ritual chamber. Find a nice theater or university auditorium in Huntington up ahead. It is a large enough city to have what we require."

Vassily, who had listened in on the phone conversation, nodded. "With pleasure."

CHAPTER TWENTY

As soon as the front door was open, Milena stepped in and narrowed her eyes. "Someone has been here," she observed. "There are tracks in the dust, and at least two of the traps have been sprung. We will look into it in a moment, but first..."

She stood aside and flourished her hand. Daniela, holding the kidnapped girl firmly and keeping a hand clamped over her mouth, came in first, followed by Hana. Milena shut the door.

Hana's brow furrowed. "The intruder was here not long ago. Yesterday, perhaps. I believe it was someone with the gift. There are traces of magic here that are not of our coven. Something foreign and amateurish."

Milena tensed at that. Who could it be? It was physically and logistically impossible for Kera or whoever the young woman on the train was to have arrived here before they did.

"Strange," Milena conceded. "There are many eccentric people in this city. Perhaps a hedge-witch, a fortune teller, or some such person sensed the spells laid here and blundered in out of dumb animal curiosity. It would seem that our defenses drove them out, but we must re-fortify. Kera will be here soon."

Raising a hand, she mapped a pathway up the stairs that

would avoid the remaining traps and curses, both the magical and mundane ones. Then she turned to Daniela. "Give me the girl. I will see to her for now. Go fetch my altar and the rest of our things. I can begin the ritual of power transference in advance and keep it in stasis while you and Hana prepare for our guest's arrival."

Daniela shoved Jessica Trammell into the smaller witch's arms. "Yeah, understood." Looking annoyed at having to once again do all the grunt work and manual labor, she stomped to their car.

Milena looked down at the child. They had cast a relaxation spell on her to keep her from panicking and crying out or trying to run away. There was still a vague sheen of fear in her wide brown eyes, but otherwise, she was as placid and compliant as a young child could be.

"Come, my dear," Milena told her in English, beginning to ascend the stairs. "We are going to take a rest while I show you the room you'll be staying in. One of my friends will be coming over soon. Does that sound fun? After I talk to her, you can go home and see your parents again. All will be well."

The girl's head moved a half-inch to indicate that she had heard, but otherwise, she did not react.

Milena carried her up the stairs, avoiding the hole where one of the steps had collapsed and prancing her way through the web of spell-traps. She set the child on her feet once they reached the second story.

Leading her by the hand, Milena took Jessica to a storage room near the back of the house, essentially an oversized closet that had no windows.

"Stay here," she said. "I will be back with a chair and a pillow." She did not consider herself a monster; there was no reason for the girl to be uncomfortable during the short amount of time she had left in the world.

She did find it distasteful to lie to a young child and sacrifice her, but the coven's needs came before the life of any one person. And Milena's honor and reputation within the order would soar after their ultimate success.

Once she had found the necessary furniture, Milena left Jessica where she was and magically sealed the door. Then, inhaling, she went down to help Hana and Daniela haul the altar upstairs. She might also have time to help them lay the traps, but the ritual took priority, and the two of them could handle the defensive preparations.

Soon, Milena reminded herself. Everything would come together soon.

Anezka tilted her chin down, then up again in a curt and imperious gesture of approval. "This will suffice. It is not superlative, but so long as the task is accomplished, it matters little how glamorous our surroundings are."

Vassily chortled in his dry voice. "It is harder to find truly exceptional accommodation outside the larger cities. But as you say, expecting to always be coddled is the sort of thing our enemies would do. We pride ourselves on being able to make do in any setting."

He was, Anezka realized, attempting to flatter her by parroting what she had said before. She paid it no heed one way or another. "Yes. Bring everyone in and ensure that our lower-ranking people are in position to move immediately once the scrying succeeds. I am willing to give Milena an hour longer than I should for the sake of her supposedly brilliant plan, but scouts and field troops have no excuse to delay once the target is in sight."

"Of course." Vassily marched out of the room to repeat her orders to the other elder members and relay the latter portion to their reconnaissance personnel.

The temporary lodgings he had found were at a local hotel Anezka supposed qualified as being in the upper-middle range as far as quality went. In addition to securing rooms for all of them with the aid of a certain amount of compulsion and persuasion magic, they had also rented the use of a convention office which, once properly shielded from scrutiny, would make an effective ritual chamber.

Anezka arranged the chairs around the main, central table so that she would be at the head and the other elders would be able to sit in their proper position relative to their standing within the Orthodoxy as well as form an effective magical circle.

Milena, of course, could not be present in person, but she represented the other half of the working to come. If she failed, nothing the rest of the coven's leadership did today would matter much.

Vassily and the others filed in. They all had the appropriate mood of solemn focus, as was customary before the casting of a major and powerful spell, but there was a noticeable undercurrent of gleeful excitement.

Anezka did not chastise them for it. She felt the same way, and she trusted their expertise and self-discipline. None of them, she was confident, would allow personal feelings to get in the way of the passionless task that lay ahead.

Once everyone had taken their seats, Anezka looked at Vassily.

"All the scouts are in place, Grandmistress," he declared. "As you requested earlier, some have remained at points in the Northeast to secure the territory we conquered previously, but the bulk of them, around eighty percent, are poised to fan out in search of the council the instant we discern their location."

Flexing her hands, Anezka replied, "Good." Then she clapped once, causing the electric lights to go out. Another clap and the wicks of the candles on the table burst into emerald flames, first a bright profusion of fire, then a normal-sized but eerily green steady glow.

"Elder witches and warlocks of the mighty Orthodoxy," she intoned in Russian. "We are gathered here to snuff out our greatest enemies once and for all. They shall be revealed to us; they can hide no longer. Milena! Are you there? We call out to you as one mind, seeking the link to your consciousness, your power, and the lifeblood of the ones you shall slay upon the unhallowed altar of sacrifice. Milena!"

As the minds of the elders linked and the dark powers they shared began to circulate among them, they all felt the faint presence of their absent member, but it took longer than they would have liked for her to respond.

I am here, Grandmistress, and all others. Everything is ready, and Kera approaches now. Her power will be ours, I swear it. Her life and the girl's will lead us to victory.

Kera and Chris sat in their new but temporary ride, an SUV, with Chris behind the wheel. "I haven't driven anything but my Jeep," he admitted, "but this was the biggest thing they had, so it's better than trying to adjust to a goddamn compact Toyota or something."

Kera waved a hand. "Right, and I've only driven my bike lately. You'll do fine. Now go go go. I'm willing to spend time making a plan, but we can do that while we drive."

"Ha, *we*, she says," he shot back and pressed the button to start the car.

Though he was a little awkward at first, Chris seemed to have the hang of the vehicle by the time they were a quarter-mile from the train station. Once he was comfortable, he filled Kera in on the details of his conversation with Lia.

"Okay, get this. Lia and Stephanie were doing some research

on possible Orthodoxy activity around here, and they say they located a safe house in...drumroll...Jurupa Valley. Steph scoped the place out and has some intel on the types of defenses they have, though if the witches are there, they might have beefed things up further."

Kera blinked. "Guess I hired the right people after all. Okay, what's the address?"

Clearing his throat, Chris went on, "I have it, but first, another suggestion. Lia said she's coming out, and I think we should wait for her. She was at your place instead of her own, apparently, so that shaves five or ten minutes off the trip, but still, we'll need to wait for her to arrive. She's not sure if Stephanie can make it or not. And something about Stephanie being cursed to see pink spots eternally, which they hope you can help her with, though she might be able to cure herself. *And* she mentioned that she had been in touch with Pavla."

Kera scowled and pinched the bridge of her nose. "Jesus, is that all? Mothra wasn't sighted flapping over the Valley, was he? It would be nice if we could just focus on one thing at a time. A little girl's life is at stake."

Chris reached over and put a hand on her arm. "I know, and we'll save her, but let's take our time with this. Think of everything you know about these people, and on the basis of that, slow down and tell me how you plan to go into this safehouse without getting yourself burned to a crisp or turned into a dung beetle or human-sacrificed."

He had a point. Kera thought about the vision the witches had left for her, and hearing Chris' mention of sacrifice clarified the meaning of what she had seen. She recalled a passage from the book the Kims' friend had lent her about how some cultures and magical traditions believed that sacrificing a person of power would transfer their strength to those who spilled their blood.

Within the magical remainder of the psychic message were the witches' thoughts, some of which revolved around her. Kera.

"I'm the one they want," she concluded. "This is all a ruse to lure me into their clutches so they can use me as fuel. Well, they're going to fail at that, but I'm going to succeed at getting Jessica Trammell back to her parents."

Chris gave her a faint smile. "You've never been lacking when it comes to motivation, resolve, determination, and that type of thing. I think you *will* succeed, but let's make sure of it. I don't want to wake up tomorrow remembering that yesterday was the day your luck finally ran out."

"Me neither," Kera quipped, then realized how stupid that sounded. "Um, I mean, waking up in, uh, hell? Or wherever. Dammit, I can't make clever-ass comments right now."

Chris shrugged. "Nobody's perfect."

Soon they arrived at a drive-thru place not far from the address Lia had given them. It was early, and they hadn't had time for breakfast on the train, so Chris got them some food and coffee. It was not only for nourishment but also so they could wait for a while in the parking lot without looking too suspicious. The hope was that Lia wouldn't be too long in arriving.

Both their phones buzzed at approximately the same time. Kera, who was keyed up and getting into the proverbial "zone" of body-mind coordination, was able to slip hers out before Chris could. She swiped the screen.

"Oh, shit," she relayed. "It's Stephanie. She has to work later. She wants to help but is worried that her curse is going to fuck everything up since she can barely drive, has trouble seeing, et cetera. What the hell did those bitches do to her?"

Chris squirmed in his seat. "I don't know, but it sounds unpleasant. Don't let them do the same thing to you."

The rest of the message was Stephanie expressing her embarrassment at how stupid it was to be worried about an inconvenient hex, let alone getting to work on time when a kid's life hung in the balance. Kera knew how she felt.

After a moment's consideration, Kera texted her back, saying to come with Lia and they would see what they could do to help her.

"All right," she murmured. "I want to charge in, as I'm sure you guessed, but I'm going to admit that you're *probably* right about waiting for our backup to roll in."

Steph texted back, pointing out that Lia had already left but she would be coming by herself and apologized if she was late to the party.

Kera frowned. "Dammit. Forgot about that. I hope it's safe for her to drive. Still, we'll adapt." She paused. "But we can't wait for her. Once Lia shows up, it's go time."

They ate, drank coffee, and stalled for another twenty minutes before heading toward the address. A faint sense of unease crept in as they drew nearer their destination.

Though Jurupa Valley was for the most part pretty nice, the neighborhood around the Orthodoxy's safe house had a strange air of desolation. It wasn't far from the freeway or from other perfectly normal areas, so it was difficult to determine why. Kera supposed it was mostly in her head.

Chris slowed after they turned onto the street where the house lay. "Okay, this is the place, approximately. Unless you say otherwise, I'm going to wait here instead of trying to find the house yet. Don't need to clue them in that we're here until you're ready to do your thing."

Kera nodded. She was still wearing her jacket, so the witches probably couldn't perceive how close she was, but a random car slowly rolling past their driveway a couple of times would be a dead giveaway to anyone.

While they waited for Lia, Kera found her mind turning to something else.

Pavla had been an upper-middle-rank witch in the Orthodoxy, she recalled, and she and Stephanie had held their own against her in battle with difficulty. Similarly, Kera had to assume the three coven members on the train were at least as powerful as

Pavla and the petite brunette leader was quite possibly more powerful. From what the book said, sacrificial magic was a task best saved for experienced adepts.

And yet, Kera had defeated her and her two minions single-handed. Luck had played a part, to be sure. They had seemingly underestimated her, and in the narrow confines of the train, their superior numbers didn't mean as much.

Today, Kera would be storming a defended location on the Orthodoxy's new home turf, and the witches had the advantage of foreknowledge. It wouldn't be as easy this time.

But the more I think it over, she reflected, *the stranger it is that I have any chance at all. I've been a magic user for less than a year, and I haven't had that much formal training. Am I really that powerful?*

Chris was the first to answer his phone this time when both their devices buzzed again. "It's Lia. She'll be here in five minutes."

Kera nodded. *They're extremely anxious to sacrifice me, probably because they figure my talent will give the Orthodoxy a huge boost, so I suppose I'm pretty fucking special.*

CHAPTER TWENTY-ONE

Anezka's eyes, closed until this moment, flew open, and a faint red glow emanated from her irises.

"Yes," she urged. "Begin! Draw her in. Already our power is on the cusp of what is needed."

Her voice rang out, echoing through the makeshift chamber and across the astral plane to the mind of Milena.

Anezka's hands lay claw-like upon the surface of the table, her black nails digging into the wood. Milena had begun the rite of sacrifice in advance, starting the process with a single drop of her own blood. It was enough to create a small but intoxicating infusion of power and entice the ancient and shadowy spirits who were involved in transferring the magical essence of the victim into the intended vessels: them, the Orthodoxy's elders.

And since all of them were united in their intensity of purpose, focus, and self-discipline, they were at the peak of their strength before the sacrifice even took place. Each of the senior witches had come to the day's endeavors well-rested, well-fed, and confident of success.

It was difficult to maintain the astral connection to Milena and her altar hundreds of miles away while at the same time beginning the spell of scrying and holding it in suspension over the Council of Thaumaturgists, ready to descend like a bolt of lightning and crack open their barrier of invisibility. But they had done it before, and Anezka was one of the most powerful leaders the coven had ever had.

Mother LeBlanc would fail. She, the mightiest of her order, was *at best* Anezka's equal, and she presided over a small group of tired, hungry, hunted, and defeated people. They lacked the numbers, organization, and ruthless will of the Orthodoxy.

All it would take was the knowledge of where they were. Then the hammer stroke would fall, and with the deaths of LeBlanc and the others, North America would be joined with Russia and Eastern Europe in the mightiest witch empire the world had seen in ages—perhaps the largest of all time.

Milena's voice sounded within their collective consciousness.

She is here. Kera is approaching. She is strong and wily, but we are well-prepared and shall not make the same mistakes twice. Be ready!

Anezka smiled, and her hands trembled. "We are, Milena. Do it."

Kera, Chris, and Lia crouched behind the fence. Kera had risked the expenditure of a little extra magic to cloak them and their cars from sight, hearing, or scrying. By this point, she was good enough at basic spells like that for them to deplete her stamina only a little bit.

"All right," Kera told her friends. "I can't wait for Stephanie. If she gets here and it seems like I need help, send her in, but we can't delay any longer while that little girl is in danger. Lia, I skimmed the stuff you sent. Didn't have time to read it in detail, but I got enough out of it that I have a plan. Trust me."

Chris nodded. His sardonic smile implied that he was about to make a smartass remark, but he did not.

Lia wore a serious, earnest expression, as she often did. "We trust you, Kera, but telling us what your plan *is* would make it easier for us to help if need be. Remember, it's you they want. I would wager money that they're willing to wait another five minutes for you to walk through their front door, though I agree we need to move soon for the child's sake."

Kera flexed her hands in mild frustration. "Okay, here's the gist of it. What's that saying? I think the military uses it. 'No plan survives contact with the enemy' or something like that. I'll probably have to change it and make shit up as I go along. That's happened pretty much every time we've gone into battle. Nonetheless..."

She took a deep breath.

"I'm going to try a trick that's so basic they might overlook it or figure I couldn't possibly be using something so obvious against them. I'll conjure an illusion of myself and send it through the front door. Then I'll conjure like three or four more and have all of them attack the house from different angles, with the real me hitting one of the windows at the same time. They'll figure it out pretty quick, but it might throw them off long enough for me to get the edge."

Lia nodded. "Okay. Good. What else."

Kera coughed. "Find the girl and get her out of there. As much as I'd like to hang around and beat the shit out of those three, rescuing the kid is the important part. If need be, I can turn her over to you guys, and then I can hold the witches off while you take Jessica back to her parents."

Chris' eyes widened in amazement. "That's it?"

"Yeah," she muttered. "That's it. Well, if I do the illusions right, they ought to have a little more substance than usual. I used the basic version against..." She stopped herself.

Lia grimaced. "Yes, I recall. It worked well against Johnny and Sven, but as you say, it won't be nearly as effective against experienced magic users."

Kera stood up. "Trust me. Keep an eye on what's going on, and stand by to grab the girl."

Before either of them could delay her with further questions, she sprinted around the outside corner of the fence.

"Kera!" Lia called. "Dammit. All right, let's get in our cars, one of us on each side of the house. I hope no one sees us stuffing a child into our vehicles and driving away fast. Ugh."

Chris raised a palm. "Don't worry. The girl's parents technically hired us, so they can vouch for our legitimacy."

Lia stared, then her face lit up. "We have a *customer?* That's great!" For the first time in far too long, she grinned like an overexcited schoolgirl. Then she recalled what was going on and got back to business. "Yeah. Move out."

Meanwhile, Kera was halfway around the fence. Once safely out of the reach and view of her friends, she cast the spell to summon the illusory copies of herself, but this time, she did something different.

Particles of dirt, chunks of earth and rock from the barren lot, and sticks and leaves from the nearby half-dead trees floated where Kera crouched and formed small whirlwinds around her. These formed the cores, giving each of the holographic figures a small degree of physical mass and existence. The illusions shimmered into being around them.

Before dispatching them to do their jobs, Kera attempted one more thing. Recalling how the witches had spread their auras out over the whole train in a vague cloud, she tried the same thing with her magical signature.

Her mind's eye perceived a white-gold light like the sun, splitting apart and dimming as it filtered outward. It became less a single main node and more a series of shining masses. It wasn't quite the same as the uniform haze her adversaries had created, but it ought to be good enough. She tied the main light points to the doppelgangers.

Okay, girls, she said in her mind, and her thoughts became commands to the pseudo-beings she had created. *It's go time.*

One of the illusions jumped up and vaulted over the fence. Kera could hear the swirling gravel within scrape the wood, which was a good sign. The figure ran parallel to the house's side before angling toward the front door.

Kera felt rather than heard or saw the witches notice the intruder and drew a sharp breath. Then she waved her hand like a sergeant leading a squad into battle.

She and the other four copies jumped the fence in unison. She had two of them assault the closer side of the house and brought the other two with her to the rear. There was no way to be certain yet, but she suspected Jessica Trammell was being held somewhere toward the back and on the second floor.

A hunch, and my hunches are usually correct or close to it. We'll find out soon enough.

She soared down from the top of the fence, augmenting her movements through basic magic. She kept one of the doppelgangers with her while commanding the other to circle around to the house's far side, the only direction from which none of the other doubles had yet attacked it.

Within the building, she could faintly hear women's voices calling to one another in Russian. As Kera jumped toward the nearest window on the top floor, something toward the front of the house crashed loudly and set the whole building shuddering.

Damn. Must have been a hell of a trap, whatever it was. My poor fake illusion. Hope it didn't get hurt.

She sailed through the air while conjuring a shield that surrounded her body like a transparent suit of armor and smashed through the window. As the glass shattered into hundreds of fragments around her, she saw a dark, dirty bedroom that was empty of anything except a bed covered with a filthy old sheet and a wooden dresser in the corner.

Kera came to a rest on her hands and knees, thankful the shield protected her from the glass shards.

Now the girl. Where is she? There's so much magic floating around this place that I can't get a bead on her position, but it's not too big of a house. I can look for her the old-fashioned way as long as the witches are distracted.

She sprang to her feet, rushed to the door, and flung it open, ready to fight at a split-second's notice.

To her surprise, the hallway beyond was empty, but it presented more doors than she would have liked: two on the same side of the hall as the room she'd come from, and another two on the opposite side, next to the stairwell.

While trying to decide which one to open first, Kera sent her mind out to her illusory clones, attempting to discern which of them had been attacked or if any magical presences were close to them.

The feedback that returned to her was a chaotic mess of thaumaturgic impulses, astral strife, and an overall feeling of hostility. There was something beneath the noise as well, a dark, loathsome, foreboding impression tied to the house or something within it rather than to the battle or any spells being cast.

Her trio of adversaries had managed to disperse their auras. It was impossible to guess where they might be, except through logic and her physical senses.

Kera figured an interior room was more secure than one with a window, so she bolted across the hallway and pulled open the first door. Within was nothing save a few boxes filled with what looked like old photographs, rusting cookware, and moth-eaten clothes.

Before she could open the next door, two figures appeared from around the corner.

The first was her or a magical facsimile thereof, and the second was the tallest of the Orthodoxy's three agents on the train, the tough-looking one with curly hair. Her eyes widened at the sight of Kera and her mouth fell open, then something in Russian or a similar language echoed down the stairwell.

Kera kicked her in the stomach and the woman fell back a half-step, but the blow didn't seem to do much good. Her hands wrapped around Kera's ankle before she could retract her leg.

Oh, crap. She's resilient, and now she knows for sure I'm the real Kera since while the illusions might have been able to spring a trap or two, they're not capable of kicking someone, are they?

Since her athletic abilities were still partially boosted by the charms she had cast on herself, Kera jumped up, braced the foot the woman had caught against her abdomen, and swiped her other foot across the witch's face. Her head snapped to the side and a bruise appeared on her jaw, but she didn't go down.

She did let Kera's foot go, though. Kera tumbled through space and rolled into the wall, crashing there but springing to her feet in time for the witch to throw out her hands in a spell.

Kera dodged to the side as a trident of lightning bolts leapt from the bigger woman's hands and smashed into the wall, shattering boards and setting them on fire. A stray bolt, a side-fork of one of the main ones, branched off and struck Kera in the midsection, but she had enough shield left that it crackled into oblivion, although it weakened the shield and drew sparks from its surface.

This one, Kera concluded, *isn't the sharpest tool in the shed. She could have set the whole house on fire with that, and somehow she failed to notice that I had an active shield despite having her goddamn hands on my ankle.*

She summoned one of her illusions to enter the fray. It wouldn't be able to do much, but if Kera could create enough motion and disorder, the witch might get confused as to which was the real target.

But no sooner had one of the doppelgangers appeared than the woman lunged at Kera with frightening speed and force. Kera tried to twist away but took a strong blow to the side, enough to stun her and interrupt her movements. Then the bigger woman launched a punch at her face.

Gritting her teeth in pain as the torso strike exacted its toll, Kera managed to duck. The witch's fist cracked the board where Kera's head had been, and Kera kicked her in the leg while striking her with a wave of concussive force.

"Ugh!" The big woman grunted, toppling over and cursing either in Russian or her native tongue. She flung up an arm as her rump struck the floor, and a beam of fiery plasma shot from her hand.

Kera cried out in alarm, summoning another shield. It formed at the last instant, so some of the blazing ray got trapped inside it, creating a stationary fireball that Kera could feel singeing her clothes. The rest of the plasma ricocheted and refracted, igniting other parts of the walls.

Behind where Daniela had fallen, another bedroom door opened as though by itself and a woman's voice shouted, "Idiot! You will kill her or burn this place down! Kera. We know it's you. If you want to save the girl, *come here.* We have business to finish."

The big woman had risen to a crouch, ready and eager to pounce again but awaiting further instructions from what could only be their leader. This was Milena, if Kera recalled correctly, the Orthodoxy's chief practitioner of sacrificial magic.

"Yeah," Kera shouted into the room, which was dark aside from a faint reddish glow, "and I know what you want with me. Let the little girl go, then I'll come in for a friendly talk."

Behind her, she felt an obscure swell of magic and something pressed against her mind: a compulsion spell, a powerful psychic command.

Kera hadn't expected it, and at first the spell succeeded, making it impossible for her to refuse. She took two robotic steps toward the open door, then stopped.

"No!" She spun and hurled a confusion spell into the shadowy space at her back. The compulsion weakened but did not drop.

The third witch, the Asian-looking one, must be a specialist in psionic magic, which meant she'd be resistant to it.

Daniela roared and charged, knocking Kera against the wall and twisting her right arm behind her back. "Do what we say!" she barked. She yanked Kera back and drove her toward the black bedroom. Hana cast another enchantment, a spell of relaxation designed to weaken Kera's will.

She was faltering. They were winning. The witches had brought her to the threshold of the room.

Hana stepped out from behind a corner and advanced, watching Kera's back as she maintained the mental-attack magic that complemented Daniela's brute force.

Kera remembered something Pavla had said about how the Orthodoxy often made witches who were complete opposites work together in the interest of balance.

She summoned what free will she had left and blasted Daniela with every form of psychic attack she could think of: fear, shame, insecurity. The tall woman, so tough and aggressive, had surprisingly few defenses against the concentrated blast, and Kera saw into her anxieties.

Daniela is afraid that Milena will sacrifice her if they screw this up! Kera grasped. *They don't trust each other. They're all trying to skate by without getting in trouble, doing this only out of their fear of their grandmistress.*

Hana's compelling wave of discouragement strengthened and Kera felt her knees buckle, but Daniela was almost paralyzed too. Kera recalled the images of human sacrifice she had seen and placed Daniela's and Hana's faces on the victims, projecting the hideous spectacles into both their minds.

Daniela shrieked. Kera grabbed her, tripped her at the ankle, and tossed her into Hana. The smaller witch crashed into the wall.

From the bedroom, Milena shrieked, "What are you doing? Bring her in, you idiots!"

Kera faced Milena's subordinates and blasted Daniela with fear spells again, combined with percussive-kinetic force. The big woman, screaming in terror, was driven over the rail above the stairwell and crashed into the banister on the landing. The last thing Kera saw of the witch was her limping out the front door, shaking in panic.

Hana got up, but Kera was faster.

If she's the brains and Daniela was the brawn, she probably sucks at hand-to-hand fighting. Kera punched her in the face.

Hana fell back, mewling in pain, her lips bleeding. She reflexively cast another relaxation spell, but Kera had anticipated it and channeled the effects to her own advantage, settling into the calm focus that came with extensive martial arts training. Then she kicked Hana in the groin, threw her into the wall again, and dragged her back into the bedroom Kera had entered the house through.

Seeing the broken second-story window, Hana sobbed, "No! Please!"

Kera's stomach tightened. She didn't want to kill anyone, especially not a small woman begging for mercy, but then she remembered Jessica Trammell. "Sorry," she murmured and threw the witch out the window. It wasn't *that* far to the ground, and Hana managed to cast a slow-fall spell on herself halfway down. She still slammed into the dirt hard but not forcefully enough to be seriously injured or killed.

To Kera's surprise, Chris appeared from behind a toolshed and grabbed Hana as she hesitated. "Go home!" Chris shouted, shoving her away. Hana ran without looking back.

Milena screamed in rage and cursed in Russian.

Why isn't she coming out of that room? Kera wondered. *She must still have to do something to prepare for the sacrifice. Now's my chance.*

Kera dashed past the black bedroom and flung open the closet on the interior side of the hallway. It was empty except for a chair, a pillow, and a little girl with dark hair. Dashing in without thinking, Kera grabbed Jessica around the waist. "I'm taking you home," she said, though Jessica seemed to be either sedated or bewitched. She was barely aware of what was going on.

She ducked out of the closet, turning her back to Milena's room to protect the girl in case an attack came at her, but strangely, nothing did. Then she ran down the stairs, taking them two at a time and hopping over the collapsed floorboards. Halfway down, she tripped over a wire.

"Fuck!" she shouted. Kera hurled Jessica into the air and cast a feather-fall spell on her so the child drifted slowly toward the floor of the living room. Kera wasn't as fortunate and tumbled down the stairs, smashing into walls and rails. Somewhere near the bottom, she felt a magical trap ensnare her.

Her head felt like it was encased in thick cotton, and she could barely hear.

At the top of her lungs, Kera shouted, "Chris! Lia! Come get her!" She struggled to her feet.

A moment later, Chris appeared in the front doorway. He took in the scene before him in an instant, then ducked forward to snatch up Jessica, who was beginning to whine and squirm. As relaxed as she was, the chaos was starting to get to her.

Then he reached out a hand to Kera, helping her up and guiding her out the front door.

We're going to make it, Kera thought. They staggered across the lawn, and she put some of her remaining power toward undoing the spell that had deafened her. Her hearing slowly began to return. *We pulled this off. We—*

As though she were connected to a bungee cord, Kera was yanked backward and into the air. She screamed. There was just enough of her magical shield left to prevent every bone in her body from breaking as she crashed through the wall of the second-story master bedroom. The entire wall collapsed, and daylight intruded on the unnaturally dark chamber.

Kera's body was afire with pain, but she didn't think she was badly hurt, though her head spun. She looked up and rose to a squatting position.

A table had been set up in the center of the room, and near it was a hideous altar of black stone, topped with a leering gargoyle. It looked like a fountain, and the lower parts were stained with what could only be dried blood.

Milena was two feet away, straight razor in hand. Her placid, rather pretty face was twisted with fury.

Milena snarled, "Now you will die." The razor swept toward Kera's hamstring.

Kera's hand shot out and seized the smaller woman's wrist. Though Milena was not as strong, Kera was still in pain and disoriented, and Milena had the advantage of standing while Kera squatted awkwardly beneath her. The two were evenly matched at that moment.

"No!" Milena spot. "Stop it! I am a professional. I do *not* fail, especially not against people like you." She struck Kera with fear, confusion, and discouragement spells, but Kera was well-inured to resisting them, thanks to Hana's efforts.

Milena cast a charm that encased her hand in a small pyramid of heat and flame and drove it into Kera's side. Kera growled in pain, and the other witch managed to flip her toward the sacrificial table beside the fountain.

Being close to the repulsive thing, Kera could feel the stolen life energies throbbing within it. It was almost depleted but still providing a marginal benefit to the Orthodoxy. Without it, there would *be* no sacrifices.

Milena swiped again with the razor. Kera dodged and kicked the witch away, then turned and combined a concussive force spell with a simple punch directed at the fountain-altar. The gargoyle shattered into black fragments, and cracks ran through the rest. Any blood spilled into it would leak.

The malign aura that emanated from it grew weaker. Milena shrieked in horror.

"No, no, no!" she howled. "It is priceless! Even if we can't get the full benefit of sacrificing you, you are still marked for death! Nothing will stop us from—"

As she stepped forward, this time trying to slash her opponent's throat, Kera realized she meant it. Milena would never forgive her and would make killing her a personal priority until the end of time.

Kera thought, *I didn't want it to come to this.*

She caught Milena's wrist again, then a voice echoed through the room, clearly projected there by someone else. It was speaking Russian, but the cold, booming, imperious tone of demanding impatience was easy enough to understand. One of the two had to die *now.*

Kera twisted Milena's wrist until it broke. When the witch screamed, Kera seized the razor and in one motion, swept it across her throat. Milena's eyes bulged as her blood flowed down her chest.

The altar throbbed again; it was thirsty. Kera pushed Milena away and kicked her to the floor, depriving the fountain of its offering. As Milena died, none of her power, energy, or life force was returned to her employers.

The room grew quiet. Looking at the corpse at her feet, Kera's anger swelled, not only at the Orthodoxy but at herself.

"Fuck you for making me do this again," she snapped.

Anezka's voice caught in her throat as the truth of what had happened unfolded before them. The fledgling spell, held suspended while it waited for the infusion of power, was impatient to be released. All it would take to tear open the veil of magic that protected the council was a few drops of blood: Kera's, the girl's, Milena's, Hana's, or Daniela's.

But the altar was damaged. It received nothing, and it never would again.

"No!" Anezka roared. The other senior members flinched, and their contributions to the collective scry wavered and faded. "*No!*"

Anezka stood up, turned around, and faced the wall. For the next five minutes, she could think of nothing save her urge, her *need*, to rip Kera MacDonagh's heart out of her chest and crush it before her eyes.

As she stood in total silence, no one disturbed her. No one said anything.

CHAPTER TWENTY-TWO

Mary Mitchell stared at the little tree, her face lighting up with a girlish joy that Mother LeBlanc had not seen from her in years.

"It's incredible, truly incredible," Mary gushed, and she raised her hands to run them over the leaves. "I had no idea that palm trees were not truly *trees*. Well, I suppose I do recall seeing something about the order, phylum, and so forth they belonged to, but somehow it did not register in my mind until now."

LeBlanc smiled at her. "There is no substitute for firsthand experience, it's true." The sun was warm, and the late morning air was humid but curiously invigorating. It felt like home.

Mary shook her head and peered at the palm fronds and the trunk, then her eyes moved to the ground. She was likely linking her mind with the rudimentary consciousness of the plant to gain a deeper understanding of its root system.

"They're giant dandelions, only woody around the trunk and with green petals instead of yellow. In a manner of speaking. A form of 'flowering plant.' Oh, this is embarrassing, in all honesty. It brings to the fore how little I've traveled in these last few decades and how badly I have neglected the flora of the subtropics."

MICHAEL ANDERLE

LeBlanc waved a slim dark hand at the vast, swampy, almost jungle-like yard. "Well, it is my hope that we will be able to spend a reasonable amount of time here to rest in peace and safety. There will be work to do, but you should have enough free time to become well-acquainted with all the plants of the bayou. Or a good sampling of them, if nothing else."

Then she frowned. "That species of palm is not native to this region, by the way. You might want to consider moving on to something more appropriate to the history of the New Orleans area. I'm not sure who planted it. In any event, it has taken well to the climate here."

"Indeed." Mary looked up. "Surprising that the sun is so warm so early in the day and this deep into autumn. Well, no, it's *not* surprising on paper. In real life, though, it's different. I feel like a child on vacation. How could I have spent so much time in the Northeast?"

She chuckled and returned to her quasi-scientific examinations, proceeding to a patch of weeds and flowers that grew in a particularly low and damp patch of the house's backyard.

LeBlanc let her be, turning away and walking back to the building. It was an old plantation-style mansion, though it had been built only about a century ago, well after the ugliest events associated with the South had come to an end. It belonged to an old friend of hers. She had been coy about divulging his name to her fellow council members since in New Orleans, she felt an obligation to keep *some* secrets to herself.

They were outside the city in the middle of nowhere, though civilization was not far away. As such, they were protected by obscurity while still being within the massed and unique place-aura New Orleans exuded.

Most of the council was inside. The younger members, LeBlanc noted, were having some difficulty adjusting to the place. It had not undergone any renovations to speak of since it was first built, so it lacked electricity and had only limited plumbing, let alone central air conditioning. Fortunately, the worst of the summer heat was over for the year.

Crystal Green sat on an old, slightly moldy couch before a huge bay window, fanning herself with a hat. Faint particles of snow and frost appeared in the air as it moved over her face.

"Pardon me," she commented. "I shouldn't look a gift horse in the mouth, but I'm over-accustomed to the climate of upstate New York. Anything over seventy degrees combined with humidity and I start to have a rough time, I'm afraid. Or anything over eighty even when it's dry."

LeBlanc, not offended, shrugged. "Believe it or not, I don't greatly care for humid heat either, but you might say I'm used to it, given how much time I spent here when I was younger. In any event, it should not climb much above eighty, and then only for a few hours as the afternoon goes on."

Crystal's face fell. "It will get cooler in the weeks to come, won't it?"

"Slightly, yes," LeBlanc explained. "NOLA experiences three entire months of winter, although those are some weeks away yet, during which the high temperature generally stays around sixty-five. If we are here that long, you ought to enjoy yourself."

Walking past the duchess, LeBlanc went to the ground-floor guest room. Samantha had insisted on the best bed in the house for James, which was an old four-poster, a bit mildewed but otherwise perfectly comfortable.

LeBlanc asked, "How is he?"

"Good," Samantha answered with a wan look that might have qualified as a smile. "I was so worried when he had that...episode right before we crossed out of West Virginia."

LeBlanc grimaced. James had, after passing out on their first day in the moving truck, come awake in a strange panic, as though his mind was still delirious from a nightmare, and begun spitting out fragments of incantations tied to emotional echoes and general expulsions of power.

Everyone had pitched in to calm him down beside the river that flowed through Barboursville, but the damage had been done. The Orthodoxy had surely noticed the flare-up of untamed magic and picked up their trail.

But in the end, they had gotten away. Driving in shifts, they'd been able to make it all the way to St. Louis and then to NOLA virtually without stopping.

Samantha continued, "But he's improved a lot. Still needs his rest, but I can tell he's turning a corner. If we can stay here for two or three weeks, I think he'll make a full recovery."

LeBlanc smoothed her multicolored dress. "Excellent. Let's have lunch, shall we? I'll get everyone together."

She provided the food, pulling entire dishes out of the folds of her garment and serving them on the fine china and silverware that came with the house. Her fellow thaumaturgists, none of whom had ever figured out how she managed her tricks, applauded and offered half-serious guesses as to what powers she still hid from them.

She slid a casserole down the dinner table. "Perhaps one day I'll reveal it to you all, but for now, eat and be merry."

They passed a good forty minutes on the meal, everyone in good cheer for the first time in what seemed like too long. Hugh Buchanan was genuinely charmed by the old mansion, though he confessed he would miss electrical appliances and found reading at night by candlelight bothersome.

Meanwhile, Amanda and Josiah joked like high schoolers, and Rufus and Crystal got into a discussion on the transmutation of heatwaves. Ezeudo spoke to Samantha about James, and the Nigerian seemed to relax, now confident that his mentor would be fine given a little more time.

Through it all, LeBlanc had remained aloof. Not in the sense of being cold and disinterested, but in that there were other things on her mind that the others could not possibly have known about, appreciated, or understood. And though they had at long last found a place where they would be safe, there was still work to do.

LeBlanc said in a low, casual voice, "I'm going to get something to drink. I will be back soon."

Though she did not like using magic on her friends, she had placed a subtle enchantment on her words so everyone heard her but no one paid much attention. It would make it easier for her to slip away.

Which she did. The others continued their half-jovial talking as she made her way out the back of the house, losing herself amidst the weeds, willows, cypresses, moss, and muck of the encroaching swamp.

A sensation enveloped her as she felt the bayou close around her, and the house—and the entire human world of the present century with it—passed out of sight and out of mind. It was indescribable, somehow both warm and cold, dreadful and yet ecstatic. There was nothing about it that could rightfully be called thaumaturgy, witchcraft, or any other such term.

LeBlanc laughed. This, she realized, was what those without the gift meant when they said something felt "magical."

But that comparison was not valid because as the old woman advanced, seeing both the substantial changes in the vegetation that had occurred over the decades and the ancient landmarks that had changed not at all, she grasped something else. Few if any other people on the planet were capable of experiencing nostalgia in quite the same way she was since their lives were more or less capped at a single century.

For a moment, she was terrified of herself. By the standards of nearly all things that lived upon the Earth, it was *unnatural* for her memory to stretch as far back in time as it did.

And yet, the thing she sought was far older than she was. She had been a little girl when first she had heard about the Chalice of Old Jack.

Another odd shudder went through her. By now, the land was

losing the ability to make up its mind if it was dry land or water, but LeBlanc, easily casting the necessary enchantments, glided over the surface. The trees grew larger and denser, rising higher to block out all sight of the outside world even as the ground sank under the waters.

"Old Jack" was not the true name of the Chalice's original owner, of course. It was a nickname that was used out of respect and deference to the power of his real appellation. The man who'd kept the artifact safe at the time had been named Jack—or was it Jacques?—as well. There was an odd symbiotic relationship between the keeper and the thing they kept safe.

The population of birds and frogs and insects grew as she advanced into the wilderness. None of them bothered her, although many watched her pass in silence.

And although it was approximately noon, the swamp was strangely as dim as if it were twilight. A more ignorant individual than LeBlanc would have blamed it on the trees, a sudden bout of cloudiness in the sky, or haze in the air. Thinking that it was something so mundane, so readily comprehensible, would have comforted them. LeBlanc was permitted no such luxury.

At last, she came to the tree.

It had been dead for at least four hundred years, she estimated. And here in the swamp, where the profusion of life also brought rapid decay to all things, it had remained perfectly intact that entire time. It rose from a shallow pool of unusually clear water, surrounded by muck and weeds, and its gnarled branches were smooth and white.

LeBlanc closed her eyes.

"Girl," she heard Old Jacques say, "when you get to the tree, look at the sun. It's easier around noon. That one high, curling branch there will block it out, and the shadow will look like an arrow on the water. That's the way you need to head. Go and have a look at it, but don't touch it. It holds things, precious things, that people have right now but won't need till later, you understand?"

She had not understood. It was clear that the Chalice was special and important in some way, but at such a young age, she had no way of knowing what he meant.

Nonetheless, she had gone all the way to the edge of the hiding place and had glimpsed the artifact. Then a strange fear had overcome her, and she had turned back before she got close enough for a good look at the thing.

Not this time. This was the day—finally—when she would finish what she had started all those years ago.

LeBlanc followed the shadow of the great branch diagonally forward and to the right from her current position. The clear, shallow water barely moved beneath her feet. Then, abruptly, she was back on solid ground, on a winding path of mud and rocks that twisted away from the swamp and up a forgotten hillock composed of dead plant matter and out-of-place minerals.

Notwithstanding the rays of sunshine that had revealed the arrow-shaped shadow, it had grown darker still, to the point that it might have been midnight.

LeBlanc worked her way up the slope and pushed through sheets of moss, vines, dead roots, and leaves. At last, she found her feet resting in the same position they had when she was only a child.

The open space before her seemed smaller than it had back then, of course, since she was far larger now, but it had lost none of its dramatic effect. There was a bowl-shaped depression in the top and center of the mossy hillock, the base of which was lined with chalky white stone or dust or dulled crystal, and around it was a natural fence of thorns.

LeBlanc reached out. Destroying the thorns seemed unnecessary, so she commanded them to move aside. They did, retracting like masses of snakes to either side and leaving an opening about four feet wide for her to pass through.

At the center of the alabaster hollow was a petrified tree stump on which an old cup sat.

It was made of finely-worked brass. Nothing about it suggested materials that were expensive, and it lacked adornments other than the faint runic script that encircled its neck, but the craftsmanship was incredible. Having rested in the wilderness for spans of time beyond the comprehension of human beings, it was as ageless and pristine as if it had been kept in an airtight museum vault.

"Old Jack," LeBlanc began. Her voice sounded too loud though she'd spoken barely above a whisper. "I think I know what you store in this cup when you don't need it now but will need it later. And I believe that the people who want to harm us are using the same methods you told people never to use, which was why you gave them this chalice instead. With your permission, I would like to borrow it. I'm a daughter of the bayou, and I have been here before. I was afraid then, but I'm not anymore. Turn me away if you have any objections."

The hollow responded with silence, though it was not the silence of cold rebuff. It was the quiet that came with peace and contentment.

LeBlanc bowed her head. "So be it. I will return the Chalice when I'm done with it. Maybe I can find it a new keeper too since it's been so long without one."

She stepped forward, reached out, and took the cup from its place. Nothing happened, but the brass felt warm in her hand, and it smelled nice in a way she could not identify. It was a distant and hazy association from her childhood, faded almost into oblivion by the passage of time.

Shaking her head to clear it, LeBlanc turned around and left the same way she had come. The day became brighter as she got farther from the hillock and the dead tree, as though an entire night had passed while she was gone and it was early afternoon the next day.

LeBlanc stepped through the weeds and back onto the grassy lawn of the mansion. Mary Mitchell was out back again, sketching the new plants she had discovered with colored pencils in a blank notebook. She looked up.

"Oh, Mother LeBlanc. Where have you been? We were starting to worry. And..." she squinted. "What is that?"

LeBlanc held up the Chalice, noting how much brighter the brass looked under the natural sun. "Now we stand a chance."

CHAPTER TWENTY-THREE

Chris and Lia had gone only a couple of blocks away to wait for Kera to rejoin them before they all went back to the train station to deliver Jessica Trammell to her parents. Since the girl was still under a heavy relaxation spell, she did not panic, try to escape, or otherwise draw attention to herself.

"You know," Chris commented, "there's probably an APB or something out to find the kid, so if a cop drives by and sees her, there's going to be hell to pay. Yeah, we could likely get it sorted out once the parents confirm they hired our agency to help with the search, but still, ugh. I'm not in the mood to be mistaken for a kidnapper."

Lia reached out a knuckle and stroked the little girl's cheek. "That is understandable."

"And," Chris added, "I'm worried about Kera. Even with Pavla's quasi-intervention, those witches were no joke."

Lia looked over her shoulder. "Wait, a car's coming. I think it's the one you rented."

Before either of them could consider that it might be one of the Orthodoxy's agents, the car stopped and Kera climbed out, waving to them. Both relaxed.

Chris murmured, "Unless they disguised themselves magically to look like her." He opened the car door, stepped out, and shouted at the approaching figure, "Hey! What did we have for lunch that your mom made like a day or so before we left your parents' house?"

Kera stopped, staring at him dumbly. "Uh, pasta salad. I remember that. Sandwiches? Why the hell are you asking me that? Wait, you're making sure I'm the real Kera. Got it. Yeah, I am."

He nodded. "You pass the test. All right, get in the car since we'll need to return that damn thing."

When he climbed back into Lia's car, she told him Stephanie had just texted her. "Since she missed the fight," Lia pointed out, "I told her to meet us at the train station. If Kera has the strength left, maybe they can collaborate on curing her of that god-awful hex."

The two cars drove the short distance back to the station, parking near one another. Lia helped Jessica out, noting that the girl was becoming somewhat more responsive.

"Hey," she asked in her tiny voice. "Are we going to see my mom and dad again?"

Lia smiled. "Yes, baby. We're taking you to them right now. This is the station for the train you were on, remember?"

She chewed on a finger. "Okay."

Chris exhaled. "Good to see it's wearing off, so things don't look too weird. Um, is there, like, a law that we have to hand her over to the police instead of just taking her back to her parents? God, I hope not."

Kera jogged up. "I don't think so," she offered. "The cops will probably be relieved that it's all over and they don't have to keep combing the whole town. But then again, they'll probably want to go after the culprits, which could cause some problems. In fact, here comes one now. I think it's the guy I charmed earlier."

It was. "Is that your child?" he asked them.

Kera took the lead, realizing she looked like she had recently been in a brawl that had left half a house destroyed. She prepared another light spell to deflect suspicion and smooth the process.

"No, sir, it's Jessica Trammell. We're with MacDonagh Investigations, and the parents hired us to find her. We're taking her back to them." She cast the spell to be safe.

The officer blinked. "Oh. Okay, then. Great!" He wandered off.

Chris put his arm around Kera's waist as they proceeded. "Lot of magic you've been using today. When this is over, which it hopefully will be in, like, ten minutes, I'm going to buy you an entire buffet. Not a meal ticket *to* a buffet, but the whole thing."

Kera's mouth began to water. "That sounds *great.*"

As they prepared to enter the building, someone ran up behind them. It was Stephanie.

"Hey!" she called. "Sorry I wasn't here in time to help, but LA traffic did its thing, and I can't drive properly with, um, all this going on." She pointed vaguely at her face and moved her index finger around in a circle.

Kera nodded. "It's all right, Steph. I'm mostly drained, but give me a few minutes, and we'll remove the curse. Pink spots, you say?"

"Magenta," Stephanie corrected her. "Like, purplish-pink. Ugh, I'm starting to get used to the awful things."

Moments later, they found the Trammells sitting on a bench in the terminal, with a railroad worker and a cop talking to them. None of the four saw the small group yet.

Kera's brain was suddenly afire with worry bordering on panic. Without consulting her friends, she made a split-second decision and encased them all in a dome that blocked them from sight and hearing.

Chris looked at her, and so did Steph. Chris asked, "Did you just cast a spell?"

"Stop," Kera said. "I don't want my face plastered all over the news for this. I have an idea, though, and after we're done, we're heading to the nearest all-you-can-eat restaurant. Then we're banishing those magenta spots to oblivion."

Though mildly skeptical, the others agreed.

Catherine Trammell, meanwhile, sat listening to the police officer inform her that there was no sign of anyone in possession of a girl meeting their daughter's description so far. She stared blankly into space, holding her husband's hand and trying not to think about anything.

Then light footsteps approached. "Mom! Dad!" a girl's voice shouted.

Catherine exploded out of her seat, bowling aside the two men standing in front of her. Her heart felt like it was going to thump its way into her throat. She tried to say Jessica's name, but all that came out was a gasping sob as she fell to her knees and scooped the child up in her arms, clutching her close and crying.

Aaron rushed to her side. "Jessica. Oh, thank God. Are you okay?"

"Yes," the girl said. "I'm fine." She seemed oddly aloof and confused, as though she were trying to remember something. Then she reached into her pocket, pulled out a minuscule piece of what looked like plaster, and placed it in her father's hand.

Without thinking, he accepted it, and as the cop and the engineer came over to check on them and ask questions, he felt his mind go strangely blank.

The policeman remarked, "Good. Didn't you say you spoke to someone claiming to be a private detective? Do you have any information on them?"

Aaron was almost as overwhelmed with emotion as his wife was, but he had to attend to business. He turned to the officer, scratching his head. "I don't remember," he admitted. "I think someone offered to help look for her, but I was so upset and so much was going on that I'm blanking. I don't think so?"

Later that evening, he would find the card for MacDonagh

investigation and his memory would be jarred. The temporary mind-wipe spell would fade.

But for now, looking at his daughter and feeling a lump form in his throat, the most important thing was taken care of. His family could go on living.

Kera allowed herself to relax as she stepped back into the house. She didn't *want* to be here again after the ugly scene she'd been forced to deal with while stopping Milena and the others. Also, police cars kept crawling around the neighborhood, so she'd had to be careful.

But now that she was recharged and Stephanie's vision was cured of its neon confetti problem, there was one more thing to do.

It had occurred to her during their massive lunch that the recent murders Lia had investigated, which had been performed according to sacrificial procedures in the book, were almost certainly the work of the Orthodoxy. She had saved herself as well as the little girl from that fate, but the victims who hadn't been as lucky deserved justice.

It was dusk, and though orange light still burned on the horizon, the half-destroyed house lay in deep gloom. Kera could barely see. By memory and touch, she worked her way up to the second floor.

She found the closet she had opened while looking for Jessica, the one filled with boxes, including what appeared to be photo albums. Probably it was stuff leftover from the original owners and had simply remained there when the Orthodoxy had purchased the place.

But maybe not.

Kera took the box out and into the second-floor bathroom where, much to her relief, there was a working light since having to conjure a light of her own would be annoying. Then she got to work.

To her surprise, the albums turned out to contain pictures that looked familiar. One of the individuals depicted in them was a woman Kera had seen in the crime scene photos Lia had found.

"The former owner was one of Milena's victims?" Kera wondered.

She spent another hour combing the rest of the house and eventually turned up maps and personal dossiers on other people throughout the US, all of whom had been fatally mutilated with a razor blade.

Which meant their life forces had been stolen by the Orthodoxy to work its malevolent will throughout America and the world.

Kera sat on the floor, eyes closed, and allowed her mind to expand and intertwine with the residual pain lodged within the house and the items she'd found. She could not be sure, but she thought she had established a connection with the deceased, albeit a tenuous one.

I don't know much about spirits of the dead or what thaumaturgy has to say about the afterlife if there is one. But if there is anything left of these peoples' consciousness, I want them to know their loved ones will have justice. The world will find out what happened to them. I'm going to make all of this stuff available.

She opened her eyes and gathered the most important pieces of evidence. She wasn't certain if the police or one of the district attorneys would harass her for not sharing the information with them sooner. If that seemed likely, she would send the stuff to them anonymously.

If not, though, it might help the agency to finally have a case they could say they had solved. And either way, the families of Milena's victims would no longer be tormented by uncertainty about the deaths of their parents, siblings, spouses, or children.

"It's a start," Kera told herself. "And if nothing else, the horrible fact that this all happened might be what starts to unravel the Orthodoxy once and for all. They won't get away with it again."

Anezka was willing to admit to herself what she would never admit to anyone else in her coven. She had made mistakes.

They should have pursued the council immediately after taking over the Lovecraft estate and devoted all available resources to killing them. They should not have worried about trying to impress the lesser covens throughout North America or trying to hold territory in the Northeast or *anything* except hunting down and killing their chief rivals, every last one of them, allowing *nothing* to get in the way of that all-important task.

Anezka sensed that the rest of the Orthodoxy knew it or was beginning to suspect as much. Given the setback they had just suffered, it was time for drastic measures, not only to bring them closer to victory but to reaffirm who was in charge.

The grandmistress mounted the stage, raised her arms, and splayed the fingers of her hands so her long black nails pointed in ten directions, seeming to encompass the whole auditorium. The crowd beneath her hushed.

She had ordered all available personnel—everyone brought to America for the war and any "extra" witches hanging around the regional offices—to congregate here in Knoxville, Tennessee, which was fairly close to the exact center of the eastern half of the United States. The only members of the coven excused from attendance were those running the bare-minimum operations at the offices, as well as the token forces guarding New Orleans and Los Angeles.

They had rented an assembly hall at the local university,

paying the money and casting the spells necessary to ensure both comfort and privacy.

Now, Anezka stood before a small army. Three-quarters of the coven was gathered before her, and that included the minority of their members who had remained in Moscow.

"Witches of the Orthodoxy," Anezka began, her voice augmented by magic so it echoed and reverberated without a microphone. It seemed to thunder over the assemblage. "Necessity dictates that we adopt a different approach to our conquest of the North American continent. *Total war.*"

She paused for dramatic effect, allowing the words to sink in as the eyes below her widened.

Then she went on. "Milena, a member of the senior table, has been killed. Killed by the American upstart, Kera MacDonagh, with the near-certain help of Pavla. Those two deliberately sabotaged our efforts to wipe out the American Council of Thaumaturges. That means they are the council's allies and will suffer the same fate."

Not everyone had heard about Milena's death yet, and though no one was gauche enough to react openly, Anezka could tell that a few of them were shocked. The mere mention of Pavla made everyone appropriately wrathful since she was shaping up to be one of the worst traitors in the coven's history.

"This Kera," Anezka proceeded, "though crude and untrained, possesses raw power far beyond what most casters have. She might have been a great asset to us, but she has scorned our friendship a dozen times. Therefore, she must pay. This war ends when every member of the council, along with Pavla and Kera, lies dead, and I mean to end it within two months. Our dominion over this continent will be undeniable. There shall be no more hesitancy, no more half-measures..."

She outlined the rough strategy the Orthodoxy would employ. The field army gathered here would march on New Orleans, either catching and destroying the council even if it meant braving the dangers that might await them in the mysterious bayou city. If they slipped away toward California, their soldiers would be positioned so the council could not flee to Mexico or Canada.

Then, whether LeBlanc and her toadies were dead or not, the final maneuver would be against Los Angeles. By the time Anezka returned to the City of Angels, she intended that *all* their enemies would be reduced to piles of bones beneath her feet.

"There will be no distractions," she concluded. "Any peripheral activities in this country are hereby suspended. Our operations in Eurasia are of secondary concern at best. All available resources shall be bent toward the single goal of total annihilation. Do you understand?"

The witches on the floor threw up their hands in allegiance, and Anezka smiled. Whatever frustrations they might have had would soon find excellent opportunities for venting. Yes, some of them would die in the fighting to come, but she had little doubt who would be the ultimate victor. Those of her troops who fell in battle would be honored for their bravery.

Kera, Pavla, and LeBlanc would be wiped not only from existence but from memory. They would be destroyed so thoroughly that reality would regret having birthed them.

CHAPTER TWENTY-FOUR

James woke up. He yawned, stretched, and swung his legs over the side of the bed, throwing off the covers in the same motion.

"Ugh," he groaned. "Ought to have done that slower."

He found his glasses on the nightstand, unfolded them, and put them on. Then he spent a moment examining and admiring the stately, old-fashioned but rather dilapidated bedroom in which he had been lodged.

Ever since he had known Mother LeBlanc, he'd been curious about the native environment that had shaped her. They had missed out on visiting New Orleans during their cross-country trip to deal with the undisciplined casters unleashed by their book, but at last, they were here.

Mary Mitchell sat in a chair near the door, reading a book. *Tropical and Subtropical Gardening* was the title. She looked up.

"James. How are you feeling?"

He rubbed his eyes. "Better. Not perfect, but better than I have in quite some time." He looked down at his chest. Though he would have an impressive scar until the end of his days, it didn't look too bad from the outside. It was the internal damage that was still causing him lingering problems.

He frowned and looked around. "What time is it? Must be three or four in the afternoon."

Mary chuckled. "No, it's around ten in the morning. This region is a sauna. Crystal is nobly suffering through it, though she is better equipped than anyone to do something about it. She's working on a spell that will replicate the effects of air conditioning since the house is not equipped with that particular luxury."

"Lame," James quipped. "I support her in her endeavors."

Frowning, Mary added, "I only hope she doesn't accidentally kill any of the local plant life with a frost. The flora here is truly fascinating, though not adapted to winter weather, I'm afraid. Oh, LeBlanc wants to speak to you about something. There have been two important developments in our situation."

James nodded and walked to the door but stopped on the threshold. "Oh, Mary? Thank you. I don't remember half of what's happened since they turned my house into an ashtray, and..." His voice trailed off since he didn't want to talk about Damian or Zacharia. "And everything else. But I know you did what you could to keep me alive. I won't forget that."

She nodded. "You're welcome, James. I know you would do the same for me despite our minor disagreements during more peaceable times."

James went into the kitchen, where someone had set up a small generator to power a coffee pot, a microwave, and a toaster. There was still a third of a pot of coffee left, and he poured himself a mug.

At the table sat Mother LeBlanc and Ezeudo. James, still groggy, did not realize until he sat down that there was something resting on the surface between them, and it was not a thing to be dismissed. As he sipped the brew, his eyes fixed on it: a brass chalice with an inscription around the neck.

It did not give off an obvious aura of power, yet something about it set off an alarm within his brain. It was paradoxical, but

he *knew* he beheld an artifact of immense and sublime importance. It spoke to a part of him that comprehended things in
childlike intuitive terms rather than anything the adult intellect
could grasp.

"I take it," he began, "that's the...*thing* you mentioned wanting
to dig up once we got to NOLA?"

LeBlanc had been staring at the chalice, studying it, and
Ezeudo likewise. She inclined her head. "Of course. And it's good
to see you're feeling better, James. If you're up to it, there are
things you must know."

Ezeudo said, "I stumbled across one of the people from the
Orthodoxy closing in on us. Perhaps because I am not a full
member, they did not detect me until it was too late, and I was
able to drive them off. This was a day ago when I was farther
north in the state, so our location remains secure. They probably
knew we were headed to New Orleans anyway. So, while
LeBlanc says we are safe for now, they will come after us soon."

"Correct," LeBlanc affirmed. "The other thing you must know
is that this object," she gestured at the ancient cup, "might be
what turns the tide in our favor. I hesitated to speak of it before
since it had been so long since I last saw it that I needed to
confirm its existence and location with my own two eyes, but as
you can see, it is real. The Chalice of Old Jack. That was not his
real name, but 'Old Jack' will suffice."

James wanted to make a wisecrack, but the odd feeling of
superstitious awe was back. He held his tongue. "I see. What, ah,
does it do?"

LeBlanc flourished a hand and produced a muffin and a
banana from within her dress. "Here, eat something." She pushed
them across the table. "But yes, the Chalice. I know *roughly* what
its powers are, but I must be certain before we risk our future on
its efficacy. We shall determine how it works tonight. If you feel
well enough, you may participate."

James took a bite of the muffin—banana, which seemed

redundant given the fruit of the same type that LeBlanc had conjured to go with it—and washed it down with coffee. "I'm in. I'm getting tired of not feeling well enough. You have to flex a weakened muscle for it to get stronger. Hell, Ezeudo is beating up Orthodoxy goons now, and I've been in bed this whole time."

Ezeudo shrugged. "I did not beat anyone up, but thank you."

LeBlanc stayed silent for another half a minute. "So be it. Having everyone present would be best. And though we have time for you to finish recovering, I think time is running out. If we must leave NOLA, the only place left to go is—"

James interrupted, "Let me guess. Los Angeles."

Kera had allowed her head to rest on Chris' shoulder. The sunset was beautiful. "This was a great idea," she purred. "Naturally, I feel guilty about sending poor Lia and Steph back to keep holding the fort while we extend our vacation, but, um, we deserve it. I needed to clear my head after all that."

Notably, her thoughts had begun to turn gloomy as she dwelled on the necessity of killing Milena. If anyone deserved to die, it was probably her, but Kera found herself hoping for a time in which violence would no longer be needed.

Chris wrapped an arm around her waist and drew her closer. "That we do. That whole train ride was like being back at work again in an especially busy week. Not fun. Oh, and I barely got to see the countryside since we were asleep during the best parts or distracted by fighting those witches."

"Well," Kera extended her hand, "at least California isn't lacking in scenery."

Rather than go straight home, after they finished their business in Jurupa Valley and Riverside, Kera and Chris had rented a hotel room near the slopes of the San Bernardino Mountains before hiking up a trail to a scenic overlook just in time to watch the sun set over the valleys and sink into the Pacific Ocean beyond.

It felt silly to take their weekend getaway so close to home, but it would make it easier to return to their homes and jobs.

Thinking about what was to come, though, Kera felt like a dark cloud was settling over them.

"Chris," she said, "I'm worried. We killed one of the Orthodoxy's most important people, and Pavla helped us do it. I thought they might forget about us and leave us alone, but they're probably going to treat this as siding against them in this stupid witch-war they have going on with the council. Things might get dangerous."

He nuzzled the top of her head. "I'll do what I can. You know I'll stay by your side."

She clenched her jaw and let out an exasperated sigh. "I appreciate the thought, but that's not what I meant. I don't want you ending up as collateral damage. I think we need to talk about a standing order for you to get out of the way when things start to—"

"Hey," he interjected, and there was an edge to his voice that surprised her. "I thought we already agreed there *wouldn't* be any plans for me to be shut out of *anything*. I signed up to be your partner come hell or high water, which means I have as much a stake in all this as you do. I helped with everything we dealt with these last few days, didn't I?"

Frowning, she retracted her head from his shoulder. "Kinda, yeah. All I'm saying is that it doesn't do *either* of us any good if you get captured and used as leverage when I'm not there to protect you or for you to jump into a situation you're not able to deal with and get hurt. I care about you, okay?"

"I know you do," he replied. His tone was gentler, though she could sense his lingering annoyance. "But if I'm going to trust you, you need to not underestimate me. I know I don't have magic. I defer to your judgment when it comes to that stuff and let you handle it. But I've pulled my own weight with all the other stuff so far. If things get rougher, I'll adapt to deal with it. We're in this together."

Kera's gut roiled. "You're goddamn stubborn, aren't you? Let's play it by ear. If I have to shove you into a closet and lock it to save your life, I will, no matter what you say or how much you complain later. But, well, yes, I appreciate your help...most of the time. Don't do anything stupid. That's all I mean."

"I'll try," he replied. It wasn't much of a response, and she suspected they would have another version of this same argument again before long. Possibly within the week.

She embraced him. "It's a nice evening. Starting to get dark and chilly, though. Want to head back to our room?"

"Good idea," he agreed. "If things do get worse, at least we'll have the memory of tonight, right? It's one of those perfect evenings we'll look back on years from now."

If we're both still around years from now, Kera thought but did not say. *Around and together. God, I hope so.*

"Yes." She tugged on his belt. "Let's go."

CREATOR NOTES
MAY 25, 2021

Thank you for not only reading this story about a Badass Detective but also these author notes in the back!

I appreciate you hanging with us for all of the (so far) badass stories.

I think I mentioned in one of these author notes somewhere how I came up with the badass concept (just add a type (witch, vigilante, druid, etc.), and you have a series name.

I chose to break Kera's story into three trilogies mirroring her growth over time. Part of that was also to allow us a chance to explain to those who love vigilantes that Kera wasn't just a witch.

Same reason for Detective.

Unfortunately, I'm not sure that was a good decision for marketing purposes. It seems that a witch as a character has more fans than a vigilante or a detective...damn.

Live and learn!

Kera's story is finishing up in the next book...for now.

I don't know if I'll come back to her in the future or not. Feel free to drop us notes and let us know if you want more Kera!

If you enjoyed the stories, please go back and write up a review and encourage other readers to give this series a try.

Your support always helps!

BBQ and Sous Vide

So, I found a fantastic BBQ joint (ok, it was suggested by Jeff Chaney (Author JN Chaney)) called L2 in Henderson / Las Vegas area. Jeff had recently been to Florida and brought back some of his favorite BBQ sauce for me to try.

It was a bit weird to be in one BBQ place with a bottle of a competitor's BBQ sauce from Florida in the same place. It was a rough time, but I pushed through.

The meat was fantastic, so at the end, I ordered a pound of brisket and a link to go.

A couple of days ago, I nuked some to heat it up, and sure enough, I wrinkled my nose because heating the meat in a microwave was a bit rude to the meat, to be honest. It didn't have the same texture or awesomeness as eating it at the restaurant.

Fast forward to today when my wife sent me a notice about another BBQ place in Las Vegas closer to downtown. I read through the review, and all of a sudden, a strong desire for smokey meat permeated my senses.

Unfortunately, my wife was asleep, and I didn't want to just leave her without letting her know I was going to be out for a while. Then I remembered *I had the leftover L2 bbq.*

But there was no way I was reheating the goodness in a microwave again.

I have a sous vide setup. Sous vide is where you put your food in an airtight bag and heat it in a bath of temperature-controlled water. I had been using it to heat up frozen leftovers while I was working. The solution was working to perfection.

I thought, *why the hell not try it on BBQ?*

I heated both the sausage and the sliced beef in a larger bag to 185 degrees, and it rocked! The only downside was it took at least thirty minutes to heat it up and could have used another ten to get the internal temperature to 185. If I had waited that long, there was a good chance I would have started to eat my arm slathered in BBQ sauce.

It was close.

OTHER STUFF YOU CAN READ

I'm going to pitch you some additional ideas if you would like to check out other stories I've either written, been a collaborator on, or created.

The Kurtherian Gambit (21 book series) – My first series about a vampire. She saves the world and goes into space. Follow Bethany Anne on a kick-ass adventure where she has to choose death to live again.

The Witch of the Federation – Future story where Earth is a bit post-apoc, space-faring with two alien species we have as 'friends.' One of those alien species is called the Meligorns and has magic. Our story starts where a human learns she can control magic as well. Her name?

Stephanie Morgana... Of a lineage of Morganas!

Skharr DeathEater – Sword and Sorcery epic story of a man, his Horse, and the god(s) who won't let him rest in peace on a farm. They need him to do amazing things, and Skharr accepts the challenge.

There are Barbarians, then DeathEaters, and the most notorious of all is Skharr DeathEater.

Take care, everyone – See you in book 03!

Ad Aeternitatem,

Michael Anderle

CONNECT WITH MICHAEL

Connect with Michael Anderle

Website: http://lmbpn.com

Email List: http://lmbpn.com/email/

Social Media:

https://www.facebook.com/LMBPNPublishing

https://twitter.com/MichaelAnderle

https://www.instagram.com/lmbpn_publishing/

https://www.bookbub.com/authors/michael-anderle

CPSIA information can be obtained
at www.ICGtesting.com
Printed in the USA
BVHW031527070621
608939BV00003B/492

9 781649 718204